PROMISED LAND

*Also by Marita Conlon-McKenna
and available from Bantam Books*

THE MAGDALEN

PROMISED LAND

Marita Conlon-McKenna

BANTAM BOOKS

London • New York • Toronto • Sydney • Auckland

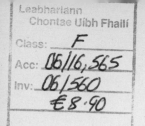
PROMISED LAND
A BANTAM BOOK: 0553 812572

First publication in Great Britain

PRINTING HISTORY
Bantam Books edition published 2000

1 3 5 7 9 10 8 6 4 2

Set in 11/13pt Sabon by Falcon Oast Graphic Art

Bantam Books are published by Transworld Publishers,
61–63 Uxbridge Road, London W5 5SA,
a division of The Random House Group Ltd,
in Australia by Random House Australia (Pty) Ltd,
20 Alfred Street, Milsons Point, Sydney, NSW 2061, Australia,
in New Zealand by Random House New Zealand Ltd,
18 Poland Road, Glenfield, Auckland 10, New Zealand
and in South Africa by Random House (Pty) Ltd,
Endulini, 5a Jubilee Road, Parktown 2193, South Africa.

Reproduced, printed and bound in Great Britain by
Cox & Wyman Ltd, Reading, Berks.

In memory of my wonderful mother Mary and Aunt Eleanor Murphy – two very special West Cork women

Acknowledgements

I would like to thank the following:

My editor Francesca Liversidge
Sadie Mayne
Alice Wood
And all the great team at Transworld
Caroline Sheldon
Gill Hess
Simon Hess and Geoff Bryan and everyone in
the Dublin office
The National Library of Ireland
My wonderful friends
My husband James and my children, Amanda,
Laura, Fiona and James. Special thanks for filling
my life with joy.

Wexford 1954

Chapter One

The land stretched out all around her, acre after acre of the finest farm land in the county. Ella could never have enough of it, never fail to appreciate the rich landscape of patterned fields, green upon green, hemmed by a ragtag border of hedgerows and ditches, which formed their farm and its surroundings. A hundred fertile acres that straddled the Wexford–Waterford borderland, with the estuary in the far distance and the dipping bowl of Lough Garvan in the middle of it all. She watched as the great grey heron rose up from its murky blue fish-pool and flew languidly out across the lake, the water below shivering in the March breeze. She shivered herself, wrapping her heavy knitted jacket about her and stomping her boots across the muddy ground. The day was cold and it was high time she got back to the house and set to preparing the midday dinner, for the old man must be starving by now. He'd have the fire cleaned out and lit and would be sitting in the armchair waiting on her. She couldn't remember the day or the time she had begun to call or consider her father an old man, but of late Martin Kennedy had slowed down. His long spine had begun to bend and his joints stiffen and swell. Every day more work seemed to fall to her as he no longer had the power or the energy needed to run the place.

''Tis all yours, Ella girl!' he'd console her, when she was soaked to the skin, or frozen cold, spattered with dung, her fingers raw with heavy work, her muscles aching with fatigue, the promise of the land keeping her going.

Returning to the whitewashed farmhouse that nestled snug in the curve of the hillside Ella noticed no comforting dash of smoke from the chimney. Inside, the embers of the previous night's fire still lay warm in the grate and the bread and soft butter sat on the table where she'd left them that morning, the butter melting, the bread hardening and the full teapot up beside the Rayburn untouched.

'Daddy!' she shouted, alarmed. 'Daddy, I'm back!'

Panicked she took the stairs two at a time, making for the master bedroom at the front of the house. Her father was sitting on the edge of the bed, bent over, the green sateen coverlet lying on the linoleum.

'Are you all right, Daddy?'

His heavy brogues and socks lay on the floor before him, and she could tell he'd been trying to put them on.

'What is it Daddy are you sick?' Rushing over, she sat down beside him, hugging him. He didn't answer, couldn't answer, the words wouldn't come out the way he wanted and she could read the fear in his eyes.

'Can you stand?'

There was no reply and she noticed the dribble of saliva that ran from the corner of his mouth and down his chin.

''Tis all right Daddy, I'm here now. You'll be all right, honest you will.'

His skin felt cold and she realized that he must have been sitting like this for hours, as she'd heard him dressing himself when she'd left the house that morning. His untied pyjama bottoms gaped loosely from his hips; embarrassed, she fastened them, touching his chicken-cold skin.

'Let's get you tucked up Daddy, you're freezing cold.'

Her father was a big man and it was as much as she could do to turn him round and lift up his feet and legs and lower him onto the pillows and bolster, pulling the sheet and blankets over him.

'You stay there Daddy and I'll go get help. I won't be long, I promise.'

She'd go up onto the main Wexford road, hoping that a car would come along or that one of the neighbours would appear on a tractor, anything, anyone that would get help. She cursed the Department of Posts and Telegraphs that had said it would be years before telephones would be installed down this way, for it was at least a three-mile walk to O'Connor's Bar where there was a public phone. Perhaps the Flanagans might help! She began to half walk and half run the mile or so towards their place, without seeing a sinner. Panting, she had to stop to get her breath when she noticed the work crew of men at the road's edge, picks and shovels in their hands, chipping at the grey stone face of a curve in the hillside, scooping out the earth and stone to create a hollow. They were working on the parish grotto to Our Lady and St Bernadette that was being built for the Marian year celebrations, and downed their tools when she approached them. Running towards them she begged the labourer seated in the van to drive to the pub and phone the local doctor, or call in to his surgery and tell him that he was needed urgently up at Martin Kennedy's. She thanked the workman and turned to race back along the gravel road, praying that her father was not in pain.

Her father lay staring up at the bedroom ceiling, his body awkward, his face contorted, as she prattled on trying to reassure both of them that all would be well. She fixed up the bed and patted his bolster, trying to make him reasonably comfortable. In readiness for the doctor's visit she tidied the bundle of clothes abandoned on the chair in the corner and stacked the pile of newspapers that had accumulated beside her father's wide bed, and using a corner of a sheet wiped the dust and tea and milk stains from the mahogany table.

'There you go Daddy, that's much better.' She sighed, catching a glance of the scared-looking woman that she was in the dressing-table mirror. He must be thirsty and she offered him a sip of water, not knowing if that was the right thing or not, holding the china cup to his lip as if he were a baby, the water spilling down his neck as she tilted it between his lips. Then she sat waiting, stroking his arm till the doctor came.

'It's a stroke, Ella. We could try and get him down the stairs ourselves but it's safer to let the ambulance boys do it. I'll organize it.'

Martin Kennedy tried frantically to speak and make himself understood.

'It's all right, Martin, you have to go to the hospital, you've had a stroke. I'm going to organize a bed for you in St Joseph's. Don't worry, Ella and I'll look after everything.'

Ella could see that her father was agitated. He hated St Joseph's, and she hated the thought of his going to the old County Hospital.

'Could he not say here?' She gesticulated at the stuffy front bedroom, which her father loved.

'No,' said Paddy Walshe emphatically.

Ella saw the doctor out. He was about ten years younger than her father, but with his grey hair and tired green eyes could have passed for the same age; both of them drank in O'Connor's pub of a Wednesday and a Friday night.

'You'd best send for your brother, Ella. Get him home as soon as you can. Martin would like to see him.'

'Is he that bad?'

Paddy shrugged. 'You can never tell, but it's best to be on the safe side.' The local doctor, although an infrequent visitor to the house, had always been a good friend to the family, stitching cuts, easing pains, lancing boils. He had too a directness and honesty about him that garnered respect.

'I'll get him so,' sighed Ella.

'Try not to worry! Martin will get the best of care in St Joseph's, and I'll see the both of you tomorrow when I do my rounds. We'll be better able to assess his condition by then.'

Back upstairs she could sense the dismay in her father's face; avoiding his eyes, she busied herself about the room fetching pyjamas from the chest of drawers, and his razor and toothbrush and a fresh towel, relieved when she finally heard the trundling ambulance pull into the farmyard below.

It had taken an age to get her father from the bed and down the stairs on a stretcher, she trying to keep out of the way as the ambulance men manoeuvred the reluctant patient out to their van. She clambered in beside him, and rode the long stretches of potholed and bumpy country roads, her father, a scared, old man, holding her hand all the way.

*　*　*

Inside the old red-bricked hospital building, calm red-faced girls took over the care of her father, making her sit down and have a cup of tea in the corridor. She watched as they bustled up and down, their crisp starched uniforms rustling as they passed, shiny hair pinned tightly under their nurse's veils. They'd pulled the green curtains around the cubicle where her father lay and a young pimply-faced doctor was attending to him.

Ella hated St Joseph's with its green half-tiled walls, cream-coloured paintwork and myriad of overhead pipes, its pinkish marbled floors and that strange hospital stench that filled your nose the minute you stepped into the place. Her mother had died in this hospital. The doctors and nurses had been unable to stop the spread of septicaemia from her burst appendix.

'We'll be admitting your father,' the sister told her after more than an hour's wait. She had followed them up in the clanking iron lift to the male ward of St Paul's, which was a long narrow room that contained about eighteen beds. The patients ranged in age from the elderly wizened figures propped in worn armchairs to two young fellahs sitting on the edge of a bed, playing cards.

'Visiting time is at seven o'clock,' remarked the ward sister, dismissing her. 'It's best you leave it to us to admit your father and get him settled in. You may return later this evening.'

*　*　*

She'd kissed her father and tried to placate him, sensing his disorientation. 'The nurses will look after you, Daddy. I'll be back after tea, once I've fed the animals and checked the place. Honest, I will!'

He tried to nod and she wondered if he understood at all what she was saying. She hugged him clumsily, feeling guilty at leaving him in that place that she knew he detested.

'It'll be fine, Daddy!' she promised, trying in all honesty to reassure herself as much as him. Relieved, she left the place and went back home.

Chapter Two

The old farmhouse was lonesome without him, and Ella wondered if she'd ever get used to not having her father about the place. The two of them had been constant companions for more than ten years, keeping house together, sharing the workload and minding each other, sitting up at night discussing the next day's work and planning for the weeks and months and years ahead.

Their black and white collie dog Monty had pestered her, following her around like a shadow as if she had somehow or other spirited the old man away. She knew that he just missed his master. She was behind in the work too, late doing everything. The hens were scratching outside looking for food clucking worriedly at the ground, waiting for their meal. The cowshed was in a state and she'd have to muck it out, as it smelled something awful. She'd meant to check the sheep and lambs up in the back fields, first thing in the morning, but hadn't got round to it yet. The pots and pans needed washing and she'd hardly a stitch of clean clothes to put on her. She'd wash a few bits and pieces first, and then set to, once she'd hung the washing on the line. Nowadays between the hospital visiting and the farm, she hadn't a spare minute. Doing the work of two wasn't easy.

There had been no improvement in her father's condition and if anything he appeared worse to her. He had lost his speech and seemed paralysed down one side of his body. She hated seeing him like that, one side of his strong face pulled different from the other, one arm and hand useless, unable to walk or move around. She'd noticed, too, that once or twice he had seemed not to recognize her when she sat down in the chair beside his hospital bed.

'He's a sick man, and everyone on the staff is doing their best to keep him comfortable,' was all that Dr Walshe consoled her with, though she noticed he made no mention of recovery.

Ella had rifled through her father's bedside table drawer and found the bundle of her brother's letters. The old man had kept them all. The last one Liam had sent was from an address in Liverpool and that was a few years ago. There was very little information in the letter and she'd read it and reread it to try and discover more about her brother. She'd written to him, telling him all that had happened and what the doctor had told her; that was over a month ago and there still had been no reply. She was angry with him. How could he not come home and see his father when he knew how ill the old man really was? Liam had walked out of the house over ten years ago after a blazing row. She remembered her brother's white face and furious temper as he'd packed the old brown suitcase, flinging everything into it.

'Don't go, Liam! Don't leave us!' she'd pleaded, begging him to stay, grabbing hold of his jacket, crying, scared of the rows between himself and her daddy. She had just been a schoolgirl then with no say in anything, least of all the ways of men. Her brother had left for England the next morning, his cap pulled down over his curly hair, his eyes red-rimmed and sore-looking. The old man had shaken his hand and wished him well, neither of them prepared to say sorry or climb down. They were stubborn, the Kennedy men, pride parting the pair of them.

So it was that she had been left with her widowed father. The two of them lived alone in the old farmhouse at Fintra. In time she had learned to cook and clean, her father showing her how to gut a fish and skin a hare and make light crusty pastry, the way her mother used to, but nothing she could say or do or make or clean could return the farmhouse to the way it used to be when her mother was alive.

Fair-haired Helena Kennedy would sing or hum as she worked, her bright eyes shining as she spotted another chore that needed doing. Folding clothes, washing the Delft, cooking the meals, tending the animals, sowing and planting and hunched over the heavy spade digging into the earth; even at night as she sat by the fire her hands never stilled, knitting a heavy woollen sweater for her husband, darning the socks, or mending the tears in their clothes. Yet Ella knew that her mother was totally contented, happy with her life. The house had always seemed warm and cosy then, filled with the smell of baking and the sweet freesia scent that her mother wore.

Ella's heavy winter coat now hung on the peg beside her father's at the back of the kitchen door and her boots nestled under the pine rack. The two of them worked side by side, tending the cattle, minding their sheep and planting with the seasons. She'd left school at fourteen. The land was her education; that's where she was needed, school could teach her no more. At times she wished that her brother was there to share the workload and help with the farm but knew that it was useless to voice such hopes. Tom Brennan, a local man, was hired at times by her father and besides there were plenty of casual farm labourers always looking for work. She herself worked as hard as any man, her hands hard and callused from using the spade and hoe, her skin wind-burned, her long light brown hair pinned up out of her way. She grew strong and tough and wiry. A good farmer's daughter.

'Martin, you're raising the child like a tomboy!'

her Aunt Nance had complained. Her father would stop whatever he was doing as if suddenly noticing her, paying heed to his older sister. 'Helena wouldn't like it!'

The very mention of her mother's name was enough to change the expression on her father's face from argumentative and annoyed to a reflective one as he considered whatever his sister had to say on a subject.

'She's the living spit of her,' was all her father would murmur and Ella would blush, knowing that excepting her light brown hair and taller frame she was a constant reminder of the woman he loved, with the same large blue eyes and full lips and skin that freckled in the sun. A visit to Aunt Nance and Uncle Jack's dairy farm at Rathmullen about five miles away would be organized and she would spend a few days with her five cousins, Teresa, Constance, Kitty, Marianne and Slaney, who like steps of stairs were around her own age, with Kitty only six months older than herself, and their older brother Brian. The influence of 'the ladies', as her Uncle Jack referred to his daughters, was bound to rub off on a gauche young girl who spent far too much time on her own. Their brother Brian would be kept deliberately busy on the farm and out of the way of their giggling and whispering and racing around playing silly games that Kitty and Connie invented.

There was always fun and laughter and plenty of female company up at the Kavanaghs'. She loved

23

visiting them and being considered part of their family but, when the time came, was glad to get back to the peace and comfort of home, entertaining her father with stories of all their goings-on as he sat and smoked his pipe in front of the fire. Often they would both drive over to join Jack and Nance and their clan for Sunday lunch. Her kind aunt would fuss over the two of them and send them home with fresh-baked soda bread, and sweet cake and whatever else was left in her pantry.

Ella sighed and dragged on her boots tentatively. She'd found a field mouse in the left one once, and her father had checked them for her ever since. It had only been a tiny mouse but the memory of it still made her cringe. Pulling on her warm coat, she walked up the back fields, Monty racing along beside her. Her breath formed clouds of steam it was so frosty out, and she dug her hands in her pockets and was glad of the thick knit hat and scarf that she'd decided to don. The grass was greening up and bunches of wild daffodils spattered the ditches. The ground was heavy underfoot, rain-soaked and muddy as she turned her back on the lake and clambered over a turnstile and up towards the hill fields. She could see the white fleece of their ewes and lambs in the distance. It was only as she came closer to the flock that she could see the cluster of worried-looking ewes, huddled together, the lambs bleating plaintively.

Monty made a run at a mass of black crows pitched on the grass, scattering them with his barking. Dread coiled in her stomach as she spotted the bloody carcasses of two young lambs, their entrails stretched along the ground.

'Jesus!' she said aloud, closing her eyes as nausea washed over her. There were three more, she discovered as she surveyed the field, and two of the ewes were injured where they had obviously tried to fight off their attackers. Monty sat at her feet, unsure of what to do. Who could have done this? What should she do? What would her father do? She knelt down to examine a ewe. She had a deep gash on her leg, but the blood had caked and although she was limping slightly, it looked like it should heal up. The dried blood soaked into her fleece was probably that of one of her lambs. Ella patted her, trying to comfort her. The poor thing was still dazed with shock.

'Ella! Ella!'

She turned round to discover Seán Flanagan climbing over the ditch. His father's farm bordered on theirs and the families often shared the cost of wire fencing and digging ditches and putting in drains.

'So they got you too! How many lambs did you lose?'

'Five,' she replied angrily.

'We lost nine.'

'Who did it, Seán?'

'Bloody dogs! O'Sullivan's dog is half crazy, it

would nearly take the arm off you if you step into their farmyard, and they always leave it out at night. You see it roaming around the place, and the tinkers have a few half-starved bitches that probably joined in. Jim and the da are gone down to the sergeant to complain.'

Silently Ella thanked the Lord that Monty slept stretched out in front of the fire every night, guarding the house, for the dogs involved would have to be put down.

'How's the da?'

'Much the same, Sean.' She stood up, brushing the dirt off her knees.

'Do you want me to bury them for you?'

She nodded, not trusting herself to speak. In situations like this she realized just how alone she was, and was grateful for the good neighbours.

'I'll wait till the sergeant has seen them, so don't be worrying yourself, Ella.' He reached for her hand clumsily and gave it a squeeze. She didn't draw away.

When she was about fifteen she'd had the biggest crush ever on Sean, following him around and finding excuses to visit Flanagan's farm whenever she could. Sean had pretended not to notice despite some fierce slagging by his two older brothers. Now the boot was on the other foot, and he somehow or other always seemed to be over at their place. He had a sturdy build, with broad shoulders, and long legs and body, making even her feel small when she stood beside him. His straight dark hair was in sore need of a good cut, his eyes were a hazel-brown colour, his face strong and almost handsome. She supposed he was good-looking compared to most of the men she knew, with a quiet reserved manner that made him easy to talk to. Her father liked and respected him, and she knew he held her father in high regard too. She was still mad about him and was glad that it was now being returned, the two of them often attending the local dances and parish socials together. When Sean escorted her home in the moonlight, his kisses almost made her weak.

'Is it all right if I call over later Ella, after tea?'

'I'll be going to the hospital.'

'Then I'll drive you! My da won't mind me driving you to see Martin.'

She nodded, pleased. Sean had brought her to the hospital a few times. Twice on the way home he had pulled the old Ford Prefect into a quiet spot off the lake road and courted her. She had been glad of his kisses and his hands pulling her close to him. She had responded as eagerly as he had and returned home red-faced and swollen-mouthed, glad that her father was not there to witness her passion.

At the rate things were going one night she would end up bringing him inside, and up the stairs to her bedroom.

'Sean Flanagan fancies you like mad,' said her younger cousin Slaney.

'Sean Flanagan wants a wife and a farm of his

own,' murmured Marianne, 'and you'd be a great match.'

'And you have him if that's what suits you Ella love,' added her aunt.

Ella blushed, glad that men couldn't read women's minds. She wasn't stupid and knew that it was high time she made a match and settled down. She was twenty-one and with her father sick, the farm would need a man about the place. The Kennedys and their farm were no doubt already the talk of the place.

'See you later then Ella, pet.'

She watched as he crossed back over the hedge. He'd called her pet. She wanted to run after him and fling her arms around him but instead began to walk.

Honest to God she was like a bitch in heat with all the dogs after her, what with her father sick and the running of the farm to be sorted out. Every local bachelor was coming out of the woodwork considering her a good prospect. Men she didn't give a toss about like John Mannion, who'd insisted on giving her a lift home from the village last week and was a skinny galoot of a fellow, and Tim Murphy, who made her laugh with his jokes, and Kevin O'Leary, all seemed to have become obsessed with her father's welfare of late and were always enquiring about him. As far as she was concerned there was only one man in her mind and that was Sean Flanagan; none of the rest of them were even a patch on him.

Her head full of such considerations, she made her way back down to the outhouse. She'd fetch a bucket and some disinfectant back up to the hill field and wash the sheep's cuts and grazes. She didn't want the animal getting sick on her. What if the dogs came back tonight? Maybe she should sit up in the field keeping watch, or move the sheep to the small paddock at the back of the house. She should have asked Sean what to do. There was no point worrying her father about it as he had enough to contend with. He just had to get better. The farm needed him and truth to tell so did she.

Chapter Three

Ella had scarcely slept a wink, tossing and turning all night. Her bones were so stiff and sore she could have sworn that she was an old one, instead of a twenty-one-year-old woman in her prime.

Martin had been in a bad way the night before. He had never opened his eyes once to any of them and had developed a strange heavy breathing.

'He's just resting.' Her aunt had tried to reassure her but she could see the worry in Nance and Uncle Jack's faces. Sean had gone out to sit in the hospital waiting room.

'Do you think your father would like the priest?' the staff nurse had asked.

Ella had seen the look that passed between his sister and her husband. She had just nodded in agreement. She had sat by his bed for an hour, watching the rise and fall of his chest and the easiness that now filled his face. Her father was a religious man; he'd want the priest to attend him.

'If he doesn't get in tonight I'll leave word for

Father Tom to come up to the ward in the morning,' the staff nurse added gently, squeezing her patient's hand.

'Come home and stay the night with us, Ella?' her aunt had offered.

'No! No thanks! I'd prefer to go home.'

She was adamant about going back to Fintra, not wanting to leave the farmhouse empty. Sean was waiting to drive her. Understanding her need to be in her own place, Aunt Nance had wrapped her plump arms round her and held her close, while Ella forced herself not to break down and cry.

Sean was quiet on the drive home along the dark country roads, both of them enveloped in silence. She was in no mood for kissing and courting and was glad that he didn't attempt to pull off down towards the lake shore. Outside the house he turned off the engine; she was exhausted and in no humour for chatting.

'Thank you for driving me, Sean.'

'Are you all right, Ella?' he asked, concerned.

She shook her head, not trusting herself to speak as tears began to stream down her face. Sean pulled her towards him, cradling her against his chest. 'It's all right Ella, I'm here. You're not alone.'

Strange, but there in his arms she felt safe and secure and not at all embarrassed. She relaxed against him, sniffling as he stroked her hair and the side of her face.

'Ella, you are so beautiful.'

She sniffed, knowing that her eyes were red and scalded and her nose running and Sean was the only one who would still consider her beautiful.

'You and I have known each other a long time and you know I'll do anything for you. Should anything happen to your father, you can count on me. What I mean is that I'm here for you, Ella, I always have been.'

Ella studied his broad strong face in the darkness. He was as kind and as good a man as a girl could ever expect to meet. She'd known him all her life and knew in her heart he'd make a good match, a good husband, a good father and a good farmer. Was he offering to marry her? She didn't want to think that far ahead, not with her father lying so ill in his hospital bed.

'Thank you, Sean.' Her breath shuddered as she opened the car door. 'But Daddy's going to get better. He's as strong as an ox. Daddy will be fine again, you just wait and see!'

She sat at the kitchen table waiting for the kettle to boil. She'd boiled an egg for herself and out of habit had put on two; she'd have the other hard-boiled later. Two slices of her aunt's soda bread lay buttered on her plate. She had no appetite but knew she must eat. The warm April sunshine filled the room as the birds sang outside in the trees, oblivious to her distress. A car pulled up out in the yard and, fearful, she jumped to her feet and ran to the door. She didn't recognize the black Ford Anglia. A man and woman were getting out of it, and looking up at the house. She was in no mood for visitors. Most likely they were trying to sell the latest vacuum cleaners, or other household appliances. She'd be polite but firm, and get rid of them. She opened the door as they came towards her. Something about the man was familiar.

'Ella! Ella!'

Immediately she recognized him and flew across the yard to meet him. It was Liam, her brother Liam. He'd come back!

'Liam! Liam! I can't believe it!' She found herself screeching with excitement like a little girl as her older brother scooped her up in his arms and hugged her.

'You're all grown up Ella, a real young lady! I just can't believe my eyes. When I left home, why, you were just a skinny schoolgirl in pigtails and now you are as pretty as a picture.'

She punched him gently in the chest, and tried to get a good look at him. He'd filled out and there were fine lines round his eyes; his hair was now tightly cropped. He was still handsome, like she remembered, but had a look of someone who had experienced much in life with a repressed sense of anger and disappointment.

'Oh, I'm forgetting my manners,' laughed Liam, pulling the young woman standing behind him forward. 'This is Carmel, my wife. We got married last year. I know that the two of you will be friends.'

Ella couldn't believe it. He was married and hadn't even bothered telling them. She looked at the rather plain-looking girl who only seemed a few years older than herself. Her fair hair was cut to just below her chin, and her rather pale broad face was covered with a smattering of light freckles. A gold wedding band shone on her finger. The two girls hugged each other awkwardly, both unsure of what to say.

'Come inside. You must be jaded! I'll make a fresh pot of tea and would you like some breakfast, I've a few back rashers and a bit of pudding?' she offered.

The three of them stepped into the kitchen and she noticed her brother's eyes hungrily devouring every corner of the place: the tiled stone floor; the wooden dresser laden with plates and cups and saucers and all sorts of knick-knacks; a plaster cast statue of Our Lady in the centre of it all; the white Belfast sink, and the draining board; the range which filled the kitchen with heat; the two chairs pulled up to one side of it; the dog's bed in the corner, and the wide pine kitchen table where they sat down.

'It hasn't changed a bit,' said her brother, 'not one blooming bit!'

Ella thought he sounded almost relieved.

'Can I show Carmel about the place?' Grabbing his wife's hand, he disappeared, and she could hear the two of them racing all over the house as she melted a bit of lard in the pan and set to frying the bacon and setting the table.

'I'll fetch in the luggage,' said her brother matter-of-factly, when they returned to the kitchen.

'Is there anything I can do to help?' offered her sister-in-law kindly.

'No, you sit and relax. The breakfast will be ready in a few minutes.'

She could see the other girl run her eyes over the kitchen and cursed herself silently for not having the place a bit cleaner. The dresser was dusty and crumbs littered the floor. She lifted a bowl of sour-smelling milk off the floor; sometimes Monty liked a lick of a bowl of milk, and she should have remembered to empty it.

Liam returned with two heavy brown cases, which he deposited in the hallway.

The three of them sat around the table eating breakfast, her brother relishing the thick slices of white and black pudding that she had fried. They had always been a favourite of his. She was pouring the cups of tea and thought it strange that Liam had still made no mention of their father.

'You got my letter about Daddy?'

'Aye, that's what brought us home, Ella. How is the old man? What do the doctors really think?'

She told him as much as she knew, her eyes welling with the relief of having her brother back home sitting across the table from her and sharing what was going on.

'Daddy's bad, real sick. Seeing you will be the best thing ever Liam, I know it will.'

'Do you think so? We parted on bad terms, Ella. I was a selfish young pup then, and he was such an old bastard, he wanted me to slave for him and I just couldn't take it any more. I told him what I thought of him.'

Ella studied the blue and white willow pattern on her plate. 'That doesn't matter any more, Liam. He's sick and old. All that matters is that you are here now; you came back to Ireland, back to see him.'

'Aye, I suppose so.'

'Honest Liam, seeing you will be like a tonic. It's just what Daddy needs. He kept all your letters by his bedside, in the drawer. Promise there'll be no more fighting between the two of you.'

'Of course! I'd better go to see him. Will you come to the hospital with me, Ella? I don't want to face him on my own.'

'Sure, I will,' she agreed. 'There's visiting time this afternoon.'

It felt good the three of them sitting at the table and Ella felt an overwhelming sense of gratitude that her lost brother had finally returned to Fintra.

'Will we sleep in my old room?' Liam asked, draining his mug of tea and standing up to move the cases.

Ella blushed, embarrassed. She hadn't even thought of the sleeping arrangements now that her brother had a wife. There was only a single bed in the room, which had been used for storing things for the past few years, once her father had given up any hope of Liam's return. There were her father's fishing rods and tackle box, as well as the old sewing machine of her mother's, a jumble of old clothes and shoes, piles of *Ireland's Own*, and annuals and books that she had read, along with broken household objects that might be used some day in the far future. On top of all that the room was musty and needed a good airing.

'The room's been empty for years, Liam; Daddy used it to store things. It's a right old mess and will take a day or two to clear out.'

'I see! What about the big room?'

'Well you know that's empty, with Daddy in hospital.'

'That should do us fine, then, Ella. It'll only be while he's there.'

She hesitated, for a minue unsure if she was doing the right thing or not, then making a decision, sorted fresh sheets and pillowcases from the hot press and carried them in to the large double bed in her father's room.

'Listen, I'll make the bed and unpack,' her sister-in-law offered in that strange half-Irish, half-English accent of hers.

'No! I won't hear of it, Carmel,' insisted Ella. 'I'm delighted to have you both home and will make up the room for you.'

'Maybe I'll show Carmel the farm while you're getting things sorted,' suggested her brother.

Carmel shot her an apologetic glance and Ella watched from the window as the two of them walked down the driveway and set off across the fields. She still couldn't get used to the fact of her brother having a wife, and them having no idea about it.

She had soup and sandwiches ready when they returned.

'It's huge,' murmured Carmel. 'I wasn't expecting the place to be so big. Liam always told me he grew up on a small farm in Ireland.'

'How do you think the place looks?' Ella asked, wondering what her brother thought of the low field which had been drained about five years before and all the other work she and her father had done on the place since he went away.

'Aye, 'tis grand!'

She noticed her brother avoided discussing all the changes that had happened since his absence. Why, he hadn't even mentioned all their ewes and lambs and their increased headage of cattle.

'Why don't you two go to the hospital and I'll clean and wash up here,' offered Carmel. 'Liam, you father's probably much too ill to take in the shock of a new daughter-in-law. I think it would be better for just the pair of you to go.'

'Are you sure you'll be all right here, love?'

'Aye.' She nodded, kissing his cheek.

Ella followed him out to the car, slipping into the passenger seat. To be honest she was glad to have some time on her own with him before they reached St Joseph's.

She could feel the tension and strain between them, knowing that this stranger who called himself her brother had made no effort to keep in touch with her at all. He'd walked out of her life just as surely as he'd abandoned their father and Fintra. He drove along the narrow roads that cross-crossed the countryside, barely looking at their land or making mention of the farm.

'Why did you go away, Liam?'

'I told you already,' he replied, barely lifting his eyes off the roadway.

'No honestly, tell me why?'

She had waited more than ten years to hear the full reason why her brother had taken himself off to England, disappeared out of their lives. She could remember bawling her eyes out, curled up in her winceyette nightdress wondering why her brother had left her, and her father stroking her hair and drying her eyes, and telling her that they'd be grand the two of them on their own. She was inconsolable, still grieving for her dead mother and then her lost brother. At the time it had seemed to her that everyone she loved had left her, and her father remained the only constant presence in her life.

'I had to get away Ella; I just had to get away from this place and from him. You were too small; you don't remember what he was like. He had me working that bloody land since I was a lad of about seven. I wanted to stay on at school but he wouldn't hear of it, oh no, he had to drag me out of the Christian Brothers after Mammy died and make me stay home and help with the farm. I'd him arguing and shouting and bullying me day in, day out. What kind of life was that! I couldn't stick another minute of it. In the end I warned him, tried to get him to cut me a bit of slack, like the Flanagans and the other farmers did with their lads. He'd have none of it, I was his slave and by God was I going to work for every shilling he threw me! I packed my bag and left, Ella. All I could think of at the time was getting away from him and this bloody place. That's all he cares about you know, that bloody land of his.'

Ella stared out the car windows as the landscape spun wildly by. Liam was still angry with their father. Nothing had really changed.

'I got a job in London straight away, and when the war ended there was massive reconstruction going on. I'd a job on a building site as a brickie and found a nice digs for myself.'

'Didn't you miss home?'

He shrugged his shoulders. 'There were thousands of other Paddies over there. We had a bit of a laugh on the building sites and the money was good. One good thing was that the old man had got me used to hard work. After about two years I signed on for the merchant navy because I'd decided it was high time I got to see a bit of the world.'

'Where did you sail to?' she asked, full of curiosity.

'Spain, Italy, Germany, Egypt and Morocco. You name it Ella; I probably got to see them. I saw the pyramids, and rode a camel in the desert.'

'Like the sheik of Arabia.' She giggled, picturing her brother like Rudolph Valentino or one of the other film stars.

'Something like that.'

'Go on!' she pleaded.

'Well, Greece was another of our regular stops, and Naples too.'

'Did you go to Rome?'

'Aye, I did that too. Saw the old Roman Empire temples and the Colosseum and the like and the fountains. 'Tis a beautiful city, I had a week's leave there.'

Ella stopped her questions, suddenly awkward remembering that he had never found the time over all those years to visit home.

Liam blushed slightly and she knew he had read her thoughts.

She filled him in with small talk of the neighbours and locality as they drove the rest of the way, directing him through the town of Wexford towards the small local hospital. She could sense his nervousness at the thought of his impending visit to their father. She had no pity for him. The prodigal had returned, and she could only witness their first meeting.

Chapter Four

Their father was awake. Ella was very relieved to see his eyes open and take in the sight of Liam standing at the end of the bed. Agitated, Martin tried to speak, to express all the words lost to them over the past number of years. However the stroke had left his speech useless and unintelligible.

'Hush, Daddy! Liam's here, he knows you're glad to see him.'

'It's all right, Daddy, I'm back! Everything's going to be all right.'

Ella noticed her brother neither made any apology nor gave any reason for his long years away. Martin Kennedy's eyes raked over his son's features as if trying to reconcile the man who sat beside him with the angry young lad who had run away to England years before.

Clumsily father and son embraced. Seeing him circled in Liam's arms made her realize how frail their father had become, how wasted his muscles. He took a grip of Liam's hand and would not let it go, her brother sitting hunched over on the edge of the hospital bed. Once or twice her father tried to speak, the two of them bending close trying to decipher what he was saying.

'Is it about the farm, Daddy?' sighed Ella, running her fingers over his cheekbones, wondering what he was so concerned about. 'Don't be worrying about the farm, Daddy, everything is fine there, honest to God it is.'

'Ella,' he kept repeating. She could tell how fretful her father was; seeing Liam had obviously upset him, and he must be frustrated from trying to tell them something and not being understood. She hated seeing him in such a state, the saliva dripping from his lips and at times barely able to swallow it.

''Tis all right Daddy, Liam and I are here together. All we want is for you to get well again,' she said, trying to soothe him.

Her father looked exhausted, all the colour drained from his face, with the effort of trying to talk to them. They passed the rest of the afternoon by his bedside, the nursing staff diplomatically ignoring them. For the most part Martin slept and the two of them kept a vigil, reminiscing about life at Fintra and filling each other in about their lives.

They talked and talked. She wondered if their father heard. At times he opened his eyes and twice they welled with tears. Ella, unsure if he was crying or not, wiped them away and gently kissed his forehead. The hours dragged by and the other visitors began to trickle into the ward, laughter and noise disturbing the earlier peace. Martin snored heavily, his face turned to one side, his grip finally loosened.

'We should go home,' she suggested. 'He's too tired, Liam. We'll come back in again tonight.'

Driving home Ella reflected that she was glad to have her brother back; at least there was someone else to share the worry of her father's illness, and make the house a little less lonesome. She knew that Liam must be weighed down with guilt and regret after seeing the old man, but she was not prepared to comfort and absolve him of the neglect he'd inflicted.

Back home, she was glad to busy herself with routine chores, checking on the ewes and lambs and filling the water troughs, with Liam insistent on helping her. He hadn't a clue about farming and seemed to have almost forgotten anything he'd ever learned.

'I'm used to being away at sea, Ella, but just you wait, I'll get my land legs back!'

The seed potatoes were ready to go down, and the top field needed turning. At least Liam would be able to give her a hand with some of the jobs. Ella set the table for three and prepared a simple meal of ham with potatoes, cabbage and carrots. She'd no time to be making fancy desserts and was glad of her aunt's confection in the pantry, serving the tart with a dollop of cream. Carmel praised her cooking and once again offered to clear away the plates and do the washing-up afterwards; Ella made no objection as she pointed out where everything was stored to her new sister-in-law.

Carmel came to the hospital with them later that night, as she was keen to meet her father-in-law for the first time. She pinned up part of her hair, and patted her face with tinted powder, and used a cheerful red lipstick to make her lips look even fuller and bigger. She pulled a shiny silk red and ginger scarf from her handbag and wrapped it gaily round her neck. She suddenly appeared much younger and prettier than she had first seemed, and Ella could understand how Liam had fallen in love with her.

The English girl had hugged Martin the minute she was introduced to him, and treated him as if he were at home sitting in front of his own fire instead of an invalid confined to a hospital bed. She told him about England and how she'd been born in Liverpool, the daughter of a Galway woman who'd fallen for an English shipping clerk.

'Five children they had, Mr Kennedy, and I'm the youngest. I like big families, coming from one myself.'

Ella could tell that her father had warmed to Liam's wife, as he was concentrating hard trying to take in her words. He was attempting to show some sign of approval for his only son's marriage. She was glad that the old man had been given the opportunity to meet this daughter-in-law.

'So the prodigal has returned!' murmured Una Flanagan when she heard that Liam was back home. 'Let's hope that he's not left it too late to make his peace with your poor father.'

'Daddy saw him in the hospital, Mrs Flanagan, and they seemed to be getting on just fine,' Ella insisted loyally.

The neighbours were an inquisitive lot, wanting to know what was going on in the Kennedy household, and how long her brother was going to stay. He and his bride were the talk of the place. At Sunday Mass the whole congregation nearly fell out of their pews when Carmel and Liam walked in and sat down in the seat beside her. Carmel's face looked white and strained and Ella was so annoyed with them all that she could have screamed at them to stop tormenting her sister-in-law. Those good Christians, staring at them over their prayer books and watching them all through the mass!

Father Hackett made mention of Liam's return after his sermon, saying how it made a change to welcome an emigrant home instead of saying yet another farewell to a parishioner taking the boat to England.

Afterwards, outside the church, a crowd had gathered round the two of them, seeing for themselves how Martin Kennedy's boy had turned out. Sean Flanagan joined them.

'Sean, this is my brother Liam, do you remember each other?'

The two men looked at one another, Sean standing a good bit taller than her brother as they shook hands. Ella noticed the slight enmity between them.

'I'm sure Martin's glad to see you,' said Sean politely. 'You've been away for so long.'

'Too long,' agreed her brother, 'but at least I found this wonderful lass on my travels.' Carmel smiled as she was introduced to Sean, realizing immediately who he was and his importance in Ella's life.

'Sean, isn't it great to have Liam back home,' sighed Ella. Her brother had moved away slightly and was engrossed in conversation with the parish priest.

'Aye, great if that's what you call it, him turning up out of the blue when Martin's so sick! More's the pity he didn't remember Martin and youself before now.'

Ella was surprised by his sarcasm and could see her brother annoyed him. A few minutes later he made some lame excuse about having to get back to the farm; Ella felt furious with him for not staying and talking to her or even offering her a lift home, wondering why Liam's return home to Kilgarvan had upset him so.

*　*　*

Liam and she visited the hospital as often as they could. Ella sat and let Liam talk, and make up those lost conversations. She watched as their father slipped in and out of sleep, day by day letting go of his grip on life. The colour bleached from his face, his skin turning the colour of yellowed newspaper, shadows painting the contours of his face. Only his eyes stayed the same, piercing and blue, the eyes of a young man not ready to leave the world of earth and roots and green grass, not believing in his fate.

He died on a Tuesday, both of them bearing witness to that last breath of life.

Martin Kennedy had died with dignity in the way he wanted, he'd had full absolution and Ella was sure he was relieved to have seen his family reunited.

Afterwards she had clung to Liam, broken, craving his strength and acceptance in her wild-eyed grief. The pain of it tore her to bloody bits as she looked at that husk left behind by her father's spirit, knowing that she would never see him again.

Good-hearted Aunt Nance and Uncle Jack had taken over, organizing the removal of the body, and the funeral. She was grateful to them for doing what was needed and expected. She had no stomach for it. Carmel had made sandwiches and baked cakes and polished, and cleaned the front parlour and hall and kitchen till they gleamed. She was grateful to this stranger who had known to do the right thing.

*   *   *

They had brought her father home to Fintra, laying him out in the parlour for friends and family and neighbours to pay their respects. Ella could hardly bear to be in the room with his corpse, as she still wanted to believe that he was somewhere off out in the fields working, and would appear in calling her name at any minute.

The Kennedy clan had come from every corner of the country. Her Aunt Maeve who had arrived from Edinburgh with her husband Tom. Some of her mother's people had come too, Shipseys from West Cork. Ella was glad to see her long-lost cousins and hugged them all fiercely.

'He was a good man!' said Tom Brennan over again. 'As good as you'd ever find.'

'What a worker! From dawn to dusk, digging and ploughing and tending the animals, sure he put the rest of us to shame,' murmured Fergus Flanagan, who had held his neighbour in high regard.

Ella took some comfort in their words. The house was packed with people and she longed for peace and quiet to grieve her father on her own. She watched as Liam went around shaking the men's hands and introducing Carmel to their wives.

'Blessed is the corpse that is rained on' had been one of her father's sayings. Well, he must be truly blessed because rain soaked the mourners escorting the coffin from Fintra to their parish church in Kilgarvan. She had never seen such rain, drenching rain running down the mourners' faces, soaking coats and hair and skin, everyone having to shake themselves off like dogs as they entered the small grey stone church.

Father Hackett was there to greet them. He and Martin had been great friends and she could hear the emotion in his voice as he welcomed his old friend's remains to the altar.

Somehow or other she had got through the funeral day. Listening to the Latin Mass, the small church packed with everyone she knew as well as old acquaintances of her father's. Aunt Nance, wearing a navy suit, bosoms heaving, kept blowing her nose loudly as tears streamed down her plump face.

Liam sat beside her, his hand gripping the wooden church bench, his knuckles white.

Ella just sat there letting the words and the music and the smell of incense wash over her, as the rain lashed against the church windows and rattled on the roof.

It was a short walk to the parish graveyard and Ella held Liam's hand tightly as they followed the coffin. The wet didn't bother her, not at all. A low stone wall edged the graveyard and at one end a deep hedge of whitethorn and fuchsia clustered together. It was a peaceful spot, the gravestones standing in quiet rows. Father Hackett led them all in the prayers as they laid her father in the grave, the people around her snuffling and crying. She concentrated on the blackbird singing on a bush, not wanting to hear those final parting words as Martin was reunited with her mother Helena.

Back at the house afterwards she'd run upstairs to change, as the rain had soaked through her blouse. Liam stood at the front door welcoming their relatives and friends and neighbours to Fintra, thanking them for coming to his father's funeral, organizing drinks and getting young Slaney Kavanagh, their cousin, to take the coats and umbrellas and put them away as the visitors laughed and joked. The men took hot whiskeys to warm themselves up, the women sipped glasses of amber-coloured sherry and ruby port.

Ella washed her face, and brushed her hair, which the rain had made wavy. She took a few big deep breaths before rejoining them. Liam suggested she give Carmel a hand with the food. The guests ate everything she, Aunt Nance and Carmel put in front of them. Her cousins Constance and Teresa served the food, the others running in and out with plates and glasses and salt and mustard and cups of hot tea. Every now and then she caught Sean's eye, or would find him standing near her protectively.

'Are you all right Ella?' asked her cousin Marianne, all concerned. 'You look a bit tired.'

'I'm fine.' Ella nodded.

'I don't know what I'd do if anything happened

to Daddy,' Tears welled up in her thirteen-year-old cousin Slaney's eyes. Her fair wavy hair was pulled back into a controlling chignon that was already beginning to unravel.

'Uncle Jack's fine, Slaney!' said Ella nodding in the direction of the corner, where her balding uncle, dressed in his best dark suit, stood with a bottle of Guinness in one hand busily discussing the merits of some racehorse with two other men.

Slaney's sister Kitty was sitting close by, on the arm of the couch, chatting to one of the neighbour-hood farmers and his son. Her rich red hair cascaded down over her shoulders, her green eyes flashing as they always did when someone paid her attention. Her lips curved into a constant smile. Kitty didn't believe in mourning and had put on an apple-green dress that she knew her uncle had liked on her.

'Man-mad! Even at Uncle Martin's funeral she's flirting,' sighed Slaney, raising her blue eyes to heaven, though a tone of admiration could be heard in her voice. Marianne pursed her lips, wishing that she hadn't been burdened with such good-looking sisters, while Ella smiled, glad of the friendship and banter of her cousins.

'Girls, what did I tell you, circulate!' ordered Aunt Nance, interrupting them, her cheeks flushed with the heat of the room and with tending the oven and the fire. 'That Scottish uncle wants another drop of whiskey, and Father Hackett has had nothing to eat yet, see if there's any cold meat left in the kitchen for him. Go on now, Ella's enough to be doing!

'Are you all right pet?' You know your daddy would be right proud of you, and how well everything's gone. Martin's had a grand send-off, thank God!'

Ella didn't trust herself to speak. Her Aunt Nance was always the one to hold her and comfort her. Her aunt squeezed her hand. 'It'll all be over soon, pet, honest it will. It doesn't seem right, a young girl like yourself burying two parents, but then that's God's will. You know that you always have Jack and myself and the girls and Brian. We all care so much about you, we always have.'

Ella hugged her aunt, relishing the comfort of the familiar smell of her lily of the valley cologne and warm skin.

'I'm glad that the rogue Liam has come home. It'll be good for you to have him around the place, and that wife of his seems a nice sort of girl. Martin was always worrying about him; you know he felt your mother's death unsettled him. Anyways that's all water under the bridge now and the two of them had made their peace, which is the main thing. The farm needs a man, it's too much for a girl on her own to run.'

Puzzled, Ella drew back and was about to quiz her aunt when the two of them got caught up in a discussion about her father's prowess as a boxer with an old school friend of his.

'A Wexford champion so he was!'

'He had his first fight when he was sixteen!' murmured the old man proudly, 'and I was the one who tried to floor him.'

It was well into the night when the funeral party finally ended and the last of the neighbours made their way home. Liam insisted on escorting most of them to the front door, though he hadn't spoken to many of them since he was a young fellow and it was Ella that they had come to pay their respects for Martin to.

Sean had hugged her closely on the doorstep as they said goodnight, his lips clinging to hers, wanting more.

Ella began to lift cups and saucers, and glasses and ashtrays.

'Leave it, Ella,' suggested Liam. 'We can do it in the morning.'

She watched as Carmel and he, arms wrapped around each other, made their way upstairs. She turned out the lamps and checked that Monty was safely asleep in the kitchen before going to bed herself. Through the stone walls she could hear their grunting lovemaking, and turned her face to her pillow, tears scalding her eyes.

Chapter Five

Ella cleared out the wardrobe in his bedroom, his suits hanging to the left, his tweed jackets and his trousers to the right. The shirts she had ironed were still stiff and suspended; he didn't like too much starch in the collar. The jacket smelled of him – soap, sweat, skin and tobacco. In the pocket she discovered a mint humbug, his favourite sweet. He must have been saving it. She had already parcelled up his vests and socks and pyjamas to give away, and taking the garments from the metal bar placed them carefully in the brown box her aunt had given her. Someone would benefit from her father's demise.

His shoes were too big for Liam and carried the shape of the way he walked, his footfall. Someone else might be glad to wear them. She didn't put the jacket away into the box; she couldn't. It reminded her too much of him and like treasure was secreted and buried in the back vaults of her own wardrobe.

*   *   *

Ella walked the fields for hours. She knew every hill and hedgerow in the place, every stick and stone of it was precious to her. She remembered each fence her father had laid, each ditch he'd dug. The land he'd deliberately left fallow, believing every piece of earth had a time and a season. The livestock that he'd bred and raised; did the animals know he was gone? She doubted it. Monty grieved him. The old collie had adored Martin and had been his constant companion for more than twelve years. Dogs were loyal. She would be his master now, a poor substitute.

'Come, Monty!' she called, leading him down by Lough Garvan. It was so peaceful down there, she had forgotten how much its still blue waters soothed her. The long thin rushes caught in the breeze, setting a dancing wildness rippling like a wave along the shore. She watched as a pair of wild swans glided by, long white necks arched. Soon there would be cygnets, dabbling in the lake. When she was small she used to think that their swans were 'the Children of Lir' and had kept hoping to catch them one day returning to their human form. Her father had never disillusioned her.

It must have been hard for the old man raising a daughter on his own, though he had never complained. He'd been content to sit in by the fire with her night after night, until she was old enough to

be left on her own. He'd helped her with her home-
work, listened to her spelling lists, read the
newspapers out to her, listened to programmes on
the wireless with her. He'd never courted another
woman after the death of her mother, never even
looked at one. He'd been a good father, no matter
what Liam thought. Her experience of him had
been totally different from that of her brother. It
was as if they had been raised in different house-
holds by a different parent. She was glad to have
Carmel and Liam staying but was curious that they
had made no mention of returning to England now
that her father was buried. She supposed that
neither of them was in a hurry to return to the
rented flat they'd told her about. Death seemed to
have frozen everything and it was probably the
same for them. She couldn't imagine her life
returning to normal without her father.

Monty began to bark furiously. Ella turned round
and grinned, seeing her Uncle Jack tramping across
the damp grass towards her. Monty leapt on him
enthusiastically, whirling and whining.

'Get down boy! Get down!' ordered her uncle.

'He misses Daddy.'

'Aye, we all do. Nance is above with Liam but I
thought I'd find you down here.' She linked her
arm with her uncle's, the two of them falling into
step automatically. ''Tis peaceful here. There's
some huge row going on at home and the ladies are
all sulking with each other. I thought it best to get

Nance out of the house in the hope that they'll either kill each other or make up. That's usually the way with sisters.' He sighed aloud.

'They're not that bad!' she teased him.

'Aye, I know that! How are you doing, Ella?'

She stopped and looked across the lake. 'I'm fine, Uncle Jack. I miss Daddy, that's all.'

'Ella, I don't know if Nance said anything to you the other day but Maurice Sweeney the solicitor wants us to meet him in his office in Wexford town . . . the day after tomorrow. It's about reading Martin's will.'

Ella didn't want to hear about wills and the like when her father was barely cold in his grave, but she knew that her Uncle Jack was not normally an insensitive man and was only doing his duty.

'I believe that I've been named as his executor.'

She wasn't sure of what to make of this information. Probably it had been a wise choice by her late father, as he and her uncle had been close friends for more than forty years.

'Should we be getting back?'

Ella nodded. She wanted to get back to Fintra and thank her aunt for all she'd done. She didn't know what she'd do without both of them.

Maurice Sweeney sat at the large mahogany desk positioned close to the window of his office overlooking the harbour. It had been his father's, and his father's before him. He was a great believer in tradition. The chair that supported his overlarge body had been stuffed with horsehair and wadding and then covered in leather. His arse fitted snugly into it and it gave him a bird's-eye view of the busy quays and the town bridge, where the Slaney River entered Wexford's harbour estuary. He watched the people, down below, going about their business. Wexford town with its narrow winding streets and alleys was one of the oldest towns in Ireland, known long before the fierce Norsemen captured it and made it a trading post, the quays the lifeblood of the town as ships entered and sailed from them over the centuries, his ancestors signing required documents and contracts for generations of locals. Many were clients already, others would be eventually, for such was the way of a solicitor's profession. Humankind was always destined to need the good offices of law men like himself. He took a sip of the dark strong tea that he liked. His secretary had already informed him of the arrival of the Kennedy family. He had got out the file on the last wishes of a Mr Martin Kennedy, now deceased. It all seemed straightforward enough.

The Kennedy brother and sister were shown in accompanied by an aunt and uncle and a sister-in-law. Luckily there were enough chairs for everyone to be seated. Joan his secretary offered them all a cup of tea before disappearing down to the kitchenette on the lower landing. Why the woman had to make every business meeting of his into some kind of tea party was beyond him. She said that clients appreciated it, especially those that had been recently bereaved. Experience had taught him it was better to wait till the tea had been poured and all concerned had a slice of Madeira cake, before getting down to business. He always hated being disrupted midway through reading a legal document.

He made polite small talk about the weather and the price of cattle and expressed his regrets at the death of his client. Joan had arrived back with the tea tray, clattering plates and cups. He supposed it was the only chance the middle-aged spinster got to fuss and act like a genteel hostess. His own wife, Lillian, usually plied their guests at home with gin and tonic, or stiff whiskeys. She wasn't much of a one for teapots and the kitchen.

He watched as the family relaxed, then clearing his throat began to read. 'I Martin Kennedy of Fintra, in the town land of Kilgarvan, a farmer, make and publish this my last will and testament hereby revoking all former wills and testamentary dispositions at any time heretofore made by me. I appoint Jack Kavanagh of Rathmullen House to be executor of this my will and I direct him to pay all my just debts, funeral and testamentary expenses.'

Maurice could see that Mr Kavanagh was content with his responsibility and guessed that the two men must have enjoyed a friendship which had merited a mutual trust and respect, which relatives did not always necessarily earn. Now came the important bit, the part that they were all waiting for.

'I give devise and bequeath the antique sideboard which stands in my parlour to my sister Nance. It was our mother's and now should be hers.

'I give devise and bequeath all the jewellery belonging to my late wife Helena to my daughter Ella. I also give devise and bequeath to her the sum of nine hundred pounds which is held in an account with the Munster and Leinster bank.

'I give, devise and bequeath my house at Fintra and all farm lands attached to my son Liam for his own use and benefit.'

Maurice Sweeney ignored the gasp of disbelief from his client's daughter and read on. 'In the event that my son Liam has predeceased me, I give, device and bequeath these properties to my daughter Ella.

'In witness whereto I have signed my name the day and year herein written. Dated twenty-fourth day of January 1949.'

Maurice Sweeney finished off, leaving Martin Kennedy's signature clearly visible on the bottom of the document. He wondered if the property concerned was a large farm or just a few poor acres.

'No! I don't believe it. My daddy never wrote such a will!'

He watched dismayed as the young woman with the light brown hair and pale face grabbed at the document and began to peruse it line by line.

'I do assure you, Miss Kennedy, that this is your father's will made in this very office over five years ago. As far as I am aware he did not make another one.'

The brother was hugging his wife, barely able to contain his excitement. The older couple stood up awkwardly and thanked him for his diligence. He had pity for the girl; obviously she had expected to inherit more. In his opinion nine hundred pounds was a fine inheritance for any single young woman, and he considered her late father had been more than generous towards her. Still, it was not his business to reason the ways of family, his job was only to convey the wishes of his client and this had been done satisfactorily. A copy of the deeds of the aforesaid house and farmlands rested snug and secure in his safe. Coughing and standing up he tried to convey to the family party that indeed his appointment with them was ended, but none of them seemed aware of the pressures on his time.

Joan knocked discreetly on his door, signalling the arrival of his next client Philip O'Brien, who was left to sit in the waiting room.

'My apologies, I know this is difficult for you all but I'm afraid my next appointment has arrived. If there is anything I can do, please rest assured that I will and, Liam, if you wish to come back and talk to me or need any advice I am at your disposal.'

He shook the men's hands and out of courtesy held the door open for the women. His stomach growled with hunger and he tried to push thoughts of his regular Tuesday lunch of roast beef and horseradish served in the Talbot Hotel to the back of his mind as he escorted them to the stairs. Today was bread and butter pudding day, he felt sure of it.

Ella clung to the polished wooden banister, unable to see the steps, somehow or other managing to arrive at the ground floor and step outside and into the street. She felt giddy and disorientated, her mouth dry. She couldn't believe it. Liam had got it all. Liam, who hated Fintra, hated the farm, had been handed it on a platter. It felt like the flesh had left her body and only a bony skeleton remained. That fat legal old fart hadn't a notion of what was going on, not a notion! How could it be that her brother would inherit the land and farm when he had only set foot on the place in the past two weeks? That couldn't be right. Liam had left Martin, abandoned the farm, left Ireland. He couldn't just walk back into her life and steal everything away from her. She wouldn't let it happen. Her daddy had promised her the land, promised her the farm. She couldn't believe that her father would do such a thing. He knew how much the farm meant to her, how much she loved it.

'Nothing will change Ella, honest!' broached her brother, trying to hug her awkwardly, as they walked outside in front of the solicitor's office. 'Fintra's your home. I know that and so do you. I

63

have no objections to you living with Carmel and me.'

She could see the look of triumph flicker in his eyes, hear it in his voice. He was his father's son inheriting his property as generations of sons had done before. Daughters when it came to it didn't count for much! Bile rose in her stomach and throat and she felt like she was going to be sick.

Carmel's eyes were shining with happiness and anticipation as she linked her arm through Liam's. Uncle Jack was already involved in some sort of serious discussion with her brother and only in her aunt's eyes was there any sympathy. Strangers pushed past them en route to the bank and shops and along the quays, totally oblivious to her situation. What did Liam mean saying 'nothing will change'! Everything would change, everything had changed already, her father had seen to that.

Chapter Six

Inheritance had changed everything, shifting and altering the delicate relationship between herself and her brother. Liam had become the winner, which meant that she was the loser. Carmel and he were beside themselves with joy at their good fortune, at finding themselves now the owners of Fintra and all its adjoining lands. Ella was sick to her soul with the unfairness of it all. She was no hypocrite and could not bear the pretence of letting on she was pleased for them. In secret she scoured the house hoping to find another will that her father might have written and hidden away. Her search was to no avail, and she had to accept that the farm and house were no longer hers no matter what her late father had promised. His words had meant nothing when that treacherous legal document had been left safe in his solicitor's office, disinheriting her from all she loved.

'This is your home, Ella!' Liam repeated over

and over again, but somehow she chose not to believe him.

'Liam and I are happy to have you here living with us Ella, honest we are,' her sister-in-law had added, an earnest expression in those blue eyes of hers. 'Sure you know more about running the farm than either of us! We'd be lost without you. Fintra will always be your home no matter what happens.'

She had bitten her tongue, and swallowed her pride. She had nowhere else to go for the moment and was too upset to even begin to think straight about her future. At times, looking at her brother she felt a deep hatred for him and wished that she had never sent the letter that had brought him home, but of course that would still not have altered the contents of her father's will. She had no intention of staying under their roof, a spinster sister dependent on them for her livelihood. She couldn't bear it. He and his bride were ensconced in her parents' bedroom, the old dressing table from the spare room placed near the window and a new set of bed linen and pillows purchased. Day by day Carmel was taking more of a role in the running of the house. She'd already moved some of Ella's mother's furniture and ornaments around and had taken over the shopping and housekeeping.

'I think a nice piece of lamb for the dinner on Sunday, Ella, and I must get another bag each of sugar and flour from the shop, and remind me to order some of that nice pickle that Liam likes from Nolan's.'

Ella didn't say a word, as her position of mistress of Fintra was now usurped.

On the farm things were different too. Liam had all sorts of plans and notions about modernizing the farm. Their father was barely cold in his grave when he wanted to go and change things, run things his own way.

He had insisted on sowing barley down by the lake field.

'Daddy was going to put turnips there!' she reminded him.

'Well Daddy's not here now, Ella, and I'm telling you that barley's the thing for that field.'

Ella sighed to herself, remembering how the field had flooded two years previously and they'd lost an expensive crop, the ground remaining marshy for months after. Liam had even told her to cut back on the amount of meal she fed the hens with, as it was expensive. Already she could see a slight drop in their laying and wondered if her brother had noticed it too. She had to bite her tongue constantly trying not to argue with him and asking herself what would a man who'd been away at sea for years know about farming anyway. Why, he was even talking about getting rid of their cattle and switching over to a bigger dairy herd.

'Uncle Jack does well with that dairy herd of theirs, maybe I should be considering it.'

'Daddy always kept cattle,' she'd reminded him. 'He made good money from cattle.'

Ella could see that her brother wasn't really

willing to listen to advice from anyone, leastways his younger sister. He wanted to put his own mark on the farm. Ella longed to give him a good clout on the head and tell him to have a bit of sense.

'Carmel and I are going into town to see the solicitor Mr Sweeney; will you keep an eye on the place, Ella? I want to go to the bank too, and have a word with the manager about taking out a small loan.'

'Liam, Daddy always said that you should be lodging money into the bank, not trying to borrow it from them.' She remembered the time when her father had gone cap in hand to the bank manager and had been turned down, making up his mind only to use the services of the bank for the safe keeping of his money and nothing else.

'I don't give a damn what he said, this is Carmel's and my business. We don't have a nest egg of money sitting in an account like some people. If we want to run this place we'll have to borrow!'

Ella ignored the jibe, watching angrily as they drove away from the farm and in towards town. She hoped that the bank manager would turn them down.

She was out in the yard sweeping when Sean Flanagan pulled in on a tractor.

'How's it going?' he asked matter-of-factly.

She kicked at the straw and dirt and wished that she was wearing something a bit better than her thick old cardigan and a washed-out-looking cotton skirt. Her hair was pulled up and pinned to the top of her head.

'Grand!' she lied. She had scarcely seen him since the funeral and was annoyed with him for avoiding her.

'Yeah! They look it! Where's the brother?'

'Gone to town to see the solicitor,' she said, swallowing hard.

Sean had silenced the tractor and climbed off.

'I heard about that,' he said gently.

'Who told you?'

'My da.'

'I suppose the whole bloody place knows by now what Daddy did!'

'Aye.'

A heavy silence fell between them.

'Listen Ella, I'm sorry about the farm. I know how much this place means to you.'

Ella looked across at the outhouses. She wasn't going to break down and cry in front of Sean, no matter how she felt. She longed for him to put his arms round her and say it didn't matter at all, that nothing mattered except the two of them, but he didn't. She could see the unease in his face, and almost recoiled when he took her hand, dropping the yard brush to the ground.

'We've got to talk, Ella, you and I.' His voice

was serious and she wondered what he wanted to talk to her about.

'Come into the house then,' she suggested, walking ahead of him. 'Liam and Carmel won't be back for ages.'

She pushed open the back door and led him into the warm kitchen, washing her hands at the sink. He came up behind her and embraced her, pulling her close to him. She could feel his hot breath on her neck, and out of instinct let herself lean against him. He turned her round swiftly and catching her chin in his hands bent down and began to kiss her. She responded eagerly, relieved that at least the attraction between them had not changed. She returned his kiss, breathless and excited. They kissed and kissed for what seemed like an hour, neither of them wanting to talk, only interested in being as physically close as they could. He pulled her onto his lap as he sat in the fireside chair, his fingers pulling at the buttons of her cardigan and underblouse. She could barely wait for his mouth to touch her breasts as she stroked his chest and ribs.

Ella wrapped herself in his embrace, not caring that his hand had slipped under her ruched-up skirt and was stroking the inside of her thighs; she longed to rub herself against the base of his thumb. She began to tug at the belt of his trousers, loosening them. For a second he held her hand, then pushed it away, reclosing his belt, pushing the metal prong back into its hole. Stunned and confused she stopped, looking up at him.

'I'm sorry, Ella. I shouldn't have let things go so far,' he breathed out heavily.

Embarrassed and rejected, she tried to straighten herself up on his lap. She tried to pull away and stand up, but he had a firm grip on her wrists.

'Don't!'

She blazed red. She didn't understand him at all.

'Ella, this isn't the right time or place for this to happen between us . . . honest it's not!'

'Why? What are you talking about, Sean? Don't you want me as much as I want you?'

'You know that I do.'

'Then what the hell is it, Sean?'

He stared down at the ground.

'Is this about the farm, Sean, is that what this is all about?'

His eyes immediately flew to hers and she could see truth there.

'Well that's bloody it!' she said, furious, jumping away from him. 'I'm not quite the catch that you thought now that I've no farm or land of my own!'

'No, Ella,' he said, trying to grab hold of her. 'It's not that. Don't say such things!'

'Let go of me, you bastard! Let go!'

'Not till you calm down and listen to me, Ella.'

He was too strong for her to fight against and seemed impervious to the kick she gave him in the heel.

'Listen Ella, how could I ever ask you to marry me, when I have no place or land of my own? Jim is getting the farm, I've always known that. I've no money, no savings, no land, I couldn't afford to marry you at the moment no matter how much I want to.'

'Ask me anyway,' she whispered, so soft she wondered if he'd heard.

'How can I?' he said slowly. 'Where would we live? What could I offer you?'

'Offer me! I wasn't expecting you to offer me anything but yourself, Sean Flanagan! Obviously you were the one expecting more. Well, I'm sorry for your bloody disappointment, about not getting this farm, but if that's all you care about, you can shag off out of here!'

'Ella stop! I love you, you know that,' he said, trying to calm her down. 'Maybe if I go away and work and save, eventually we'll be able to . . .'

'People who love each other get by Sean, they find a way to be together.'

She stood there facing him. If he'd said to her, there and then, to come upstairs and lie down and let him prove his love for her, she'd have gone with him. If he'd asked her to walk out of the farm door and travel ten thousand miles to the furthest corner of the earth with him, she'd have done it. For she loved him.

Instead he got up politely and began to tuck his shirt back into his trousers.

'Get out!' she shouted. 'Get out of my house!' She began to laugh almost hysterically. 'I mean get out of my brother's house, Sean Flanagan!'

She banged the kitchen door closed after him

and stood still, listening as a few minutes later he started up the tractor engine out in the yard, leaving her alone in the old farmhouse.

It was almost nine o'clock that night when Monty lifted his head and began to bark as her brother's car pulled up outside. Ella sighed to herself; she was still upset after her fight with Sean and their arrival seemed almost an intrusion. Carmel came in first with her parcels of groceries. Ella made no attempt to get up and help her, and pretended to be engrossed in the newspaper she was reading. Liam followed in a minute later. It only took a minute for her to get the strong smell of porter off her brother.

'We stopped off for a pint,' he said, slurring his words.

Ella didn't give a damn what he did.

'Liam's a bit upset,' murmured Carmel, a worried expression making her frown.

'The bloody bastards in the bank!'

'They wouldn't give him a loan today,' added Carmel. 'They told him to come back in a few months' time.'

'Bastards!' shouted her brother. 'Money men, my arse! Misers more like! I've got this place now but oh no, they wouldn't listen to me. I'll show those fellahs what I think of them, by God I will!'

'Liam, I think it's time you went to bed,' suggested Carmel, putting away the few bits of groceries and heating a mug of warm milk for herself. 'I'm away to bed anyways!'

Ella waited for her brother to argue back, but instead he sat down in the chair and refused to budge.

'I'll stay up all bloody night if I want!'

She sat quiet in the chair opposite, watching him. His eyes were staring into the firelight, when suddenly he sat up, running his fingers through his hair like he always did when he was nervous, and glanced in her direction.

'Ella, you could give me a loan,' he said.

'What do you mean?'

'I mean that you have hundreds of pounds just sitting in a bank account, money you're not even using, and I need capital to run this farm.'

'That's my money, Liam. Daddy left it to me. It's all I have, you know that! You're the one got the house and the land.'

'What good is the land if I don't have the money to farm it and keep going? I'll pay you the same interest as the bank gives.'

Ella thought about it, knowing all the plans her brother was making. She wasn't even sure if she'd consider him a good investment.

'Liam, sell me some of the land, a few acres will do, and I'll make over so much of the money to you.'

'No!' She could see his expression change to one of fury. 'This farm's mine now Ella and don't you forget it!' he shouted angrily. 'I'll not go fecking breaking it up or give a piece of it away, leastways to you! You can piss off with your money and keep it!'

She could see there was absolutely no point arguing with him. Besides, he was drunk.

'We'll talk about this again,' she ventured.

Liam's head dropped back against the chair and he began to snore heavily.

Ella watched her brother, his mouth wide open. He was deep in sleep and not likely to stir all night. Asleep, he reminded her of what he'd looked like before, when they were younger. She listened to him for a while before getting up and going to bed. The kitchen got cold during the night and she hoped he bloody well froze.

Chapter Seven

Liam made no mention of their conversation over the next few days, whether because he didn't remember it or had deliberately chosen not to discuss the matter any further she couldn't tell. Annoyed with him, she broached the subject again.

'Liam, I'm willing to give you nearly all the money Daddy left me if you give me a few acres for my own. Sell me some of the land! God knows I'm the one who's worked this plae and you know by rights I deserve to own a piece of it. Daddy should never have done what he did, he should have left it between us. He promised me this farm, and if he hadn't got sick . . .'

She could see him staring at her, cutting himself off from her emotionally, treating her like a stranger.

'I told you already, Ella, that I'm not willing to split the farm and break it up piecemeal. I'm honouring our father's will. You keep your part of your inheritance, keep your money, for I don't want it!'

'You bastard! You know you're going to end up taking out a mortgage with the bank, they'll end up owning the place. My money is as good as theirs!'

'I'll deal with the bank when I have to and that's none of your business, Ella!'

'Why won't you sell it to me? A few acres, Liam, that's all I want. If I'd inherited the farm, I'd have seen you and Carmel right.'

He laughed at her. 'Sure you would! You want a bit of land for yourself and that Flanagan fellow you're so mad about. I bet he's not quite so much in love now that your situation has changed, am I right!' he sneered.

The palm of her hand caught him with a stinging slap on the face.

He caught her tightly by the wrist, furious. 'Remember Ella, Daddy left me the farm. He had his reasons and I'm just carrying out his wishes and there's not a thing you can do about it!'

She felt like flinging herself at him and wiping that smug look off his face. A few acres would have been enough for herself and Sean, the start they needed. The only reason Liam had been left the farm was because he was a man. Her father's son! She cursed her father for his stupidity and prejudice.

The more she thought about it, the more determined she was not to give up Fintra without a fight. She didn't trust her father's solicitor to act in her interest, and asked her uncle to help if he could.

As a favour to her Uncle Jack set up a meeting with a solicitor friend of his in Waterford, driving her over to meet Vincent O'Malley at his home on the Dunmore East Road. The solicitor studied Uncle Jack's copy of the will, reading it line by line, and making notes. Ella was not sure if she should ask him questions, or just sit and wait for his opinion.

'Was your father in good mental health at the time that he made this will?'

'Of course he was.'

'More's the pity!' murmured Mr O'Malley.

He asked her all sorts of personal questions, trying to discover more about her father and brother and her relationship with them.

'Miss Kennedy,' he announced after over an hour of deliberation, 'it would be foolish of me to pursue this case, and even more foolish of me to let you do so. Your father was of sound mind and in good health when he made provision for you and your brother. He did nothing untoward in passing his estate to his son. That was after all his prerogative. By law he did not have to provide for you, an adult daughter. Jack, I'm sorry but there is nothing to be done in this case, nothing to be gained from going to court.'

Ella sat on the plump couch listening to his opinion, devastated by his words, and finally accepting the fact that Fintra was gone from her, and there was absolutely nothing that she could do about it.

Uncle Jack insisted that she come back and stay in Rathmullen, and truth to tell she was glad not to have to face Liam and Carmel after getting such bad news. She'd already brought a change of clothes with her, and everything else she needed she could borrow from her cousins over the week-end.

'You're as welcome as the flowers in May, Ella pet,' chuckled her aunt, leading her up upstairs to the bedroom she would share with her cousin Marianne. 'You may as well have Kitty's bed as there's no chance of her coming home for the weekend. She seems to be having much too good a time in Dublin.'

Ella smiled to herself. She'd already heard plenty of stories about her cousin's behaviour in Dublin. Apparently she'd broken her boyfriend John Prendergast's heart when she'd left Kilgarvan, and promises to remain faithful to him had long since been forgotten as Kitty went from one attachment to another. She was such a flirt, thought Ella as she hung up her things in Kitty's still-crowded section of the wardrobe and put her nightdress under the pillow. Kitty would never let anyone or anything get her down for long and Ella envied her that quality.

She ran downstairs to join her aunt and cousins in the large farmhouse kitchen where Marianne was curled up in a corner with her long thin legs tucked under and a worried frown on her face as she read the latest Agatha Christie novel. Her eighteen-year-old cousin was a real bookworm and you could almost tell how good or bad a book was by her involvement and the expression on her fine features and the way she curled her fingers in her short fair hair when she got to a good bit. Slaney returned from her convent school and dramatically tumbled her school books out on the table.

'Sister Angela wants us to do an essay on the life of our favourite saint, it's such a pain!'

'Who are you going to do?' quizzed Ella, curious.

'They're all awful! Utterly awful!'

'What about St Patrick, our patron saint,' suggested her mother.

'Mammy, half the class are doing St Patrick!'

'Well what about St Brigid then?'

Slaney tossed her mass of wavy strawberry blond hair, which was caught in two bunches. She was quite an actress and always ended up the centre of attention; Ella supposed it was because she was the youngest in the family and they all spoilt her rotten.

'I want to do someone interesting, not just another boring bloody saint! There must be one or two!'

'Slaney Kavanagh, I'll not have that filthy language at my table, do you hear me.'

The three girls looked at each other suppressing their giggles. Aunt Nance was known by the whole family for her own use of rich language.

Ella laughed and relaxed. It was so good to be back at Rathmullen, safe with her cousins and family. The Kavanaghs had become her second family when her mother died. At eight years of age she hadn't understood the explanations about septicaemia and blood poisoning, only the fact that God had robbed her of the person she loved the most in the world. Her aunt had done all in her power to provide some of the support and love and care that she so desperately needed. Teresa, the eldest, had become like a big sister to her, always minding her and making the rest of the girls accept and be nice to her.

Ella was glad to give a hand preparing the meal. Aunt Nance was a great cook and always hoped that her good example would somehow or other rub off on her five daughters and their cousin. Ella was sent scurrying to the pantry to search for cherries and raisins to add to the fruit loaf that her aunt was mixing.

'Have a stir for luck!' urged her aunt. 'Go on!'

Ella didn't feel very lucky at the moment but knew how superstitious her aunt was. Besides, she might get to lick the spoon at the end. Grabbing the wooden spoon she closed her eyes and wished hard. Her wish was secret and her aunt knew better than to ask. Satisfied, her aunt took over.

The peace of the kitchen was disturbed by the arrival of her uncle and cousin Brian for tea.

'Good evening, ladies!' joked her uncle. 'Marianne, get up and throw a log on the fire and let your poor old dad sit down for a bit of warmth.'

Marianne, putting down her book, obliged.

Brian disappeared off out to the scullery to wash his hands. Ella was very fond of her male cousin. Although he was very different from his sisters, much more reserved, shy even, he still possessed the Kavanagh sense of humour and an easy-going manner. At twenty-five, he was tall and lanky with a mop of brown hair, the exact same colour as her uncle's, his cheeks constantly ruddy from working outside in all weathers. He was a born farmer and she knew how proud her uncle was of him.

The six of them ate tea together, the butter from the hot potato scones running down Ella's chin.

'Teresa'll be along after. That nice young man that works in the bank is bringing her for tea to that new hotel in town.'

Slaney gave a big wink, which Marianne pointedly ignored.

'How is Kitty?' asked Ella, deliberately changing the subject.

'Kitty is Kitty!' sighed Uncle Jack. 'She'll never change.'

'And thank God for that!' added her aunt loyally. 'Kitty is having a wonderful time in Dublin. Her job in Lennon's is going really well.

She said that Mr Lennon himself promised her a raise if her sales continued. She's an excellent sales-woman, you know!'

Ella could imagine that Kitty could charm the birds off the trees if she put her mind to it.

'Well hopefully I won't have to keep on funding her then,' added her uncle, cutting into his sausages.

'Jack, you knew she had to pay a hefty deposit on that new flat of hers. You wouldn't have your daughter living in a tenement for heaven's sake!'

After the tea was cleared away Brian slipped out to meet his girlfriend Anna, who lived about a mile and a half away. She was a pretty little thing and all the family were fond of her. The rest of them settled down to play cards, twenty-one and whist, shouting and laughing at each other. Looking around her Ella realized that this was probably the first time that she had relaxed in weeks. She fell asleep listening to Marianne describe the plot of the novel she was reading and the various ways of poisoning someone and not being detected. Snuggled up in the bed she felt safe and comfortable and slept.

She didn't wake till midday the next day.

'Why didn't you wake me?' she groaned, embarrassed by such a show of laziness.

'Mammy said you looked tired, and that she'd murder me if I woke you up. Marianne and Teresa and I have been tiptoeing around the place all morning like a couple of cats,' sighed Slaney.

'You look a lot better,' declared her aunt. 'You needed the rest, sure back home you're up at cock's crow every morning, working.'

Ella smiled. Teresa arrived and hugged her warmly. With her shoulder-length dark wavy hair and large blue eyes and cupid's bow lips, she was a stunning younger version of Aunt Nance.

'How are you, Ella? How are you really? I still can't believe what Uncle Martin did!' Teresa stared at her. She and her older cousin had always been close, and she remembered that when she was a small girl it had been Teresa who had made Kitty and Connie be kind to her and let her play. Good sweet Teresa had always looked out for her. Ella just squeezed her cousin close. Teresa would know exactly how she felt.

'Did you talk to the solicitor yourself? Maybe there's something you can do to change things.'

'No,' she sighed, 'there's not a damn thing I can do, believe me.'

'Teresa, don't go upsetting Ella! God knows she's had enough to cope with over the past few weeks.'

Teresa looked at her mother, and giving one of her big smiles dropped the subject.

'Tell me about school?'

Her cousin taught in the small local national school about two miles away. She loved her job and was adored by all the children roundabouts.

'Oh Ella, I've had such a week. I got some of the children to bring in frogspawn a few weeks back.'

'Frogspawn!'

'For Nature Study. Well, we had it in jars on the shelf in the classroom and we watched as it changed to tadpoles, and then I don't know what happened, whether it was that the weather got warmer or some of the water had evaporated, but when I went into the classroom on Tuesday morning, they'd all grown and hatched or whatever you call it, and I had all these awful things hopping all over the place. The children went wild, trying to catch them and put them back in jam jars and get them out from under the desks. Oh Ella, it was just awful and of course the principal Mr Maguire stepped in to see what all the fuss was about. I was mortified. We had to gather them all up and go across the fields with them and put them in McMullen's pond. Then to cap it all Old McMullen's son, Finbarr, the one who works in the bank, came along. It was the most embarrassing thing that has happened so far in my teaching career.'

'And he asked you out!'

Teresa blushed. 'I know, can you believe it! If it wasn't for the frogspawn we might never have met.'

'Is he tall, dark and handsome?' giggled Slaney, interrupting their conversation.

'That's for me to know and you to discover, Miss Nosy Parker.'

Slaney retreated in a huff, leaving them together.

'Good riddance!' murmured Teresa under her breath.

'Is he nice?' urged Ella.

Teresa's eyes shone and the dimples in her cheeks became visible, which was answer enough. Ella was glad for her cousin. She'd had a bad let-down two years before when the fellah she had been going out with had suddenly married someone else.

The weekend passed too quickly, with Aunt Nance cooking her usual Sunday lunch of roast beef, roast potatoes, carrots, cauliflower, horseradish sauce and Yorkshire pudding. They all ate far too much, including a large portion of queen of puddings at the end. Connie and her husband Paddy had joined them. Their six-month-old baby Sean Patrick became the focus of everyone's attention.

'God bless him for he's such a fine healthy grandson!' murmured her aunt proudly.

Ella looked wistfully at her cousin, who was only two years older than her and yet already had a husband and a child and a farm to run, all the things that she had hoped and planned for herself. With her dark hair and sturdy build Constance was the image of her mother and Ella sensed she and Paddy would likely want a large brood of children running around their farm.

Ella almost wished that she could stay with the

Kavanaghs for ever, and never bother going home to face Liam again. She supposed she couldn't help feeling sorry for herself after all that had happened.

Somehow or other her aunt managed it so that the two of them were eventually left on their own together. She was a dab hand at arranging such things. Ella remembered when Aunt Nance had prepared her for her first monthly when she was about thirteen years old, and the time she had sat her down to explain the facts of life to her, forgetting totally that Ella was a farmer's daughter.

'Ella, you and I need to talk,' said her aunt, patting the stool beside her.

She sat down.

'I know that you're upset over your father's will, but you getting yourself in a state isn't going to change things one bit, you know!'

Ella took a deep breath. Her aunt was always honest and direct with her.

'Jack and I have made a will.'

Ella stared at her aunt, trying to read her expression.

'We've left the farm to Brian. It's what Jack wants, that our son inherits the farm.'

Ella gasped.

'It's not that we don't love the girls, you know how much we adore them. It's just that Jack doesn't want the farm split up, the land divided. It's been in his family for generations. We don't want any fight over it, so the best thing is to let

Brian have it. He loves Rathmullen, all he has ever wanted was to work this farm with his daddy, you know that.'

Ella didn't know what to say. There was sense and logic to what her aunt was saying. Already her cousins fought over the stupidest thing, so she couldn't imagine what it would be like if her uncle and aunt were not around to keep the peace between them. But how would Teresa and Constance and Kitty and Marianne and Slaney really feel about it when the time came? Had her aunt and uncle even bothered to get their opinion?

'My daddy, your grandfather, did the same to myself and Maeve. He left Fintra, the farm we grew up on, to Martin. Maeve and I were mad about it at first. I wept buckets, I was that hurt and upset. You know how attached I am to the old place, Ella. I suppose it's only with time I've realized and accepted that decision. The farm and land are important, don't get me wrong. I'd kill anyone who laid claim to Rathmullen, but do you know something Ella dote, if one of my children had cried or called for me, I wouldn't have given a damn about the stock, or the crops in the field, or the hole in the roof of the barn, for my children are more precious to me than anything else in this life. If little Sean Patrick had screamed or got himself upset over something today, why likely there might have been no roast dinner for you all to enjoy. Do you understand what I'm trying to tell you, Ella? There'll be other things to fill your life. The land might have made you hard, killed that fine spirit of yours. Let Liam have it.'

Ella didn't know what to say, she felt cold and shivery. Her aunt didn't understand at all. There was nothing else in her life now except for the farm. She would never forgive her father for what he had done, for the choice that he had made.

'I don't know what to do, Aunt Nance. I'm not sure I want to stay living with Carmel and Liam any more.'

'I hope they haven't been trying to put you out of the place. Jack and I wouldn't stand for it, Ella.'

'No, it's not that. I love Fintra, but I just don't think I can stay there any more now I know that it's theirs. It hurts too much.'

Her aunt stroked her hair. 'Poor old pet. You know you are always welcome to stay here for as long as you like, but that's not really the answer, is it?'

Ella took a deep breath, for she knew that too.

'Would you go away?'

She had to admit she'd been thinking about it.

'Kitty loves Dublin, would you consider moving there? You know that she's just got this new flat, which is costing her an arm and a leg, and is looking for flatmates. Would you share with Kitty?'

Ella thought about it. Even though she and her cousin were very different, they had always got along fine over the years.

'Jack says things are bad in Dublin, doom and gloom and unemployment, but Kitty managed to find something. If everyone's getting the boat to England and emigrating surely there must be some jobs left! Ella, maybe you'd be lucky like Kitty and find something you like. Moping around here is going to do you no good; unless there is some reason to stay!'

Ella shook her head. 'I've no reason to stay.'

'Are you sure, pet? Did I hear something about you and that Flanagan boy?'

Ella swallowed hard. Slaney and her gossip. 'Sean and I are just good friends, that's all, Aunt Nance.'

'Then there's nothing holding you back, pet. You were so good to poor Martin, looking after him. I've never seen such a devoted daughter, honest to God I haven't, but now it's high time you thought of yourself. I'll write to Kitty straight away and tell her to expect you.'

Ella smiled, almost laughing to herself at what she had agreed. Moving to Dublin and sharing a flat with Kitty, she must be mad!

'And do you know something, Ella, love, Jack and I will be so happy to think of you there keeping an eye on her.'

Chapter Eight

Ella couldn't hide the growing anger and resentment she felt at her brother as day after day he told her a list of jobs that needed doing as if she were a common farm labourer. At least a labourer would get paid for his work, yet Liam had made no mention of wages or even given her a penny since he took over the farm. She was the one who knew about Fintra but he wasn't prepared to sit down and listen to her views at all. He was annoyed with her and had somehow or other discovered about her visit to the other solicitor; she suspected her young cousin Slaney had let it slip.

'You can spend your money on all sorts of legal people, Ella, but it won't change a damn thing. Maurice Sweeney assures me that Daddy's will is sound and I'm only carrying out his last wishes. You haven't a leg to stand on legally.'

She said nothing as they finished the potato drills and were thinning out the cabbages, for there was nothing like the rich green, almost blue-tinged head of a full-grown cabbage, sitting close to the earth. The two of them bent down working in silence, separating out the weaker ones, their long leaves already misshapen.

'There's plenty of work to be done on the farm, Ella,' he grumbled. 'You know, you just can't take off over to Rathmullen whenever you feel like it, without a by your leave to anyone!'

'I'll do what I like, Liam, you don't own me!'

'Not when you're living on this farm and I'm the one providing the roof over your head,' he reminded her sarcastically.

'That won't be for much longer!' she muttered under her breath as she bent down again.

'What did you say?' He rounded on her, his head and broad shoulders twisting towards her.

She cursed herself for blurting out her plan to leave in a temper like that.

'You heard me, I'm gong to Dublin, just as soon as I can!'

'And what about the farm?'

'Well! What about it? This is your farm, Liam. You own it now.'

'Who's going to help out? You just can't go off and leave me like that, Ella!'

'That's your problem. Maybe Carmel could help.'

'Carmel knows nothing about livestock and farming. She grew up in Liverpool docks, her father was a docker!'

'Then maybe you'll have to hire someone.'

She could see his jaw tighten. She knew well there wasn't the money to pay a farm worker.

'You're not bloody leaving, Ella! This is where you're wanted and needed. What in God's name would a country girl like you do in the city anyways?'

'I'm not staying here,' she insisted, ignoring his insult.

'What the hell do you think you'll be doing in Dublin? Half the population of the place can't find work and have had to take the mail boat to England. Jobs are few and far between there, I'll have you know!'

'I'll find a job and I'm going to stay in the flat with Kitty.'

'You'd be far better off staying home, here on the farm.'

'Home!' she screamed back at him, enraged. 'This isn't my home any more, Liam! It's yours and Carmel's. I don't belong here!'

'You've gone mad! Of course you belong here, haven't you a nice room and a roof over your head and your keep and yet you're prepared to jack it all in and go off to Dublin with that lunatic cousin of ours.'

'Kitty's a nice girl, so you just leave her out of it!'

'She's as wild as a March hare and Uncle Jack is always going on about all the messes she gets herself into.'

'I'm not interested in gossip and tittle-tattle. As far as I'm concerned Kitty and I get on grand and for your information it was Uncle Jack and Aunt

Nance who suggested I share a flat with her.'

Ella was furious with her brother. Obviously Liam expected her to stay home and give a hand with the running of his farm. Since her father's death he'd obviously given no thought to her future or how she was meant to survive. She supposed he and Carmel wanted her as some sort of cheap labourer, to whom they would supply bed and board. She had no intentions of ending up a dried-up old spinster working on the farm dependent on the two of them for her keep.

'It doesn't matter what you say, Liam, I'm going and I'm not changing my mind.'

'Do ye know something, Ella, when I met you when I came home from England, I thought that you'd turned out a grand girl, that I was lucky to have such a sister. But since Daddy died you've changed into a right selfish bitch. Fintra will be better off without you! I don't want or need you on this land! So as far as I'm concerned you can piss off to Dublin and stay there!'

Flinging his spade to the ground, Liam tramped back across the field and along the narrow boreen, leaving her to finish what they'd started.

Shocked and hurt, she wondered why fights with Liam always had to end with him flinging things and screaming and shouting. Little had changed since they were younger.

Ella felt like she'd been kicked in the guts and knew that any possibility of remaining on the farm she had grown up on was finally gone and any doubts she'd had about leaving Kilgarvan had been viciously pushed aside.

'Don't leave, Ella! Please don't go!' Carmel pleaded, when she heard. 'Liam doesn't mean it Ella, honest to God he doesn't.'

'I can't stay here any more, Carmel, I just can't,' she insisted.

'Ella, you don't know how hard it was for Liam to come home to Ireland and your daddy and the farm after so many years away. He's all upset about things at the moment. Half the time when he says something he doesn't mean it, honest he doesn't! He won't admit it even to himself but he misses the sea. He's a sailor, not a farmer. Farming is different from what he's used to and it's going to take him a time to settle down her in Kilgarvan. He's worried about the money and trying to make a good job running the place, honest he knows that you're a much better farmer than he is but he's so stubborn he just won't tell you. He needs you here Ella, we both do!'

Ella could sense that Carmel was only trying to make the peace between them, for she was a gentle sort of girl who didn't like rows and upsets. But no matter what she said or did this time there were no excuses for her brother.

'He shouldn't have said what he said,' apologized Carmel again.

How things had changed so much and fallen apart so quickly at home since her daddy's death was beyond her. Desperate to get out of the house she pulled on her jacket and wellington boots.

'Monty! Come on for a walk! That's a good boy,' she called, opening the back door and setting off across the farmyard, her hands dug deep in her pockets, willing herself not to break down and cry.

Liam and she had managed to avoid each other for the best part of two days, and alone in her bedroom she packed her bag, an old brown suitcase that had belonged to her mother and father. She folded the best of her clothes into it, stacking them neatly on top of each other. She wondered if her few dresses and skirts would be suitable for a city like Dublin as they were hardly what you would call stylish. Kitty had led her to believe that the Dublin girls were all very glamorous and spent every penny of their money on fashion, hair and make-up and the like. She worried whether she'd fit in or not.

She walked the fields of Fintra, acre after acre, noticing the way the sun slanted down along them at different hours of the day, the yellow gorse and the blaze of purple heather that bloomed up by Finns Hill, the boggy land known as Kennedy's Keep, where her father used to cut turf for the winter, and all the things that made up her own place. She was glad that she'd got the seed potatoes down in time, for now it would be up to Liam to spray the drills and keep an eye on them. She'd also seen to it that the O'Gradys had mended the length of fencing destroyed by their Jersey cows. Liam wouldn't want those grazers crossing into his fields and eating everything around them. Their own cattle were fattening up well and their sheep were doing nicely, with plenty of young lambs in the flock. She'd told Carmel the names of two local shearers who would do the job for them, and showed her the sheep dip mixture that was kept in the outhouse. Carmel, although she knew nothing about farming, was a good listener and took down notes and reminders.

She walked up to the local graveyard where her mother and father were laid to rest. She couldn't bring herself to pray for her father, not after what he had done and the hurt and pain he had caused her. The funeral flowers still lay scattered on the grass, all withered and dead now, reminding her of the grief of his passing and the ensuing un-happiness he'd caused her.

Row or no row, she decided that she had to see Sean before leaving Kilgarvan, and cycled over to Flanagan's farm. His mother Una insisted that Ella have a cup of tea in the kitchen with her while she waited for him, while her daughter-in-law Bernadette busied herself preparing the family meal. Una quizzed her perceptively about what was happening up at Fintra and how she was feel-ing after Martin's death. She'd always liked Sean's mother even if she was a bit of a curiosity box, who loved a bit of local gossip. Her arthritis kept her tied to the house nowadays and she relied very much on others to fill her in on what was going on in her locality. Luckily she and Bernadette appeared to get on fine, neither of them objecting to sharing a kitchen.

Sean was surprised to see her there when he came home twenty minutes later. Making excuses the two of them slipped outside, walking down by the garden wall where a lilac tree in full bloom shaded them from sight of the house.

'I've come to say goodbye, Sean,' she told him.

'Goodbye!'

She could read the utter disbelief in his face.

'I'm going to Dublin to stay with Kitty.'

'Dublin! For how long? When will you be back?'

'I'm going to stay there, Sean, look for a job.'

'Jesus, Ella, don't do this. Don't just go away!'

'I have to, Sean, I can't stay here any longer, not with the way things are between Liam and me. There's nothing left for me at Fintra, not any more.'

'Don't go Ella, for God's sake don't go! Just stay! Give it another year, give me a chance to sort things out. I'll explain things to the da and try and get another job somewhere roundabouts, even if I have to go in as far as Wexford town. Just don't go and leave me.'

'I can't, Sean. I can't wait another year. Liam and I are barely speaking, he wants me off the place and now to tell the truth I just want to go,

98

my mind's made up to it. Everything's all organized.'

He stared at her angrily. 'So I can't make you change your mind and stay.'

She shook her head, swallowing hard. 'No.'

He ran his hands over his face and eyes, dismayed. 'What about us, are you just going to up and off and leave me Ella, is that it?' His eyes stared straight into hers, searching for the truth.

'I'm sorry,' she said, almost whispering. 'But you could come to Dublin too Sean, there's nothing to stop you, we could still see each other. You could get a job there!'

She wanted him to say he'd go to Dublin, London, it didn't matter at all once they were together, that he wasn't prepared to let her slip out of his life. Instead he looked silently at her making no romantic declarations, no suggestions, both of them suddenly awkward and strained.

'I was never much of a one for Dublin, Ella, you know that.'

Ella looked at his face. She couldn't even begin to read his thoughts. Obviously he didn't really care or love her enough; maybe he never had. Perhaps Liam was right after all. She tried to disguise her own hurt; she was likely the one who had imagined more between them. They were just two close childhood friends talking to each other, saying goodbye, the pain of it almost choking her.

'I'll miss you,' he said simply. She noticed he made no offer even to come to Dublin to visit her, nor did he ask her to come home at the weekends to see him.

'I'll miss you too, Sean,' she said, trying to appear somehow light-hearted, as against heartbroken at the thought of their relationship finally ending.

They hugged quickly, and Sean insisted on walking back home with her as she wheeled the bike along the laneway.

'When are you going?' he asked matter-of-factly.

'Tomorrow morning.'

The sun beat down on them and she licked a line of perspiration from her lip, nervous. He walked her as far as the gateway to the farmhouse, both of them ill at ease, Ella trying not to cry or let him see how upset she really was. She supposed it was out of habit that he smoothed the long hair back from her face and bent down and kissed her gently. The smell of sweat and grass and fresh air clung to him and she could feel the warmth of his breath as she closed her eyes trying to fix that one kiss in her memory. When she opened them seconds later he'd gone.

Chapter Nine

Leaving Kilgarvan was likely the hardest thing that she'd ever done in all her twenty-one years. She had never stayed away from home for more than a few days and was beginning to feel nervous about sharing a flat in the city. What if Liam was right and she couldn't find a job, what would she do then? She still felt shocked and bruised after saying goodbye to Sean, not believing it was really over between them and wondering if she had ever really meant that much to him. Or had it always been that she was just a good catch?

Carmel knocked on the door that evening and came in and sat down on the bed, Ella rubbing at her eyes so that her sister-in-law wouldn't see that she'd been crying.

'Are you OK, Ella?'

Ella nodded.

'Honest?'

'I'm just a bit sad, Carmel, that's all. I've slept in this bedroom since I was a little girl. They're the same curtains and flowery pale blue wallpaper I've always had. It'll be strange waking up somewhere different.'

'I felt like that when I was getting married, Ella. Imagine, I shared a tiny bedroom with my two sisters, the three of us all on top of each other in an old brass bed. We'd torn lino on the floor, cracks in the windowpane and we still had our blackout curtains long after the blackout, and yet I missed it, missed them. I was used to a family living on top of each other, to never having peace and quiet. There wasn't much of that where I grew up. When Liam and I moved into the flat I was lonely at first. It seemed so quiet and I missed them all something awful.'

'You must miss them now, being so far away from England!'

Tears welled in Carmel's eyes. 'That I do, but we keep in touch.'

Ella had noticed that the postman Tim O'Reilly seemed to come a lot more regularly of late, Carmel racing to the door to greet him when he cycled up the path, her eyes shining when he took an envelope with an English stamp from his bulging postbag. Ella knew that it must be hard for Carmel, with her English accent and ways, for it would take time for her to make friends locally and be accepted by the neighbours.

'I wish you didn't have to go, Ella. Everything that has happened is so unfair. I tried to talk to Liam about it, tried to make him see sense, but you know what he's like. He won't listen!'

Ella sighed. She knew that Carmel was being

sincere, for even in these few weeks they had come to understand each other. A farm could be lonely, especially when the dark winter days came and the woman of the house was left to her own devices. If circumstances had been different she knew that the two of them could have, would have been close friends.

She hugged her sister-in-law tightly before she went to bed.

The next morning Liam drove her into Wexford to the train station. You could have cut butter with the tension that existed between them in the car, and she could tell by the set of her brother's jawline that he was not going to ask her to change her mind and stay. Poor Carmel sat embarrassed between them.

The Kilgarvan grotto was almost finished, the local stone carved to resemble something from Lourdes, a statue of the French peasant girl Bernadette looking upwards to the spot where the statue of Our Lady would be placed. Railings protected it and an altar rail of stone and iron was being erected around it.

'Sure you'll be back for the blessing and the special Mass,' murmured Carmel.

Ella doubted it. She had no plans to return.

In Wexford town the shops were only starting to open and the place had that drab sleepy early-morning air about it as the shopkeepers swept their front steps and threw buckets of cold water onto the path. Canopies were cranked open and window blinds rolled up in readiness for the day's business as they drove up along the quays. The sunlight lit up dusty windows and faded sale items.

Aunt Nance had given her the address of the flat that Kitty was renting and the big fashion shop that she worked in, in Grafton Street. Ella was nervous about leaving the life she was used to and the place and people she knew but her change of circumstances meant there was nothing to tie her to Kilgarvan any more.

She had put on a good light wool navy suit that she had barely worn and a pair of nylon stockings and low-heeled court shoes that would be comfortable for walking and the journey. The station was not too crowded or busy and Liam parked outside it. He lifted her case from the trunk of the car but didn't even offer to come inside with her, and bending down pretending to fuss with the stiff handle and her handbag, she refused to give him the satisfaction of seeing how upset she really was.

'There you go, Ella. Have a safe journey!' he said abruptly.

She watched him walk away and get back in the car, without giving a further thought to her or her situation. They might have been complete strangers instead of brother and sister.

'Promise that you'll keep in touch,' pleaded Carmel, holding her.

Ella just nodded, not really saying anything.

'You could come home some weekends, get the bus or the train down. We'd both love to see you.'

Ella wasn't even thinking of anything like that.

'Will you get in the car, woman, I'm blocking the entrance here!'

Liam hooted the horn impatiently to hurry her up. Carmel was all apologies for his rudeness and refusal to see her off properly; Ella watched as her brother and his wife drove away, Carmel waving farewell.

Ella purchased her single ticket to Dublin and joined the crowd on the platform. There was a delay on the line and she pushed to the front of the platform when the train eventually appeared, flinging herself into a window seat. She stored her case away and made herself as comfortable as she could. The carriage smelled of stale tobacco and was none too clean. Ignoring the people around her she concentrated on the countryside that tumbled past the window, the fleeting glances of back yards and farmhouses and derelict-looking building sites with their rusting piles of old machinery and the cluttered kitchens and scrappy vegetable plots that flew by. Every mile was taking her further and further from home and she tried to push thoughts of Fintra out of her head.

Wexford, Enniscorthy, Gorey, Arklow, Wicklow, Greystones and Bray, Killiney, Dalkey; mentally she ticked off the names of the stations that they passed. Glimpses of sea and coast tantalized her; children waved as the train rushed past them, some trying to run along and chase it.

It was almost lunchtime by the time they reached

Amiens Street Station in Dublin, crossing over the River Liffey. Taking her aunt's advice Ella walked as quickly as she could, dragging her heavy case along the platform, bashing into fellow passengers who stepped in her way as she rushed to find a taxicab. She gave the driver the address in Grafton Street where Kitty worked.

It was years since she'd been to Dublin and she had to admit she hadn't a clue as to her whereabouts. The first time she'd visited the city she'd been only eight years old, when her mother and father had brought Liam and herself to Dublin for a night, staying in a small hotel near the station. She remembered them visiting the famous Dublin Zoo in the Phoenix Park and the keeper letting her feed a sticky bun to a wrinkled grey elephant, its trunk snuffling her hand for crumbs. Liam had dragged them all off to climb Nelson's Pillar afterwards and her mother insisted on the reward of a large glacé ice cream in a tea rooms close by. The only other time she'd been was when Aunt Nance had insisted she join herself and the girls on a trip to Dublin to get an outfit for her cousin Constance's wedding. She recalled trooping along after Teresa and Connie and Kitty as they tried on almost every dress in Arnott's ladies' department. Her father had given her a twenty-pound note and told her to treat herself to something nice. How she'd agonized over the spending of the money!

She looked out of the window as the driver passed the Custom House and went along the city's quays, turning up by the gas company showrooms. Students thronged outside the gates of Trinity College, the Protestant university, and she caught a fleeting glimpse of cobblestones and its central courtyard. The driver slowed as they neared Grafton Street and its huge department stores, Brown Thomas on one side of the busy thoroughfare and Switzer's on the other, finally stopping outside Lennon's, the lifelike mannequins in the plate glass windows dressed in the summer season's bright colours and prints.

'I have to go in and get the key to the flat from my cousin, do you mind waiting a minute?'

The Dubliner shrugged his shoulders, taking up a crumpled newspaper folded open at the racing page. Ella hoped she could trust him to mind her heavy old suitcase though there was little enough of value in it save for her clothes and underwear. She knew that Kitty would be busy working in the fashion department but was hoping she wouldn't mind letting her have the keys so that she could deposit her case back in the flat.

There was an air of hush inside the door and soft carpet underfoot. Ella wished that she hadn't the yoke of a suit on her and as she could see some of the staff staring at her. Aunt Nance had said Kitty worked on the ground floor, so Ella scanned the counters all around her looking for a glimpse of her cousin's familiar chestnut hair and pretty face. There wasn't sight or sound of her and Kitty generally managed to stand out from the crowd.

'Excuse me,' she asked, approaching the woman behind the glove and bag counter just inside the door.

'Yes madam, may I help you?'

'Thank you. I'm looking for one of the assistants here, Kitty Kavanagh. It's just that I can't see her.'

Recognition filled the other woman's face and she gestured to Ella to move closer to her. 'Kitty's home sick, laid up with something. She hasn't been in since the weekend.'

Ella couldn't believe her bad luck. 'I suppose I'd better go to her flat then. Is she bad?'

The other woman with her manicured nails and well-made-up face was dismissive. 'How would I know?' she said, turning to attend to a customer intent on buying a patent-look handbag.

Ella managed to get back to the waiting driver outside and give him the address of the flat in Merrion Square, imagining all kinds of calamities having befallen her cousin. She already felt hot and flustered and was glad not to have to carry her case such a distance as the driver passed through Dublin's Georgian streets, the once-magnificent houses with their tall stone and redbrick façades and long narrow windows glinting in the afternoon sunlight now converted from town houses for the wealthy and aristocratic to flats and offices.

The driver slowed down as they tried to guess which one was Kitty's, finally depositing her near the railings by the granite steps leading up to Kitty's doorway. The number was missing, and paint peeled from the ornate glass and wood fanlight over the door. She studied the list of names scrawled alongside the hall doorbell, and recognizing what looked like her cousin's name and loopy writing she pressed hard. From somewhere inside she could hear the noise of the doorbell and awaited her cousin's appearance. There was no reply. She rang again and again, without success. A mounting sense of panic began to overwhelm her. What if Kitty was really sick, and gone to the doctor or even the hospital. What would she do then?

Eventually defeated, she sat on the steps ignoring the glances of passers-by and those who crossed over the road from the railed park opposite them. The smell of cooking drifted from an open window in the basement below, chips, fried liver and onions, bacon; an old woman in a faded overall glanced up at her suspiciously.

She had forgotten how hungry she was, and wished that Kitty would return soon and let her in. All around her people walked up and down the street, busy, minding their own business, not the slightest bit interested in her quandary. She rang the bell again and again. Where the hell was Kitty?

A good-looking young man took the steps two at a time and almost fell over her case. She watched as he let himself in with a key, and quickly managed to push the door in after him before it closed on her. Kitty's flat was up on the fourth floor, right at the very top of the house. She dragged the case up stair after stair, over the threadbare carpet from land-ing to landing until panting and breathless she reached the top. She knocked on the heavy wooden door.

The sound reverberated all through the big old house and Ella almost imagined she heard noises coming from inside the door. It was useless; she would just have to wait for Kitty. Annoyed, she rang again, and this time she definitely did hear something. She recognized her cousin's giggle.

'Open up Kitty! It's me, it's Ella!'

'Christ!'

Well, she heard that sure enough. Ella stood there on the landing as the bolt was pulled back and the door was opened.

'Ella!'

There was shock, surprise, and disbelief in her cousin's voice but no welcome. Kitty's long hair was all tousled and she was holding the door slightly ajar, clad only in a multicoloured silk dressing gown, her bar legs and feet and chest all exposed. She looked really flushed, her green eyes drowsy, and Ella wondered if she might be running a temperature.

'I thought that you weren't coming to Dublin for another few days,' sighed Kitty, trying to wrap the dressing gown round her modestly.

'Can I come in? I'm exhausted and I'm just dying for a cup of tea.'

Kitty wouldn't open the door any further and Ella wondered what her cousin was trying to conceal. It sounded like there was somebody else inside in the flat.

'Oh Ella, there's not a drop of milk in the kitchen. Be a pet and run to the shop on the corner and get some. It's only across the road.'

Ella was flabbergasted, but then maybe Kitty had been too sick all day to go out.

'Here, take my case and this time don't forget to let me in! Why didn't you let me in before?'

'Sorry about that, Ella, but I must have been asleep.'

She felt immediately guilty and without any further ado agreed to get the milk, arriving back to the flat a few minutes later. She was just about to ring the bell when the front door opened and a handsome man with wavy black hair and a sports jacket stepped through, nodding at her as if he knew her. She watched as he crossed over the roadway.

This time when she got upstairs, Kitty had the door wide open for her and welcomed her with open arms.

'Are you sick, Kitty? I called to the shop and one of the ladies there told me that you hadn't been in work for a few days. What's the matter with you?'

Kitty had led her into the large living room with its clutter of chairs and a sagging floral chintz-covered couch.

'I'm grand, Ella, I just felt like a few days off. I've been working my fingers to the bone for the past few weeks and I needed a little holiday. You know what it's like!'

Ella didn't. Farmers never got holidays.

'Here, let me show you the place,' offered her cousin, anxious to change the subject.

There were two small bedrooms; obviously part of the large room had been partitioned off. Ella's room had a small single bed, a mahogany wardrobe, a bedside table and a lamp. It looked out over the back of the house and a long narrow concrete yard. Hardly luxurious! Kitty's room was larger and looked like some sort of hurricane had recently blown through it as bedclothes and clothing lay scattered all over the place. The wardrobe was so full of clothes that the door could no longer close, and Ella was surprised to see a photo of Kitty and the man in her life on the bed stand.

'Isn't he gorgeous!' boasted Kitty proudly. 'His name is Tom Donovan and he's an engineer.'

The two of them sat on the bed looking at the photograph. Ella recognized the wavy hair and handsome face.

'Kitty! He was here!'

At least her cousin had the grace to look shamefaced. 'I just can't resist him Ella, honest I can't.'

'And you sent me off like an eejit for milk.'

'No, honest to God Ella, there isn't a sup of milk in the place . . . really!'

Ella sighed. Living with her cousin had seemed like a good idea, but now she wasn't so sure. She could see Kitty was thinking the same thing.

'Come on down to the kitchen and I'll make you a cup of tea and something to eat, you must be starving.'

The kitchen was tiny, a small poky room off the lower landing, the shared bathroom for their part of the house across from it. There was only one chair and Kitty put a cushion on top of an upturned orange box to create another seat. Ella sat considering what she was going to do as the kettle boiled.

Kitty pulled at tin boxes and two or three wonky-looking kitchen cupboards. 'I've eggs, bacon, tomatoes. The sausages are gone off, the bread's gone green. We'll have to get some more in the morning. I could do us an omelette, would you like that?'

Ella was so hungry and tired she'd have eaten anything. She watched as her cousin dropped a knob of butter into a blackened frying pan and set it over the gas flame. The eggs were whisked together deftly in a blue bowl, as the tomatoes and bacon were fried quickly. Seconds later the two of them gulped down portions of the fluffiest omelette ever.

'You know, tomorrow it will be your turn to cook.'

Ella looked up from her plate. 'Are you sure about me staying, Kitty?'

The other girl nodded. 'As long as you don't go tittle-tattling on me to Mammy and Daddy, agreed?'

They hugged each other.

'Now Ella, tell me about home and what the hell is going on at Fintra!'

Dublin 1954

Chapter Ten

Kitty Kavanagh was awake half the night talking with her cousin. She couldn't believe the state that Ella was in, all agitated and tense, and she looked absolutely wretched. Her mother had written her a long rambling letter telling her of the situation and warning her to be nice to her cousin. She'd always been nice to Ella, they all had. She could still remember that awful day when their mother had arrived home with Ella, and the news that her mother had passed away in the hospital and that she'd be staying with them for a few days. Even Slaney had been good and not demanded her usual attention.

Constance had explained to them all what had happened to Auntie Helena and how Ella would never ever see her mother again. They'd all cried for their cousin and the enormity of her loss, thankful for their own mother and each other. So Ella had in time become a part of their lives. Kitty supposed that growing up together, and spending all those hours and hours of childhood in each other's company, meant that she and Ella could be good friends without the burden and rivalry of sisterhood.

'Liam's a bastard to take the farm from you!' She couldn't help but speak her mind, seeing the misery and hurt apparent in Ella's face. 'You worked that farm and slaved on the place and this is your reward, him telling you to feck off and go to Dublin!' Kitty always believed in plain speaking and telling the truth, even if it did get her into trouble. She wasn't going to try and palaver her cousin and pretend this was nothing.

'It's just that it's so bloody unfair, Kitty! Farming and the land is all I know. I can't imagine myself not living and working at Fintra.'

'I hated the farm and the blasted farm work,' Kitty admitted honestly. 'Daddy was always complaining and trying to get me to do more. If he'd had his way I'd still be down there, queen of the milking parlour and married to some local farmer's son.'

'That wouldn't be too bad.'

'Bad!' Kitty sighed. 'It would be fecking awful, Ella! I'm not like you. Do you remember when Daddy used to make me walk the cows home in the evening for milking? I hated it! I'd pretend to be doing anything else but walking those stupid animals back to the parlour. Sure I'd walk nearly half a mile behind them, pretending that I hadn't a clue how this herd of dairy cows had managed to get out on the Kilgarvan road, and that I was only out for a stroll myself. One time I even managed to lose five of them and it took us hours and hours to find them. Daddy was like a lunatic, he nearly killed me! Another time one of the stupid yokes fell into the ditch and I had to wade in to get her and pull and haul her out of it. I was knee-deep in shite and stagnant water. The smell of dung off me was only desperate! And didn't I meet the Corish brothers on the way home and the jeer they made of me. I was puce! The youngest fellow used to hold his nose every time he ever saw me after that. I was mortified, Ella, plain mortified.'

Ella couldn't help herself laughing. And Kitty was glad to cheer her up. She had no regrets about leaving her farming roots behind her and had big plans to make something of herself here in the city and find the man of her dreams, who would when the time was right sweep her off her feet. It was tougher on Ella, because all her hopes and ambitions had always been tied up in the farm, and even Sean Flanagan had been part of that dream. Kitty hoped that Ella would start over again and make something of this new life in Dublin. She was welcome to share the flat and Kitty hoped that the right sort of job would turn up just when her cousin needed it.

Kitty had to go to work early the next morning but had run over to the shops and left a loaf of crusty fresh bread and a pint bottle of milk for Ella. For the next two days her cousin slept and slept, not stirring from the flat at all. Kitty made no comments, only ensuring Ella ate and supplying her with constant cups of tea and a mug of hot whisky at night to make her sleep. It was as if her cousin was sick or injured, she seemed so exhausted and tired.

Ella had little or no memory of the weekend, only that the blonde and dark-haired girls from the room across the landing, Terri and Gretta, seemed to be in and out of the flat all the time and she felt too tired to talk to any of them. On Sunday Kitty had made her get up and dressed and the two of them had walked through almost empty streets to mass at the church in Clarendon Street, Ella only realizing when Kitty passed her a cotton handkerchief that she was actually crying. Afterwards they had sat in the city centre park, St Stephen's Green, watching a mother duck and her young ducklings swim up and down the lake, as Kitty told her all the things they would do together and the places they would visit. In only a few short days she began to feel somewhat better. Gretta, who was petite, with large doe-eyes, was like a mini whirlwind in the flat and had shown Ella how to use the temperamental cooker in the shared kitchen; Ella had surprised Kitty and the girls by having a big saucepan of stew ready when they came home from work.

The four of them had sat down together at the

small table in Terri and Gretta's bedsit and shared it, burning their mouths on the potatoes and gravy. Gretta was from Cork and worked as a nurse in the nearby St Vincent's Hospital up on the Green, while Terri worked as a hairdresser in a salon on Wicklow Street. They were good friends and flatmates and were much the same age as Kitty and Ella though Terri was very glamorous and had her hair bleached blond like Marilyn Monroe.

On her day off Kitty had insisted it was high time that Ella saw some of the city and they'd walked down to O'Connell Street, the statue of Daniel O'Connell, 'The Liberator', at one end of it and the Rotunda Hospital at the other. They had climbed Nelson's Pillar right to the top getting a look over much of the city. Ella loved the way the River Liffey wound its way right through the city, the courthouses and Customs House and second-hand booksellers all set along its quays and the crowded bridges that spanned it.

'When the tide's out it smells something awful!' warned Kitty.

They went into the G.P.O. and Kitty posted a letter to her mother and bought some stamps. Ella could not believe the size and grandeur of the place and that she was actually standing in the same post office building where the men of the 1916 Rising had fought against the British Army. They looked in Clery's and Boyer's and Arnott's, just some of the big department stores, Kitting making Ella try on skirts and blouses and jackets, reminding her, 'You're not back in Kilgarvan now!'

She had tried on a figure-hugging black skirt with a kick pleat at the back and a matching jacket with a detailed collar.

'You've a great figure, Ella, and you should show it off more.'

In the mirror it made Ella look different, like a film star, all curves. Her stomach looked flat, and her neck seemed longer.

'You've got to buy it, Ella, it was made for you.'

Kitty didn't even bother looking at the price ticket but told the lady that her cousin was buying it. Ella got a shock when she had to take the money from her purse and pay. It was the most expensive piece of clothing that she'd ever purchased, she confided. Her old shoes and blouses would not go with it and Kitty coaxed her into buying a pair of tiny narrow-toed black shoes that she assured her looked divine, and a white blouse with a soft collar and a simple pink and white print one that would also go with it.

'No more Kitty, honestly I can't afford any more. You'll have me broke.'

In Switzer's Ella added a summer button-through dress in a bright print with a tiny waist and lovely full skirt, a simple pale blue cotton skirt which swung out from her waist that she just couldn't resist. Looking in the shop mirror she was pleased with the new impression she was trying to create.

'I always find that shopping is the best cure when you're feeling blue,' confided Kitty, linking arms with Ella as they went back out into the bright sunlight.

They shared a pot of tea and had a scone and a sticky bun each in Bewley's Oriental Café before walking home to the flat.

'I'll have to get a job. I'll start tomorow. There's bound to be a job that suits me.'

Kitty and Terri had said nothing, both of them remembering how long it had taken them to find work. There was no point disillusioning Ella by telling her how hard it was to find gainful employment in the city, and of the vast numbers of friends and acquaintances who had only recently gone to Liverpool and London and Manchester in search of jobs. Why, the only reason Kitty had an empty bed in the flat was because Maureen, the previous girl she shared with, had left to work in Birmingham. Ella had no work experience that was of any use to her in the city unless she was to consider going into service with a wealthy Dublin family, doing cooking and cleaning and running the household or minding children. However this sort of job held no appeal for her and would probably have meant living in.

'I'll find something! I know I will.'

Ella applied for positions in all the shops and offices and hotels without success and even tried the Civil Service and the hospitals, but to no avail.

They wanted someone with typing and shorthand skills, previous sales experience, a good reference from their last employer. She had none of these things. At night Kitty and the girls did their best to stop her getting downhearted, and kept telling her that a good job was only round the corner. Secretly, Kitty had made enquiries about the cost of the ferry fare to Liverpool and to Holyhead, and the train fare to London, as in all likelihood Ella would have to join the thousands of other emigrants going to Britain if she didn't get a job soon. De Valera's Ireland was in a terrible state, still caught in the grip of a post-war depression that was forcing so many people to leave the country they loved. They were deserting the drab farmlands and grey tenements for higher-paid work and opportunities in England and America.

On Thursday night, Kitty, bursting with excitement, flung herself in the hall door of the flat calling, 'Good news! Good news, Ella!'

Ella felt curious as to what it was all about.

'Sally Sheridan is pregnant!' Kitty could see her cousin still had no idea what she meant. 'She's expecting a baby and has to give up work. Lennon's won't employ married women, or women who are pregnant. It's written into our work agreement.'

'What'll she do?' exclaimed Ella.

'Well, she'll have to give up work and try and get that boyfriend of hers to marry her. But the good news is that Lennon's need a new drapery assistant. It won't be advertised until next week, but I told Mr Harry's secretary Denise that I already knew somebody who was interested in the job!'

'Me! You told her about me!' cried Ella, jumping up and down with excitement and kissing Kitty.

'You've an interview on Thursday at ten o'clock sharp. Remember, Mr Harry hates people who are late.'

Chapter Eleven

Terri had taken the scissors to her head and clipped at least three inches off her long brown hair. Her fingers moved deftly, lifting and angling Ella's hair as she snipped. 'Ella, this length and shape will suit you much better,' she promised. 'It will show off your bone structure and those huge brown eyes of yours, with your long eyelashes.'

Ella tried to appear completely trusting as the young hairdresser washed and combed and cut her hair, attempting to hide her dismay as pieces of it tumbled onto the bathroom linoleum. But already she felt lighter, more feminine even. Terry styled and side-parted it, creating a soft wave flowing over one ear. Ella looked in the mirror, scarcely believing the change.

'Please, let me!' begged Terri. She took a small pair of tweezers out of the bathroom cabinet and began to pluck and shape her eyebrows. Ella's eyes watered with the pain, but afterwards looking at herself she realized that it was worth it. Her eyes looked enormous and her face had more definition.

The girls made her try on every stitch of clothes she possessed and came down enthusiastically in favour of her new skirt and blouse.

'Classic!'

'Simple and businesslike.'

'Mr Harry doesn't like frills and flounces on his staff, after all, Lennon's is a quality shop!' jeered Kitty, lying stretched out on the bed watching her.

Sitting across from Mr Harry Lennon was slightly disconcerting as she could feel the sixty-year-old man's gaze rest on her crossed legs; she was glad of the sheer nylons that Kitty had lent her.

His partner Mr Sylvester, his brother, was writing down notes on a pad on the large mahogany desk, in front of them. Kitty had told her to lie and invent jobs where she had worked, but Ella was one of those people who was unable to fib without giving herself away, and decided not to even try. She was already nervous enough of the interview without making things worse by turning bright red and appearing shifty.

'I'm sorry but I've never had any experience other than farm work.'

Mr Sylvester wrote in his book and her heart sank.

'Whereabouts was this farm?' he asked, not even bothering to look up.

'Kilgarvan, sir, down in the Wexford–Waterford

border area. 'Tis only a small place but my father had a good farm there.'

'Did you like that work?'

'Aye, I did.'

'Our father was a farmer, from the midlands. You might not think it looking at the two of us, but we're both farmer's sons! So we know exactly what it's like to rise early and milk cows and feed animals and work every hour God gave us. There's no harder grounding for a young lad or lass.'

Ella didn't know how to respond, and decided to stay silent in case she said the wrong thing.

'Because of your lack of experience,' murmured Mr Harry, 'it would only be the most junior of sales positions that we could offer you. However, we do train our people well, ask any member of our staff and they'll tell you that.'

'There is a good pension scheme, sales commission and a lunch room at the top of the house,' added his brother.

She sat in the chair flabbergasted, wanting to throw her arms round the two rather plain-looking bespectacled men, but instead just shook their hands. She'd got the job! She just couldn't believe it!

'Since you do not have to work out a notice period with another employer, we would expect you to start next Monday. There is a uniform of grey skirt and cardigan and white blouse which is issued to all staff, and is expected to be kept neat and clean. Any additional blouses etc. can be purchased at a special price from Miss Ganley, our head of sales. You will start work on the second floor, in our ladies' lingerie department.'

'Welcome to Lennon's!' they both added in unison.

Kitty had shown her where everything was, and Miss Ganley had seen to it that she was fitted out in the correct uniform of a drapery assistant. She was put working at the very back of the shop on the second floor where the range of women's lingerie was discreetly displayed. Nightdresses, dressing gowns, bedjackets and silk robes all hung along one wall. Glass cabinets held a display of brassieres and Ella thought that she would go through the very ground with embarrassment the first time a customer asked to be shown one. Julia Cullen, the senior sales girl, cracked up with laughter watching her. There were undergarments of every shape and size and she thanked the Lord that she was not expected to fit the customers as that was left to Miss Byrne, her department manager, and Julia to do. She could not have faced measuring some poor girl's breasts and deciding what cup size she was, or trying to fit a rather plump woman customer into a roll-on girdle that refused to roll on. It was embarrassing enough to be handling knickers and discussing the benefits of interlocking stitches around the gusset, or lace trims.

'You all right, junior?' Julia enquired, when a rather irate customer kept insisting she was only a size sixteen when she was clearly an outsize. Julia came over and got her to try on a much larger size by reassuring her that French factories always marked their sizes too small, and having room to move around in the bed was a prerequisite of a nightdress.

'You'll learn,' she advised Ella, 'that the customer is always right, and if not, well, it must always appear that way.'

Ella was back and forwards to the dressing room, removing stock to be hung up, and spent the rest of her time folding and refolding things. The only thing that she could sell with any confidence was pairs of nylons, where girls came in and just rustled through the box, checking their colour and size, and then went and paid for them. She met Kitty briefly at lunchtime and her cousin gabbled about a dozen introductions, few of which she managed to catch. She was glad to sit down and rest.

The afternoon saw her snowed under as a bride-to-be and her mother spent over an hour assembling bits and pieces for the honeymoon. Miss Byrne sent her up and down to the stock room looking for garters and a broderie anglaise nightdress in a size ten, and boxes of co-ordinating lingerie that might appeal to the young lady, including a fitted corset of Italian lace. Two mothers-to-be were in buying nightdresses and nursing brassieres for their confinement; she hadn't even known such items existed.

Walking home to the flat that evening with Kitty, her feet ached and she longed just to sit down. 'My ankles are swollen and my feet are killing me,' she protested, holding onto her cousin, as she felt otherwise she might have flopped down on the pavement of Grafton Street and not budged.

'You'll get used to it!'

'I feel like I've been ploughing for hours, every bone in my body aches so.'

'It's because you've been standing in much the same position for most of the day. A lot of the girls have varicose veins you know. I'd bloody die if I get those yokes.'

'Why can't we sit down if we're not serving any-one, even just for a few minutes?'

'If you want to get the sack let Ita Ganley find you sitting down, she'd have you out of the shop in two shakes of a lamb's tail. The old rip's got legs of iron herself and expects everyone else to be the same. "Customers expect staff to be alert and attentive at all times," that's her dictum. The holy customer has got to be looked after no matter what! We could be hobbling and on crutches and it would make no difference to her.'

Ella laughed; she loved the way Kitty got angry and annoyed about things and was always so out-spoken. She envied her that capability.

* * *

Gretta and Terri were delighted for her and insisted they all go to one of the pubs in Baggot Street that evening, to celebrate the start of her new career. She was relieved to be a working girl just like the rest of them. They roared with laughter when they heard which counter she had been put working on.

'Now we all know where to go to buy our underwear,' slagged Gretta.

'Don't you dare!' begged Ella. 'I couldn't handle dealing with any of you lot!'

A group of handsome-looking young men up at the bar glanced over, one of them approaching the group of laughing girls. 'Hi Gretta!'

'Oh hello, Rob. I thought that you were on night duty tonight.'

'No. That was last week.'

Gretta introduced the final-year medical student to the rest of them and he encouraged his group of friends to come and join them. The girls shoved over making space for them all.

Rob generously ordered a round of drinks for the whole table and they all toasted Ella's first day of proper employment. She yawned as the night went on. She was tired. Back home in Kilgarvan she would have been wrapped up in bed with a hot-water bottle hours ago instead of sitting up late in a pub making conversation with some students. One of them, Mike, even insisted on her slipping her feet out of her shoes and examining them.

'Beautiful! Beautiful!' was all he kept saying but then he was after downing a few pints of Guinness.

Chapter Twelve

Ella felt like a right 'Amadan' handling the small lace items that made up a proportion of the stock of the lingerie department, with her big farmer's hands and unpolished ways. Often she felt uncomfortable with some of the customers, city women with their airs and graces and keen sense of style about what was the right thing to buy or not. She wouldn't have dared offer them any sort of fashion advice as she could see in their eyes that she only ranked as a country girl to them. By contrast she held the girls and women from the country in high respect and did her very utmost to help them. The farmers' wives who had saved their money and come to Dublin on an outing could sometimes only afford a day trip on the train, or if they were lucky would have booked into the Wicklow or the Clarence hotel for a short stay. Their husbands had usually managed at the last minute to find an excuse not to come and left them to the mercy of the

Dublin shop girls and assistants with regard to purchases of immense importance. She could sense their unease and guilt at spending hard-earned money, yet also the need to have some kind of recompense for the long hours and interminable toil of heavy farm work. Their faces were round and pink, eyes trusting like a calf's, their figures full and in need of corsets and girdles and deep brassieres. Blushing, they bought silk nightgowns and pastel-tinted negligees to surprise their husbands with when they returned home. Ella did her best to be truthful and honest with them, to sell them lingerie that would be worn and not hidden away in a drawer. They relaxed with her and saw her as a friend as she ran between the dressing rooms and the rails and drawers searching for something to suit them.

Their daughters were another matter and most of the country women were prepared to lavish a small fortune on these girls.

'Isn't she beautiful in that pale pink night-dress, miss!' they'd murmur proudly, as their daughters emerged transformed looking sophisticated and sensual in satins and silk. She fetched them glasses of water from the sink upstairs and made sure they had a chair to sit on when their feet were swollen from walking in new tight shoes. Miss Byrne, her department head, pursed her lips with disdain at such unfashionable women cluttering up the lingerie section but dared not complain as Ita Ganley regularly appeared and oozing with charm led them off to try on the latest fashion in a coat or knitted suit on the floor below. Julia Cullen was the one who took the bother to show Ella the ropes and train her in. They worked well together, helping each other out with troublesome customers, Julia endlessly patient with even the worst ones. They also covered for each other when they managed to slip away from Miss Byrne's eagle eye to the ladies' cloakroom for a few minutes' break and the chance to sit down and take the weight off their feet.

As the junior in the shop Ella earned the least in salary and looked wistfully at Kitty's pay slip and the commission she earned on sales of high-priced French and English dresses and suits, while Ella only managed a paltry amount on nylons and knickers.

'It's not fair,' she'd moan on wages day.

'You're only a junior, Ella. To be honest what did you expect?'

Gradually she had got to know most of the sales staff as well as the girls in the office and the delivery department. Lennon's were good to their staff who in turn were loyal to them. Mr Harry regularly came down on the floor and patrolled around seeing what stock was moving and what goods could not be shifted from the rails. He and Ita Ganley would walk along pulling items out and studying them, discussing whether they should reorder or not.

'Them two are very close,' whispered Julia.

'Close?'

'Aye, she's got a small house on the South Circular road, and the word is that he bought it for her and that he's a very regular visitor.'

'I don't believe you!'

She couldn't imagine the tall immaculately coiffed manageress bothering with Harry Lennon, who was small and balding and not the slightest bit good-looking.

'But he's married.'

'That'd make no difference,' said Julia emphatically. 'Not a tuppenny bit.'

The summer itself was grey and miserable, with the sun always hidden behind the clouds. More often than not it rained. Ella got used to bringing an umbrella with her every time she stepped out. the wet and damp were playing havoc with her new hairstyle, which would become a mass of waves if she wasn't careful. All the rain and gales and bad weather were causing widespread crop damage throughout the country, with whole fields flattened, and she wondered how Liam was coping, hoping that their wheat and potatoes had been saved. Cattle prices had slumped too.

'Will you give over Ella and stop worrying about the bloody farm?' joked Kitty. 'Honest to

God, you're as bad as Daddy and the rest of them back home in Kilgarvan!'

At the weekends Kitty and she and the rest of the girls went dancing. Racing home from work they washed and changed and massaged each other's feet and painted each other's nails and joined the throngs filling Dublin's dance halls.

The Minister for Agriculture had made a plea for girls like themselves to stay on the land and marry a farmer, promising them romance and adventure and a higher standard of living. Didn't Mr Dillon, the Minister, know that half the population of Dublin was farmers' sons and daughters, with not a bit of land to their name, forced to come to Dublin or emigrate to Britain, in order to keep themselves? Romance and adventure, they'd find that on their own.

'Rock Around the Clock' by Bill Haley belted out as they rocked and danced till the early hours of the morning, wrapped in the arms of men whom they might never see again, sweat pouring off them as they jived and twirled and sang along with the words. Having a good time was what it was all about and Ella tried to convince herself that this was the place she was meant to be and to banish all thoughts of the farm in Kilgarvan from her mind.

Kitty was madly in love with her engineer, while she was still broken-hearted, missing Sean. She thought of him constantly. Sometimes, when dancing with a stranger, the way he held her or took her hand reminded her of him and for a few minutes she could cod herself she was back in his arms. Sean hadn't bothered to get in touch with her or send her a note or letter despite her having sent him a postcard of St Stephen's Green with her address on the back. Likely he'd forgotten about her already and was courting some other local girl.

The whole country was in a frenzy of prayer and devotion as part of the Marian year celebrations. Perhaps prayer would turn the grey skies blue and halt the tide of emigrants leaving Ireland. Down in Kilgarvan there would be High Mass and a rosary celebration for the opening of the parish grotto.

Kitty was planning to go home for it and begged Ella to join her. 'Everyone will be there and Mammy really wants the both of us to be part of it. You know how religious she is and how she loves the rosary.'

Ella was adamant that she didn't want to go, no matter how much Kitty tried to persuade her.

'Ah go on Ella, Miss Ganley is letting me take the Monday and Tuesday as my days off and she'd probably let you have the same. It'll be a bit of a laugh going down home!'

Ella shook her head. She had no intention of returning home and seeing her brother or bumping into Sean.

'Come on, you know what fun we'd have in Rathmullen. Mammy and the girls are dying to see you. The summer is almost gone and we've been stuck in the city, the break would do us both good!'

'Kitty, tell Aunt Nance that I'm sorry, but I'm not going home, not yet.'

'Honest to God, you'd cut off your nose to spite your face so you would. Do you honestly think that Liam would give a damn if you came down or not!' Kitty sighed.

Ella didn't know what her brother thought of her, but it had taken her long enough to push the daily thoughts of Fintra to the back of her mind without going down and making herself feel homesick and miserable all over again.

'No!' she said firmly.

She had the flat to herself all weekend as Terri and Kitty were away and Gretta was doing an eight to eight shift. She had gone to eleven o'clock Mass and strolled around town on her own. The afternoon she had spent sunbathing in the garden of the square, stuck in a novel of Kitty's she'd found flung under the bed. It was written by an American called John Steinbeck and made her angry as she read about the migrant workers who came to California to pick crops and had no land of their own.

That evening she sat in and listened to the radio, glad to not have to do anything or meet anyone.

She and Gretta chatted for a while. The young nurse had returned from the hospital, drained of energy, having had an awful day losing two patients.

'It's the families are the worst Ella, they want us to wave a magic wand and bring them back, they don't realize it's final and there's nothing any of us staff can do!'

Ella fixed supper for them and discovering Kitty's hidden stash of gin poured them two glasses of it, watering it down with fizzy orangeade.

'I'm off to bed, Ella, as I'm on the same shift again tomorrow. Are you sure you're all right?'

'Go to bed, Gretta, I'm fine, honest I am. You're the tired one!'

She enjoyed the peace and quiet of the weekend on her own, for she was going to be busy in work the next few days as the autumn range of wool dressing gowns and winceyette pyjamas began to arrive.

She was delighted to hear Kitty's key turn in the lock. Her cousin flung a load of parcels and bags onto the table and floor the minute she stepped inside. 'Mammy's after giving me enough food to feed an army! You'd think there are no food shops in the whole of Dublin!'

'Well, what's the news and scandal from Kilgarvan? Go on Kitty, tell me.'

Kitty pulled herself up into the armchair, slipping off her shoes. 'I told you, you should have come! Teresa's getting married to that Finbarr fellow. You should see the ring he gave her, it's only gorgeous, Ella. Mammy and Daddy are thrilled. Teresa's so lucky, they'll be so happy.'

'I must write and congratulate her.'

'She'd like that. She was disappointed you didn't come home. Anyways we met Liam and Carmel at the Mass. The whole village and everyone for miles turned up. I've never seen such a crowd in Kilgarvan and the bishop was there too and every priest and nun in the county. Mammy was in her element with all the singing and praying and everyone joining in, and then when it got dark Father Hackett organized a candlelit procession to the grotto, Ella, and honest to God it was beautiful, all of us there with our candles and the statues of Mary and Bernadette all lit up. I've never seen the like of it.'

Ella felt a pang of regret about not going and knew her aunt would be disappointed in her.

'Were you talking to Liam?'

'I was in my hat!' jeered Kitty, 'but Carmel was asking after you. She's put on so much weight with the baby.'

'Baby!'

'She's due in a few weeks' time. Mammy said she's doing far too much work on the farm in her condition.'

Ella considered the news that soon she would be an aunt. Kitty gabbled on about Slaney who was secretly seeing some boy that lived in the town and

Marianne who was thinking about being a nun. 'Mammy said she'll go to the convent over her dead body and that it's just another of her fancy notions!'

Ella laughed. Any other mother but Aunt Nance would have been delighted to have a daughter become a postulant.

Kitty rambled on about the neighbours, the O'Gradys, who had bought a new field, and Uncle Jack's thoughts of buying a new car.

'What about the Flanagans?' quizzed Ella, desperate to know about Sean.

'He's left Kilgarvan, Ella.'

'Is he here in Dublin? Oh God Kitty, don't tell me he's come to work in Dublin?'

'No, no! Jim told Daddy that he'd emigrated and that his mother was fierce upset about it.'

Ella caught her breath. Emigrated! Gone to England or America like all the rest of them, gone without so much as a word to her! Why, she might never see Sean Flanagan again. He'd get lost over there, disappear for years like her brother and if she ever did meet him again in her lifetime he'd likely be married. She bit her lip, not wanting to cry.

Kitty stared anxiously at her. 'Did I say something to upset you Ella, is that it? I thought you knew about the baby already, cross my heart and hope to die.'

'No, it's not that, its . . .'

'Sean,' added Kitty, understanding.

Ella closed here eyes. 'I'll never see him again Kitty, and I don't know if I can bear it.'

The two girls hugged and held each other as Ella gave in to her emotions and bawled her eyes out.

Chapter Thirteen

'Please, please, please, Ella! Come on the double date as a favour to me! I've nobody else to ask,' Terri pleaded.

'What about Gretta?'

'She's on bloody night duty again, and Matron won't let her swap. There's nobody else, honest!'

'Oh that sounds good, Terri. You mean I'm the last resort.'

'Ah no, go away out of that, Ella! It's not like that at all. I just think that you might enjoy yourself. Bill had booked the table for four at Jammet's. It's one of the best restaurants in the city, my clients are always going on about it and I'm just dying to see it first-hand. Go on! Be a sport and come on the double date with me. Bill is as safe as houses, I promise he's a real gentleman, and I'm sure his friend Patrick is the same.'

Ella wasn't sure about it at all. The men Terri dated were generally somewhat older than she was with a bit of money in the bank. What if she didn't fit in or if this Patrick fellow was absolutely awful? She wasn't used to dating anyone and had little experience of men, yet Terri was always good fun to be with, and they'd get a slap-up meal in a good restaurant, no strings attached.

'Listen, if you really don't fancy him and things are going badly we'll make up some excuse to leave,' joked Terri, 'but not before we get to eat dessert.'

Reluctantly Ella agreed and found herself all dressed up, her hair piled up on her head, hair pins sticking into her scalp where Terry had coaxed her brown hair into a semblance of a photo she'd seen in some magazine or other. Much too much make-up and a pair of heels that she could barely stand up in completed the picture. Terri wore a one-piece figure-hugging dress in a rich lilac colour, her blond hair hanging loose, her flawless make-up accentuating her full lips and blue eyes.

The men collected them in a taxi and dropped them at the door of Jammet's restaurant, the manager welcoming them to the plush confines of its rich plum-coloured interior.

Bill Brady was forty if he was a day and Ella raised an eyebrow at Terry's latest choice. His dark hair with its greying sides was Brylcreemed back smoothly from his heavy-set face. His skin was tanned and his large frame dressed in a expensive handmade suit. He was originally from Cavan and still carried its strong accent; by his own admission he had made his fortune building across the water after the war.

'London's East End, the West End, central London, Notting Hill, Camden. You name it girls and Bill Brady's been there and built it!' he joked, puffing on a thick Havana cigar that made Ella cough. 'But mark my words, Dublin's the place to build now. The city's getting bigger, spreading out. People are fed up of those bleeding Georgian tenements. Housing and shops and offices, that's what they'll be needing now and me and my lads will give it to them.'

Patrick Ryan sat across the table from Ella smoking and watching her. At least he was younger, twenty-nine to thirtyish at the most, and appeared well off. The waiter came and Bill ordered a bottle of expensive red wine. The girls pored over the menu which was mostly written in French, the waiter having to explain what many of the items were.

Partridge and plover! She didn't fancy the thought of them at all.

Patrick advised Ella to try the lobster cocktail to start with and recommended Jammet's speciality, fillet steak.

'That'll be fine, thanks.' She laughed. It had been months since she'd eaten a decent bit of beef and she was actually starving.

The tables around them began to fill up, and Terri kept looking about hoping to spot someone famous or one of her clients.

Excusing themselves, the girls made their way to the cloakroom to freshen up before they ate.

'Well, what do you think?' urged Terri. 'About Bill, he's nice isn't he?'

'Yes, but he's a bit old.'

'Old! What are you talking about, Ella? I think Bill's just perfect, not like those boys you and Kitty usually hang around with.'

Ella sighed, dabbing a bit of powder on her nose, which was shining.

'Patrick's nice. He's much handsomer than I imagined. He and Bill do a lot of work together. They've bought some big parcel of land outside the city and hope to develop it. You do like him, don't you?'

It was far too soon to tell but Ella shrugged, just wanting to go along with Terry and not ruin a good night's entertainment.

Refreshed, the two of them sauntered back to their table. The meal was delicious and Bill certainly knew his wines as the one he picked was just perfect. In the background a pianist played softly and Ella had to admit it was the best restaurant that she'd ever been to. Bill and Patrick kept them entertained telling stories of jobs they had worked on. She reckoned that Bill loved to dramatize and over-exaggerate things; he had them almost paralysed with laughter telling them of the antics of some of the brickies and plasterers who worked on contract for him. Patrick was quieter and more sensible in his dark suit and immaculately starched white shirt. Still, there was something attractive about him with his tightly cut black hair and blue-grey eyes. The four of them were still going strong when they noticed that the other tables had begun to clear and they realized that the restaurant staff were getting ready to close, the pianist having slipped away without them even noticing. Ella collected her coat, not believing how much she had enjoyed the night. Patrick helped her to put it on before she stepped out into the cool night air.

'Will I see you again?' he asked as they stood on the step waiting for Terri and Bill to come out.

Ella wasn't sure what to say. She had never imagined herself meeting anyone like Patrick and being attracted to him.

'Yes.' She found herself agreeing to see him five days later. Lying awake in bed that night she realized that she was actually looking forward to meeting him again.

Chapter Fourteen

Patrick had been true to his word and on the following Thursday evening he took her to the pictures. In the darkness of the cinema watching Humphrey Bogart and Lauren Bacall up on the big screen he put his arm around her. He smelled of one of those expensive aftershaves that they sold in Brown Thomas's and she found herself resting her head on his shoulder, wondering if he would kiss her. He didn't, and disappeared during the break to fetch two tubs of ice cream. She tried to concentrate on the film but found herself staring at his face in the dim cinema light, noticing the fine lines round his mouth and eyes. Escorting her home afterwards he kissed her on the lips, tracing the shape of her face with his long fingers, barely giving her a chance to respond before he said goodnight.

She thought that was surely the end of it and that she'd likely never see him again but he had turned up two weeks later and taken her to see

Dial M for Murder at the Olympia Theatre and for supper after in the Russell Hotel grill room.

'I was over in London for the past few days, I'm sorry for not getting in touch.'

She shrugged her shoulders, there was no need for him to apologize, she didn't own him or anything like that.

Terri and Bill were a different matter and were getting on famously, spending every spare hour they could together. None of them in the flat could believe that Terri had suddenly fallen hook line and sinker for the mature property man and was madly in love with someone almost twice her age.

'He's got everything that Terri wants,' explained Kitty, 'and plenty of it.'

Bill Brady was certainly not shy about spending his money and had already bought a mink stole for Terri and a small golden brooch, fashioned into the shape of a pair of scissors. She was thrilled with his generosity and adored parading around town on his arm, showing off.

'She thinks that she's like one of those Hollywood starlets, with a rich sugar daddy,' groaned Gretta. 'She's getting impossible to live with!'

Ella knew it must be hard for Gretta trying to get a few hours' sleep when she was off duty, only to have Terri come waltzing in at all hours of the night, and wake her up. Their bedsit was like a tip and Gretta, who was a very neat and tidy person, refused to clean up after her.

'That one wants a maid! Bill will have to hire her one,' jeered Kitty.

'Come to the dog races with us, Ella? Patrick is coming too. It should be a bit of a laugh as Bill has gone and bought himself a greyhound and we can all go mad and bet on it!'

Ella wasn't sure. She was tired after work and knew nothing at all about gambling. Still, at least she'd get a breath of fresh air and have the chance to see Patrick again. His visits to Dublin were erratic and she relished the chance of spending more time with him.

Pinto, Bill's dog, was like a long streak of grey misery and she'd nearly died laughing watching Bill almost burst a blood vessel when it had romped home winning its race at the Harold's Cross dog track. She and Terri collected their winnings from the funny little man behind the hatch who had given them such good odds.

'Beginner's luck, ladies! Congratulations!'

'I like this gambling lark, Ella,' smirked Terri, counting out the money. 'Having a flutter is well worth it. Beats giving a wash and a perm any day of the week.'

Ella looked at the notes in her hand, realizing that in a space of a few minutes she had won almost a full week's wages.

'Champagne!' Bill insisted the minute they crossed the door of the Cross House's public bar to celebrate. Patrick filled her glass again and again.

'Are you trying to get me drunk?' she teased.

'Maybe,' he whispered, kissing her neck.

The champagne tasted dry and strange and she wasn't sure that she liked it at all. Well-wishers came and joined their table, Bill demanding bar stools and chairs as the throng multiplied. They stayed there till late, drinking after hours, hoping an inquisitive Garda sergeant wouldn't suddenly appear at the door.

In the end Terri managed to persuade Bill to leave the licensed premises and the four of them got a taxi back into town, the driver dropping them off at Bill's home in Donnybrook. It was part of a terrace of fine-looking red-bricked houses that were close to Herbert Park.

'Sssh!' shushed Bill loudly, trying to get his key in the door. 'Don't wake the neighbours!'

They all went into the kitchen. One wall had been fitted with modern blue units and a gas cooker. Bill lowered himself into a sturdy fireside chair while Ella boiled a kettle for tea. She had a thumping headache already from the champagne and hoped the tea would ease it. Patrick kept coming and embracing her from behind, drawing her close to him. She returned his kisses, letting herself follow his lead, not caring as his hands ran up under her blouse. Bill seemed to have fallen asleep and Terri lay snuggled beside him. Her blond hair and procelain skin provided a total contrast to his rough looks.

'Bill said that I could stay tonight,' Patrick murmured suggestively.

She blushed, wondering what kind of girl he thought she was. She had no intention of letting things go any further with a fly-by-night good-looking fellow like him, no matter how attractive she found him. She wasn't that stupid and naïve.

'I'll have to go soon.'

A look between anger and disappointment flooded his face. 'Is there somebody else?' he asked, all the time letting his hands stroke the skin on her back and hips, circle after circle, the sensation of his circling touch making her feel giddy and breathless.

She thought of Sean Flanagan, imagining the way she felt when he kissed her and touched her and knew that if he had been standing in Patrick's place she would not have hesitated for one second.

'Is there?'

'No, there isn't,' she said, trying to convince herself. 'There was someone, back home, but that's over now. I haven't seen him for months.'

'Good,' Patrick said pulling her into his arms and kissing her so deeply that she could barely breathe and had to cling to him for support, both of them getting aroused. She managed to push him away eventually, her body protesting at the sudden change of mood.

'It's late, Patrick. I should be going! Kitty will be worried.'

He cursed her cousin.

Ella retrieved her coat from the back of a chair and set about leaving, not trusting herself to be another hour in Patrick's company, she was so attracted to him. Terri was plastered and objected vehemently when she shook her and woke her up.

'What the feck are you doing, Ella? What the feck!'

'We're going home, Terri, that's what we're doing. Going home before we make absolute eejits of ourselves.'

'I'll fetch you a cab,' he offered, a gentleman to the end.

'It's all right, Patrick. We'll walk, it's not that far, and beside it will sober us up a bit. We've both got work in the morning, you know!'

Dragging her friend out of the house they walked the empty pavements just as dawn was beginning to warm the sky.

She had to be behind her counter in Lennon's in less than four hours' time.

Chapter Fifteen

The country girls who didn't go down home all flocked to the National Ballroom at the top of Parnell Square at the weekends. There they did not have to compete with the city floozies and glamour girls and felt they were on their own ground. Parish news and views were expressed and if they were lucky they might meet up with someone from back home. Gaelic matches and results were shouted out in Cork and Kerry and Galway accents.

Kitty had dragged Ella along, even though she was in no humour for dancing.

'Will you shut up whinging and whining, Ella! I'm not going to sit in that bloody flat of a Saturday night while Tom is down in Limerick, by the way, working!'

'He is working, Kitty,' she protested. 'You know he told you about it! Why don't you believe him?'

'He's been in every small town and arsehole

village west of the Shannon for the past six months and I'm getting mighty fed up of it!'

'It's his job, Kitty. You know that he's working on that new rural electrification scheme bringing the electric supply to every home in Ireland.'

'I don't give a damn about them and their power supply and magic electricity. Tom should be here with me of a Saturday night, not stuck in God knows where on his own. That's if he is on his own!'

'You don't trust him!' Ella joked.

'Of course I bloody don't! Do you think I'm mad? Do you trust Patrick?'

'Of course I do,' insisted Ella. 'Patrick sees me when he's in Dublin.'

'And what happens when he's not around?'

Ella blazed. 'Then I think about the next time I'll see him.'

'So he has you dangling on a string too!'

'No, it's not like that at all,' she protested, as Kitty joined the queue to put their coats in the cloakroom, girls shoving and jostling all around them.

The relationship between herself and Patrick had been going on for months. Some weeks she saw him and then again she mightn't see him for two weeks or more. He talked a lot about his business and the hard times he'd had working as a brickie in England when he was younger.

'I earned my money the hard way Ella, and you never forget that.'

He brought her to lots of nice places, and they were regular visitors to the Theatre Royal and the grill room of the Russell Hotel. They were growing closer and she looked forward to seeing him and being with him. He made her feel all grown-up and responsible. He mentioned little about his family but she assumed that was because he too had been hurt somewhere along the line.

The Ballroom itself was massive, with seating arranged on two sides of the floor. There was a soft drinks bar at one end and the band played at the other. The girls all congregated on the right-hand side and the boys on the left.

'This place is brutal,' murmured Kitty under her breath, 'I don't know why we still bother coming.'

The band stood on the stage, the lead singer trying to make himself look like Dean Martin with his tightly fitting suit and greased hair. The music itself wasn't bad, which was something at least. Kitty spotted a group of Gretta's friends from St Vincent's Hospital and they went over and joined them. June and Aine were hoping to meet up with two fellahs they'd met there the previous Saturday. The Cork girls were great fun and Ella loved the way they made a skit of themselves. They must have kept the patients in stitches with the way they went on. Kitty and Aine went up to buy a few lemonades as June and she perused the floor.

'Any sign of them?' Ella asked.

'The lads will be in the pub having a few pints

before they come along here, they'll turn up though. Jeepers, Ella, will you look at that shower of eejits!'

A few of the fellahs were dressed in the latest Teddy Boy gear but somehow or other didn't manage to carry it off, with their quiffed hair and tightly fitted trousers and narrow-toed shoes. She hoped to God that none of them asked her to dance.

'We'll be sober as judges by the end of the night,' Kitty joked, sipping the red lemonade through a straw. The ballroom had begun to really fill up and the band had managed to up the music tempo. A few brave girls had got up to dance on their own. They all ran their eyes along the opposite side of the wall trying to see if there was any talent. Ella almost jumped with surprise when she spotted Regina O'Grady, one of the neighbours from Kilgarvan.

'Look who it is, Kitty! I'm going over to say hello to her,' she said, excusing herself. Regina waved, obviously having spotted her too.

'Ah Regina, it's so nice to see you,' Ella said, hugging her. The two of them had played and gone to school together. Regina had moved to Dublin more than three years ago and they had lost touch.

'Ella, I was sorry to hear about your father, God rest him. I couldn't get back for the funeral but Mam and Dad said you gave him a great send-off.'

Ella swallowed hard, not wanting to discuss it. 'Where are you staying, Regina?'

They swapped addresses and Ella discovered that Regina was working as a secretary in the Civil Service. 'The work is dead boring but the pay is great.'

Standing there in the middle of the ballroom they talked as if they were just chatting over the hedge. Regina's friends returned and she introduced Ella to each and every one of them, all delighted to meet someone else from Regina's home town.

Out of the corner of her eye, Ella spotted that Kitty was up dancing with some good-looking fellow in a navy suit. The two of them twirled around the room, both good dancers. Kitty had her face thrown back, her chestnut hair picking up the lights, her lips open, laughing. She might not be the prettiest girl in the place but she certainly was one of the most attractive. Her partner had eyes for no-one else and held his arm possessively round her waist. Ella wished that a bit of her cousin's style and appeal had rubbed off on her. Kitty could attract men with just a flick of her eyes or a quirk of her smile.

'I see your Kitty hasn't changed,' joked Regina enviously. They both watched as Kitty passed by them again. 'Didn't I hear something about you and Sean?'

Ella took a deep breath. 'There was something, I thought we might have ended up together but after Daddy died everything changed and I ended up coming here and the last I heard Sean's gone away.'

'D'ye still fancy him or is there someone else?'

'Regina!' she protested. She was about to mention Patrick but for some reason held back from discussing him with her old neighbour.

'So that's the way it is. Sean Flanagan's still the man!' said Regina ruefully.

Aine and June's dates had turned up, two Cork men by the sounds of it; Ella watched as they clung to their partners during the slow set. She was trying to spot Kitty amid the crowds.

'Excuse me,' interrupted a fellow about the same age as herself, touching her arm. 'Would you like to dance?'

Regina didn't mind and Ella joined him on the dance floor. He was a good dancer, able to follow the beat of the music. She hated those types that hadn't a note in their head and were all out of step and she had to lead. Bernard was a nice guy from Drogheda and good company. She noticed he wore a pioneer pin. Gretta maintained a girl was always safe with a man who wore a pioneer pin, forswearing drink for life. Regina was up dancing too. Ella loved dancing and she and Bernard kept dancing for the night, only stopping once to go and get a lemonade. She was walking past the seats when she spotted Kitty, wrapped round the fellah she'd been dancing with, the two of them kissing deeply. During the slow set when Bernard held her she imagined it was Sean's shoulder she was leaning against.

At the end of the night the band played the

National Anthem, all the couples breaking apart and standing to attention facing the stage, as the lights went full on. The glare revealed sweaty faces and pimples and facial hair that had gone unnoticed in the dimness. Bernard asked her out for a date, but she was in no humour to get involved with anyone else and it wasn't fair on him.

'The next time I'm here we'll have a dance again,' she promised.

She had to hunt around to find Kitty, who was making a show of herself again kissing her man like there was no tomorrow. She had to walk home with the two of them and glared at Kitty, daring her to stop and do anything on the way back to the flat. She left them outside on the doorstep and fell into bed so that she was fast asleep by the time her cousin crept inside.

Dublin 1955

Chapter Sixteen

Christmas had come and gone. Ella worked in Lennon's till late on Christmas Eve, sharing a Christmas dinner in the flat with an equally exhausted Terri and Gretta. Kitty chased down home for the two-day break. The January sales were upon them before they knew it and during those dark winter days when Dubliners kept their coats wrapped tightly and old men coughed and spat in the street and the tinker children begged for pennies for coal, she found herself thinking about the farm and Sean. She had to put him out of her mind and decide to forget him. There were the odd dates here and there but it was Patrick who kept calling and was mad about her while she still dithered and dreamed about someone who was long gone from her life. It wasn't fair!

She had a Mass said for her father's anniversary, thinking of all the hurt and bitterness his will had provoked, and forcing herself to try and remember the good things about him.

*   *   *

Work was going well and while Eileen Byrne was away on holiday in Lourdes, she and Julia had the run of their department.

'Who'd she go on holiday with anyway?' she asked Julia.

'Eileen always brings her mother, the two of them are great company for each other and book into the best hotels and treat themselves.'

Ella thought it must be strange for Eileen not having a husband or a boyfriend and relying on her aged mother for company. All the department heads in Lennon's were middle-aged spinsters who had forgone marriage and families. Ella hoped to God that she wouldn't end up that way.

Summer in the city was getting her down as the whole of Ireland sweltered in a July heatwave. Their flat was like an oven and Kitty never stopped complaining as the staff of Lennon's were expected to look cool and calm despite the stifling heat that engulfed them. Ella was upstairs helping on the swimwear and beach wear seasonal counter, envious of the customers who told her of the French resorts and Irish holiday spots they were visiting.

'It's not bloody fair!' she moaned again and again. Kitty brought a large Japanese paper fan into work and every now and then resorted to fanning herself with the gentle air of a geisha girl. Lemming-like, every day at lunchtime all the shop and office girls congregated at St Stephen's Green to sunbathe and eat their sandwiches, Ella among them, stretching out on the grass trying to imagine the cooling breeze blowing in off the lake, down home. The farmers all over the country were already complaining of drought and worried about the harvest and many farm animals were suffering. Some poor man had even lost a number of pigs from heat stroke.

'Will you give over!' Terri jeered. 'Pigs my eye! Think of all the poor people burnt like sausages on the beach and all them roasted red like lobsters that Gretta has to deal with in Vincent's Hospital.'

The children from the city flats paddled and jumped in the fountains in their underwear, trying to cool down, the park keepers chasing them, everyone laughing and relaxed and not wanting to work.

On Sundays, their day off, they made excursions to Bray and Dunlaoghaire and Seapoint, avoiding the massive train queues at all the stations by borrowing two bicycles from Dessie and Con, the Cork lads in the flat below, and cycling like lunatics out along Dublin Bay. The beaches and seafront promenades were packed with day trippers and holidaymakers, buying Italian ice creams and sitting in the sun listening to local brass bands performing, the music sweeping out over the water. Ella envied the small children in their bathing suits splashing and shrieking among the waves to cool down, while they just paddled and swam demurely.

Back home Liam and she used to jump in the lake when the weather got too hot. She could remember her mother standing there shading her eyes from the sun, watching them. Only once had she joined them, whooping and hollering and duck-diving in the coolness of Lough Garvan, the two of them picking up her excitement and sense of freedom and all ending up staying in the water for far too long. Ella's hands and feet had been all wrinkled when she stood on the shore. Her mother had used Liam's shirt to pat her dry, and then stretched out on the grass to dry herself off, not budging till it was tea time.

Patrick surprised her arriving out of the blue at the flat one evening. Luckily Kitty and Tom had gone to the cinema so they had the place to themselves, which was rare. Ella quickly shoved a mess of clothes on the couch over on top of the pile Kitty had flung in her bedroom. Why did her cousin always have to leave the place in such a state every time she went anywhere? Thankfully her hair was clean and she was wearing a loose pale blue skirt and a strappy sun top that showed off her golden tan. Patrick whistled appreciatively as he pulled her into his arms. She put a new Frank Sinatra record of Terri's on and ran down to the kitchen to get some glasses. The gin bottle was empty so she used the bottle of Paddy Whiskey, which was kept for emergencies. She'd pay Kitty back later. Taking a sip of it made her eyes water.

'We need some water for it,' joked Patrick. Glasses in hand they sat down beside each other on the couch. It felt strange being on her own there with him; usually they went to restaurants and pubs or Bill's. They both were unaccustomed to it and Ella didn't know what to say. Touching his hand she realized just how attracted to him she was, and did not pull back when he asked her to kiss him.

Leaning over she softly kissed his face, his brow, his cheeks, his nose, his eyebrows and his closed eyes before brushing her lips against his, then forcing him to open his mouth as they drew breath from each other. Breaking away she kissed his neck and his throat and behind his ears, getting aroused by the heaviness of his breathing and the strength of his hand on her spine. She unbuttoned his shirt and kissed the centre of his chest before kissing each side, then moved down towards his navel inhaling the smell of his skin. His eyes were closed and she sensed what he wanted. She was not ready to go that far with him. She could see him laughing at her innocence.

'What am I going to do with you?' he whispered, covering her mouth with his and making her moan with delight as he began to kiss and suck at her neck and throat. His hands pushed up the light top; she helped him to pull it over her head and to open her brassiere. She loved the way he made her feel and the rush of pleasure his kisses brought as she pushed against him. She made no objection as he slipped his hand up her skirt. She wanted him at that moment every bit as much as he wanted her. She lay down along the couch.

'God, you are so beautiful, Ella. From the first minute we met this is what I've wanted, us to be together like this.'

Ella put her arms up, pulling him towards her. 'Do you love me, Patrick?' she asked.

'Ella, you know I do.'

He began to kiss her again, so slow and deep that she was almost dizzy as he began to move against her, his body dictating the rhythm that she was to follow. She moaned feeling him ease her skirt open and off her hips as he pulled her towards him, his own trousers open. His fingers, now more urgent, pushed at her lace knickers. Everything was happening so quickly, too quickly, she suddenly realized.

'No Patrick, stop. I'm not ready. I didn't mean this to happen.' She tried to push him off her, his full weight on top of her.

'Don't be scared. It'll be all right,' he promised. 'We're almost there.'

'No! I don't want to Patrick, please!' She tried to raise herself up from under him.

He looked at her face. 'I won't enter you, Ella.'

She could feel him push and move against her, her hips and pelvis following his, wanting to meet him, only the thin piece of lace between them. He groaned and lay flat against her as she buried her face in his shoulder muffling the unexpected sigh of pleasure that ebbed through her. They lay totally still together afterwards. She didn't know what to say or do.

He kissed the nape of her neck and ran his tongue along her lips. 'The next time will be better my love, I promise.'

'I'm sorry Patrick, I'm just not ready to—'

He silenced her protest with his lips. 'I can wait, but please don't make me wait too long.'

They pulled on their clothes quickly, Ella realizing that Kitty might walk in on them at any minute. She couldn't imagine anything worse. Sitting beside him she immediately regretted that she had been so stupid and longed to lie back down beside him again.

'I'm so bloody stupid, Patrick. I'm sorry.'

They were sitting down drinking tea and eating toasted cheese sandwiches when Kitty got back.

'You two have a nice night?' she asked innocently.

Ella blushed red as a beetroot and Patrick laughed aloud.

'I think I'd better be going and let you two get your beauty sleep.'

'Patrick, we're as beautiful as you get,' quipped Kitty, kicking off her shoes.

'I'll not argue that.'

Ella walked him to the door and kissed him passionately goodbye, not objecting when his hand caressed her breast.

'See you on Monday, Ella. I've to go down and check on the plans and meet the site engineers in Cork this weekend.'

She hated when he was away at weekends.

'We'll go somewhere special, I promise.'

'You two are thick as thieves,' remarked her cousin as they were cold-creaming their faces with Ponds and washing their teeth, in their pit of a bathroom. 'It's getting serious, isn't it!'

Ella was tempted to confide in her cousin, but was too embarrassed. Kitty was always so at ease with men and her own body, she would have thought Ella was a right eejit if she'd heard what happened.

She'd see Patrick on Monday and decide how they felt then.

Chapter Seventeen

The next few days in work all she could do was think of Patrick and herself and what would happen the next time they met. She was so obsessed with him she mixed up two delivery orders, counted the cash wrong and undercharged a customer six pounds. She was lucky that Eileen wasn't around to notice her mistakes.

'You're in love Ella, you've got all the symptoms!' teased Julia.

She couldn't wait till next Monday when she'd see him again; this time she was sure of herself.

'Where's he taking you this weekend then?' Julia enquired.

'He has to go down to the building site in Cork, but I'll be seeing him when he gets back on Monday. Julia, he's promised we're going to go somewhere special.'

'Are you going home to Wexford then?'

'No, I'll just stay in town.'

'Why don't you come out with me for a change?

It's ages since we had a night out together, it'll be fun.'

Ella wasn't sure, though Kitty had mentioned that she and Tom would be going to some engineers' party in the rowing club so she'd probably be on her own again.

'That would be great Julia. Yeah, I'd love to.'

Julia and she and another friend, Eva from haberdashery, had dolled themselves up to go out on the town, and were determined to go somewhere out of their regular routine.

'Let's do something different and get a taxi out to the Fox Grill. The races were on today, so there's bound to be a good crowd. They serve late meals and I know my brother and a few of his friends will be there,' suggested Julia.

Ella wasn't sure. She'd heard Kitty mention the place but it was a good few miles out of town, up near Dundrum.

'Be brave!' begged the girls and as they hailed a taxi Ella decided that it was high time she did something different.

The bar and lounge were packed and upstairs diners sat at tables chatting and listening to a jazz pianist in the corner.

'There's Kevin!' shouted Julia, waving madly at a table to the rear of the room, almost hidden by the wrought iron balustrades. She wove her way through the crowded room towards him, her fair hair flying. Julia and he were so alike they could have been twins, and Ella could see he had the same open friendly disposition as his sister.

'Have you come to help me spend my winnings, Julia?' he joked, ordering them all a drink.

The waiter brought more chairs and they joined Kevin and his friends, who all worked in the Guinness brewery. Ella was ashamed to admit she had never seen the place, and had only smelled the aroma of hops and brewing that sometimes pervaded the city. They were all starving and ordered straight away. The plates arrived overflowing with food, Ella eating something called scampi which, even though she hadn't a clue what it was, tasted great. The pianist was taking requests and played all their favourite songs.

They'd finished eating when Ella decided to pay a visit to the ladies' cloakroom on the other side of the room. The place was packed with couples and groups of friends of all ages. It was only when she passed the window that she spotted the table for two in the alcove. Patrick was sitting there; he had his back to her but there was no mistaking his handsome looks. He was meant to be in Cork, so what was he doing in Dublin? She was about to rush over to surprise him and say hello when she realized that his companion was a woman of his own age.

Her eyes were heavily made up and she had a beautiful face; the two of them seemed totally relaxed eating their meal and talking together.

There must be some explanation and she wasn't going to jump to suspicious conclusions about him. It could be all totally innocent. She was just about to go towards the table when Patrick raised his hand to pour out a glass of wine for his companion, the gold ring on his finger catching in the candlelight. Ella stood bolted to the spot. Humiliated and ashamed, she just made it to the toilet before she got sick, waves of nausea washing over her. She stayed there for what seemed an age, the concerned cloakroom attendant asking her if she was all right. Eventually she was able to return to the table, not daring to look in his direction.

Julia and Eva didn't notice and when an hour later two of Kevin's friends said they were driving back into town she was able to get a lift with them, pleading to Julia that she was feeling unwell.

'Are you sure you'll be OK Ella, that you don't want us to go with you?'

'No!' she said resolutely. 'Once I get back to the flat Gretta will be around so I'll be fine, Julia.' She'd tell her friend in time but not tonight.

The flat was empty when she let herself in, the air stuffy and humid, and she pushed the heavy sash window open, looking out over the street and square below. She was so ashamed, disgusted with herself for believing his lies and falling for his charm. She was an absolute fool to have imagined a man like Patrick would really care about her, a country girl from Kilgarvan. She never wanted to see or hear from Patrick Ryan ever again.

* * *

He'd called to the flat on Monday night, wearing his best dark suit and carrying a bunch of flowers. Ella had kept out of sight as her cousin opened the door. Kitty told him she was out and that she didn't ever want to see him again.

There was no explanation. He didn't deserve one.

Chapter Eighteen

She returned home to Kilgarvan a month later, Kitty having persuaded her that a few days down in the country would do her the world of good. The weeks after Patrick had been wretched and miserable and the girls in the flat were as kind to her as possible. She was afraid there might be a chance that she was pregnant and had confided in Gretta. The young nurse was as supportive as any friend could be, but confirmed it was a distinct possibility. Ella had barely slept a wink with the worry of it all. Thankfully her monthly had appeared and she realized what a lucky escape she'd had.

It had been more than a year since she'd been back to her home town and she felt anxious and tense as Uncle Jack drove them from the station. The house at Rathmullen stood surrounded by fields, the driveway edged with her aunt's border of tall Michaelmas daisies and orange clumps of spiky montbretia in the late August sunshine. There was a warm welcome for herself and Kitty and Aunt Nance made no recriminations about the length of time since she had visited and just hugged and kissed her as if she had only seen her yesterday.

'Welcome home, pet!'

She supposed that was what she'd always loved about the Kavanaghs: they had invariably treated her as part of their own family and not a visitor. Everything was still the same, nothing had changed, she thought as she tucked her feet up in the kitchen chair while Aunt Nance told her all the local news about the neighbours.

'The O'Gradys are in great form. The eldest girl married one of those O'Connell boys, you know the fellah with the big farm up along the New Ross road. Vi's delighted that she made such a good match.'

'Mammy, will you stop trying to match everyone up and giving us hints!' joked Kitty, who had cut a slab of her mother's cherry loaf to eat.

'Go on!' pleaded Ella who loved the way her aunt took centre of the kitchen floor and regaled an audience, despite the heckling of her daughters.

'Old Gerry the postmaster is retiring, though they say his niece has applied to take over the place. My friend Dorothy Murphy has just had her fifth grandchild.'

'Another bloody hint!' murmured Kitty aloud.

Ella laughed. She had forgotten how alike her aunt and cousin really were with their dimples and mischievous smiles and way with words.

'How are the Flanagans?' she asked innocently enough.

'Poor Una Flanagan isn't too well. She was in hospital there a while back and Fergus was sick with worry about her, but thank God Bernadette is very good to her. Jim and herself are making a great go of the farm.'

'What about Sean?'

'What about him?' her aunt asked knowingly. 'So is that the way it is with you, Ella girl?'

'No,' Ella denied, 'I was just wondering how he is.'

'Fergus tells me that he's working in some big car factory place in Detroit, loves it over there apparently.'

It was funny how being back in Kilgarvan made her think about Sean and all the times they'd spent together. She missed those days and though she hated to admit it to herself she still missed him, finding it hard to believe he was lost to her, so far away, making his fortune in America.

Aunt Nance carried the teapot over to the table and sat down, pouring out a cup each for them, automatically milking and sugaring the tea like she did when they were children.

'Now Ella, what about you? I hear things from Kitty but tell me yourself, is everything all right?'

How could she even begin to explain the mess she'd made of things! The stupidity of getting herself involved with someone like Patrick!

'Kitty told me about your romance and likely it's for the best that it ended.'

Ella glanced furiously at her cousin and hoped she hadn't told the whole truth about the situation. Kitty stared right back at her giving her the sense that there were some things Kitty was definitely not prepared to tell her mother.

'Yes, it's for the best, Aunt Nance, though sometimes it doesn't seem so!'

Patrick had hurt and humiliated her but compared to the feelings she had for Sean it was nothing. Kitty, changing the subject diplomatically, began to talk about the shop, telling funny stories about the customers and the departments they were in.

'You two are so bold, I don't know how that Mr Harry and Mr Sylvester ever hired you both!'

'Because we're the best sales assistants in Lennon's, that's why.'

'Honestly Aunt Nance, Kitty could sell a sundress to an Eskimo and convince them it was just what they needed.'

'And Ella could take the plainest Jane or biggest lump of a woman and make them feel that we had just the thing to suit them.'

'Kitty, run upstairs with your things and make sure that Slaney made up your two beds like I asked her.'

'You want to get rid of me!' accused Kitty, hugging her mother and giving her a big kiss. 'I'll get out of your way, don't worry.'

'She's the best in the world, Kitty, but she's got no tact at all!' laughed Aunt Nance.

Ella held the teacup in her hands.

'Ella, I think while you're down here, you should visit Fintra, it's your home. You must want to go back and see it, and see Carmel and Liam.'

She didn't trust herself to speak.

'I know that you and Liam had a falling out, but he's your brother, your only brother, and you can't let this fight get in the way between you. Ours are always fighting and do you know something most of the time Jack and I don't pay them the slightest bit of notice or get involved. They all sort it out in the end and make up. You'll see, it'll be like that with you and Liam.'

'Do you really think I should go, Aunt Nance? I always thought that I'd never want to see the place again. I suppose I felt it would pain me too much.'

'Carmel is dying to see you and imagine, you haven't seen the baby yet. Mary's such a little dote. She's a real Kennedy, no doubt about it, and from what Carmel tells me she's already got her father's stubbon streak.'

'What would I say or do, Aunt Nance? I just can't go over like that.'

'Say! Fintra's your home, Ella! You don't have to say anything. You were born and raised there and Carmel and Liam aren't going to stop you visiting the place.'

'I just can't go over there on my own! Will you come with me?'

'Do you really want me to?'

'Yes, please, Aunt Nance.'

'I could go with you Ella, but I'm not sure that I should.'

Ella considered. She wanted to see the farm, the acres of crops, the livestock, and walk around the inside of her home. But what if she decided to change her mind and run away and hide at the last minute? She wouldn't be able to do that if she had her aunt in tow. Making a decision, she agreed. 'I'll go on my own.'

'Good girl, well that's settled then,' sighed her aunt, stroking her hand.

Slaney arrived in the kitchen like a whirlwind, flinging herself at Ella, hugging her madly. Her cousin had got taller and filled out since she'd last seen her. No wonder the boys were so interested in her.

'God you look great, Ella, real glamorous. The shorter hair definitely suits you and I love your new look. When I go to Dublin I'm just going to be like the two of you. Maybe I could share the flat with you and Kitty!'

Aunt Nance raised her eyes to heaven. 'I'm not sure that would be a good idea, pet!'

Borrowing Marianne's bicycle that week Ella cycled up through the village, and reacquainted herself with every favourite childhood spot, somehow in the process finding herself again. She pedalled out by the grotto. It was so still and

peaceful there and kneeling down she automatically blessed herself, and prayed for the people
close to her. Sky and earth and rocks provided the
perfect place of prayer, she thought, as she turned
the bike towards home. Her aunt and uncle and
cousins gave her the same love and support that
they'd always given her since she was a small girl
but it was Fintra and her own family now she
longed to see. She stopped along the roadside to
survey the Kennedy farmlands. She'd almost forgotten how beautiful the farm was, positioned
between the fields and the lake. Thick hedgerows
delineated the area of their lands. The sheep and
lambs that dotted the distant green fields and hills
looked clean and shorn, and she guessed that
Carmel and Liam had got the man she recommended to shear them. Below her the potato
stalks looked strong and healthy. Kerr pinks and
Queens ready to be gathered soon. The place
looked well cared for. No broken fences, no towers
of thistles or weeds. What had she expected? Rack
and ruin, in such a short space of time? A large
dairy herd moved about the rich green grass, heads
down, eating.

Getting back up on the bike she took the turn off
the road, the wheels bumping over the dirt and
gravel path that led up towards the house. She
stopped, hesitant. A line of washing caught her
eye, small dresses and cardigans and, like a ship in
sail, a canvas of white nappies that billowed in the
soft breeze. She wanted to see the baby. A long

time had passed since there had been a child at Fintra. Her father had always regretted having such a small family. He would have liked four or five at least but fate had granted him only two. Her mother had lost two other babies, one stillborn out in the middle of the fields. Liam and herself were always terrified of the spot, near an ancient alder. The other loss had happened in the hospital before she'd been born.

Dismounting from the bicycle she propped it against the wall, trying to get up her courage to knock or call at the back door. Walking around the perimeter of her home she felt as if she were an intruder.

'Ella! Is that you?'

Carmel was coming from the old outhouse behind, a baby dangling on her hips. She ran forward to greet her sister-in-law, all trace of awkwardness forgotten.

'Oh Carmel, she's beautiful, just beautiful.'

The baby stared at her, brown-eyed, her wispy hair much darker than her mother's.

'Mary, this is your Aunt Ella, say hello to her!'

The baby girl promptly turned her head away, hiding.

Ella couldn't believe how well Carmel looked, clear-skinned and with bright, almost sparkling eyes. Her figure was a little fuller than before, and her fair hair had grown down past her shoulders.

'You look wonderful, Carmel, motherhood suits you.'

'And you look stylish and sophisticated, Ella. Oh, I'm so pleased to see you. I hoped and hoped that you'd come down home and when you didn't reply to my letters I was so worried even though I knew you were sharing the flat with your cousin and Nance told me about your job.'

'I'm sorry Carmel, I should have written. It was just that so much had happened and I was so upset that . . .'

'It's all right, Ella.'

The baby lost her shyness and grabbed hold of Ella's finger, so Ella took the opportunity to stroke her beautiful soft skin. Falling into step the two of them walked across the yard, Carmel opening the back door and shooing a cat out of the way. It was only as she went inside that Ella thought about the dog. Monty must be somewhere out around the farm with her brother, for he'd never tolerate a cat taking his spot in the house.

'How's the dog?'

Carmel glanced up at her quickly. 'I'm sorry Ella, but the dog died last January. He was old and I suppose he must have missed your father. He was dead in his basket when I came down in the morning.'

Ella swallowed hard; so many changes.

The kitchen looked neat and tidy and was painted a soft creamy colour. The wooden presses were bleached and clean, the delftware on the dresser bright in the sunlight. A scatter of new cushions covered the old chairs near the fireside where they sat down.

'The place looks lovely Carmel, honest it does.'

'I did it all before the baby. I got some kind of notion about things, poor Liam didn't know what was up with me at all. I'm glad you like it.'

Carmel didn't offer to show her the rest of the house and she didn't ask.

She held the baby while her sister-in-law made a pot of tea. Mary, her little niece, pulled at her hair and played with the buttons on the front of her dress as she told Carmel about their flat in town and her job in Lennon's. Her brother was lucky to have found himself such a wife, kind and capable and able to help him around the farm.

'If someone had told me two years ago that I'd be out milking cows and sweeping up dung, Ella, I'd have thought they were crackers. Still and all I wouldn't change it.' Carmel's face suddenly blushed when she realized what she was saying. 'I'm sorry Ella, I didn't think.'

Ella rubbed her cheek against the baby's, trying to hide her feelings at seeing another female take over the role she had always assumed would be hers. No matter how much she admired the English woman, it still hurt.

The baby went down for a nap, her skin rosy with sleep; Carmel and she felt content just to sit around and chat.

'You'll stay for tea, Ella! Liam will be back soon and he'll be pleased to see you.'

Ella wasn't so sure. What would she say or do when she saw her brother?

* * *

Half an hour later Liam Kennedy arrived in. He had washed his hands at the sink and left his boots on the step before he noticed his sister.

'What are you doing here? Who invited you anyway?'

Ella could feel a deep feeling of anger flicker inside her. 'I came to see Carmel and the baby. I'm down staying with Aunt Nance and Kitty.'

'Well, you've seen them now, haven't you!'

Carmel ran towards him, imploring. 'Liam stop, please stop! There's been enough of bad feeling. For God's sake, Ella's your sister.'

Ella stood up. Her brother hadn't changed, not one bit. He'd got the farm. He'd got the land. He had it all and yet he was still that mean, angry young man who had fought with his father and refused to forgive him.

'I'm sorry, Carmel, but I'd better get back.' Ella stood up, excusing herself. She wasn't going to stay where she wasn't wanted. 'I'm sure Aunt Nance is expecting me.'

'No, Ella! Stay! Please stay! He doesn't mean it!' Carmel begged, grabbing hold of her arm.

The unfortunate thing was that Ella knew he meant every word of it.

'Liam, say you're sorry! Say you're sorry!' pleaded Carmel.

Liam got up and dragged his boots back on, calling, 'I'll not come back in till that bitch sister of mine is gone. This is my farm and tell her I want her off my property.'

Tears welled in her sister-in-law's eyes and from upstairs Ella could hear the baby start crying. She wasn't going to cry herself. Standing up she had a good look around the kitchen; likely she would never again see the place where her mother had cooked dinner and baked bread and read her stories from *The Children's Sunshine Annual*.

'I'm sorry, Carmel. I shouldn't have come. I just wanted to see you and the baby, and to see home again.'

Embarrassed, they hugged each other, then Carmel rushed upstairs to lift baby Mary as Ella slipped away.

She was so upset and shaky that she had to wheel the bicycle the whole way back to Rathmullen, not trusting herself to ride the distance.

Dublin 1956

Chapter Nineteen

On New Year's Eve 1956 Ella Kennedy found herself joining a huge crowd up at Christ Church Cathedral, in the old part of Dublin city, to hear the bells ring. All along the Liffey and out at sea ships sounded their horns to welcome another year, the crowd joining hands and singing 'Auld Lang Syne'. She tried not to think of those who were missing from her life but to concentrate on those friends around her now.

'Here's to another year!' toasted Gretta, kissing her latest boyfriend Brendan.

Terri and a crowd from the hairdressers were all hugging and kissing each other as if there were no tomorrow. Louis and Con and Dessie, the boys from the flat below, had come over to join them, fighting over who should be the first to give her a New Year's kiss.

Kitty was still down in Rathmullen, where Ella had spent two days of Christmas with her cousins. She'd managed to avoid bumping into her brother but had been thrilled to see Carmel pregnant again and little Mary when they called to see her cousin Connie.

Ita Ganley had promoted her to ladies' fashions that autumn, explaining to Mr Harry 'that she had a way with the country shoppers'. She was no longer nicknamed Junior, and was earning a higher rate of sales commision than before. Kitty was on suits, while she was at the opposite end of the floor selling coats and jackets. It was heavy enough carrying them up and down from the stock room, before even attempting to persuade a customer to try one on. She was fortunate that there had been early frosts and people were determined not to get caught out, buying the heavy wool and tweed coats that stocked the rails. There was no man in her life and she was content about that because she did not feel ready to get involved with somebody else just for the sake of having a boyfriend. There had been dates but nothing of importance or relevance, no-one to get close enough to hurt her. She sighed to herself, thinking of the new year ahead, hoping that it would bring change and fresh opportunities.

That spring she found her opportunity.

She'd always noticed the shop in Dawson Street with its tweeds and knitwear and collection of handmade clothes. It was slightly old-fashioned but was in an excellent location. The notice advertising for a manageress had only recently appeared in the window. Curious and interested, she decided to enquire about the position. The owner stood behind the counter, a middle-aged man with high colouring and white hair who was wearing one of the knitted waistcoats that she had spotted in the window.

'Can I help you?'

'Yes, you can. I want to ask about the job of manageress that you're advertising.'

He was obviously surprised by her age, but otherwise told her the kind of person he was looking for.

'I'd like to apply for it,' Ella said, deciding.

There and then Leo O'Byrne had interviewed her, asking her all about her work in Lennon's, her experience of the different departments, the stock room, and delivery rooms.

'This is a much smaller business, Miss Kennedy,' he told her. 'And to be honest it's not really a ladies' high fashion house.'

'I can see that, Mr O'Byrne, but what you have is of a very high quality. These tweeds are as good as if not better than Lennon's and your traditional knitted cardigans and sweaters are beautiful.'

Looking around, she could see the shop was stocked with an enormous array of handmade Irish goods. A lot of items were cluttered together behind counters and needed to be separated out and put on display in order to entice the customer.

'I'm afraid that the best salary offer I could make would barely match your present one, though naturally there would be commission on top of that. Also in a small shop like this there are extra responsibilities, things you take for granted in a big store.'

'Such as?'

'Such as opening up in the morning and sweeping the dirt from the front step and racing to get to the bank to make lodgements and locking up in the evenings. And there's no security or porters to help, it all just comes down to you! I need someone who is capable of taking charge if I'm away or busy at the theatre. I still do a bit of acting, you know.'

She smiled. She should have guessed that.

'Listen, why don't you have a think about it, and call round tomorrow at lunchtime.'

She didn't need to think about it. Jobs were few and far between, she knew that, but likely she wouldn't get the chance to work in a shop like Leo O'Byrne's again.

'I'll take the job Mr O'Byrne,' she said. 'But I have to give two weeks' notice at Lennon's.'

The news of her leaving Lennon's took everybody by surprise.

'Are you sure you're wise, Ella, leaving a large business like Lennon's for a much smaller shop?' Ita Ganley asked, concerned. 'Here you would have opportunities. Mr Harry and Mr Sylvester are good employers and you know in time you could well have ended up a department manageress or a buyer.'

'I know, but I think this is the right move for me, Miss Ganley. Honest I do.'

'Ella, do you realize how hard it is to find steady employment with a secure pension nowadays? Just look at all the girls and women having to emigrate to England to get work! Don't be too rash with your decision. You know, I'm quite prepared to tear up this resignation letter and it will go no further.'

Ella shook her head. She couldn't explain to the fifty-year-old manageress that she and her like were the very reason she was leaving. She didn't want to end up like them, standing behind the same counter day in day out, selling the same things, life passing her by.

Kitty thought she was mad. 'He's giving you less of a salary and you're leaving! You're totally cracked Ella, honest to God you are!'

'It's a good business Mr O'Byrne has and I'll be doing all sorts of things, Kitty. I'll only be a few minutes away from where you're working so we can still walk back and forth together.'

She finished in Lennon's on the last Friday of April, the staff banding together to give her a gift of a beautiful hand-embroidered blouse that she'd had her eye on for ages. Mr Harry came down and made a farewell speech, and when he'd shaken her hand said, 'I hear you're going to work for Leo O'Byrne. He has a good business there and no doubt you'll learn the ropes from him. Remember though that you're a Lennon's girl and we'd always be happy to have you back!'

She started in the new job on Monday morning, Mr Leo as she was told to call him making her more than welcome. The first thing he got her to do each day was to plug in the kettle and make him a strong mug of black coffee. There was no canteen or tea trolley and they took turns running to Bewley's and Fuller's for their cake or scone for the morning break. There was only one other worker in the shop, a gorgeous-looking man called Neil Patterson who worked half days. He was some sort of a writer and had already published a book. He was charming and good-mannered, with a thick curling head of dark hair and a moustache, and Ella and he immediately hit it off.

From day one Mr Leo asked her advice about everything. How much did she think the knitted stoles were worth? What colours did she think the young ladies would prefer for a wrapover cardigan? Most of the time he ignored her advice and just made his own decisions but at least he involved her, and by the end of the week he had become just Leo. One part of the shelves on the wall contained large bales of hand-woven tweed and they measured out the yards the customer needed against the brass measure on the counter.

'I'm making a good full suit, do you think that heather colour would suit me?'

The customers told her of their plans and busy

social lives as she held the materials against their skin colour or matched it with a blouse or skirt. Ella had first off done her best to tidy the enormous stock and display it to better advantage, without any interference from Leo.

The shop itself was on a busy intersection with plenty of passers-by and close to the Hibernian Hotel and the Shelbourne. Leo O'Byrne had a flat upstairs, which was very handy as when the shop was quiet he could slip upstairs for a few minutes. He kept a book under the side counter in which he wrote down all the names of good customers and any of their idiosyncrasies.

'My customers like to be remembered, Ella, so this little blue book ensures that I never forget somebody who has spent a lot of his or her hard-earned cash on these fine premises.'

The book made Ella laugh as Leo wrote down such funny things about people: the names of their pet animals, the names of their wives, the length of their arms, the nervous cough they had, the way they whistled when they talked. Leo seemed to notice everything.

'It comes from my theatrical training,' admitted Leo, 'when one is expected to know everything about the character one is playing.'

Her employer still acted and often asked her to listen to his lines as they folded jumpers and parcelled up orders.

'There aren't enough parts for men of my vintage,' he complained regularly, 'all they want nowadays is matinée idols and rock and roll stars and English schoolboy farce!'

From that first day working with him, Ella realized that she was learning more and more about the business. He showed her how to tot up the cash dockets and prepare the bank lodgements, often sending her over to the Bank of Ireland to deposit the money, things that would all have been done by the accounts department in Lennon's. Leo dealt with many of the suppliers himself and she loved seeing the latest knitwear designs they produced and the latest weave or colours they had developed. She went home from work exhausted, having helped Leo carry the parcels for delivery to the post office and then locked up.

Neil and she worked well together and the female customers absolutely adored him, flirting madly with him. Even Kitty, she suspected, thought he was cute as she often called to the shop when he was around, leaning on the counter to talk to him.

One Thursday she had come back from lunch when Leo had disappeared off upstairs. She was busy selling some tweed to a middle-aged lady who was a client of a designer called Sybil and had been sent in to pick the colours she wanted. She was stick-thin and immaculately groomed and wanted only the very best and the best of attention. Two or three more customers came in after her, and Ella did her best to pull out some sweaters for them to try on. There was no sign of Neil; obviously something had delayed him and she rang the bell connected to upstairs hoping Leo himself hadn't gone out. One customer was American and had a list of his large family and the sweater sizes that were needed. Excusing herself for a second Ella went into the back and raced up the internal stairs to Leo's flat opening the door and calling him.

'Leo! It's only me, but I'm packed out below!'

The cluttered living room was empty and she stepped towards the kitchen before noticing the bedroom door was ajar. She froze to the spot, realizing that she could make out the shape of two naked figures in the bed. Leo O'Byrne lay with his eyes closed and behind him Neil, embracing the older man. Puce with embarrassment, she stumbled through the flat and back down the stairs seconds later in a state of total disbelief as to what she had witnessed, serving the waiting customers as if nothing untoward has happened. Neil had appeared an hour later and made no mention of having heard or seen her.

Kitty, Gretta and Terri all roared laughing, tears running down their faces, when she told them that night over tea.

'Honest to God Ella, you must be the biggest eejit in Dublin if you didn't know what those two were up to!'

Ella had to laugh herself, thinking how she'd almost fancied Neil.

Chapter Twenty

She met Mac at a party in a flat in Rathmines that autumn, leaves tumbling from the sycamore trees that lined the street outside the tall red-bricked Victorian house in Dublin's famous flatland. Its former glory was now disguised as a warren of flats and bedsits that ran from the top of the house to the basement. The party was held on the second floor in a large sitting room. The fellahs that lived there worked in the bank and one of them was a friend of Kitty's.

'He looks after my savings account,' quipped her cousin.

Ella doubted that Kitty had a penny in the bank as she spent money as fast as she earned it. Still, it was nice of the young man to invite the two of them.

It was a different crowd from usual and the bank girls watched them with distrustful eyes. There were plenty of men and she supposed that they were all bank clerks and tellers. A walnut table, protected with a few well-placed mats, was laden with bottles of Guinness, whiskey, gin, a bottle of cream sherry and some wine. Over on the far side of the room two girls were engrossed putting records on the record player. Elvis Presley sang 'Jailhouse Rock' as the room began to fill. Their host Frank came over and hugged Kitty warmly, his arm sliding around her waist, which was accentuated by a wide black belt fitted snugly over the figure-hugging baby pink sweater she was wearing.

'You look great! Am I glad you could make it!'

Giggling, Kitty introduced the two of them and they shook hands politely. Frank was only a bit taller than her, but was nice-looking with a friendly face and a neat short back and sides.

'What's the party for?' asked Ella.

'It's for our flatmate Brian, a sort of farewell.'

'Is he leaving?'

'Aye, he's taking the boat on Monday. His job in the engineering works in Dundrum went and he fancies his chances in the big smoke, in London.'

Ella and Kitty glanced over at the handsome fellow with jet-black hair and a great look of the actor James Dean, who'd been killed in a car accident only the year before, a crowd of girls around him.

'The girls will be heartbroken when he's gone,' laughed Frank. 'He's a desperate man for the women!'

Ella made polite chit-chat with some of the other

fellahs and girls who Frank introduced them to. It grew warm in the room and she and Kitty moved over towards the table, feeling thirsty and needing a drink. Ella squirted red lemonade from the glass siphon into a glass for herself. Kitty did the same but had added a measure of Irish whiskey to the glass first.

'Go easy!' warned Ella, sipping her drink slowly and surveying the crowded room, hoping she might recognize a few people there. Kitty was flirting madly with Frank and she felt a right gooseberry. More and more people crammed into the party, the noise level rising; half of Rathmines must be there, she reckoned. She found herself moving towards the window where she nabbed a seat on the top of the radiator. Kitty and Frank disappeared off somewhere. Ella perused the rest of the partygoers, recognizing a girl from the hairdresser's in Wicklow Street where Terri worked and two fellahs that Kitty had introduced her to a few weeks back in the Gresham. She wished that she had dressed up a bit more for the party and put on a bit more of the warpaint like her cousin had advised; a smear of Gala lipstick and a flick of cake mascara was hardly adequate. Her hair hung to her shoulders and she regretted not pinning it up like most of the other girls there had done. It would have felt a lot cooler. Men liked women who made an effort. She supposed that was why she was left sitting like a wallflower on her own.

Mentally she groaned to herself as a few couples

began to clear the centre of the room of its chairs and table and footstool and began to dance, watching enviously as holding hands they got up and automatically fell into the dance rhythm together. Ella cursed Kitty for running off and abandoning her. Perhaps she should go and search for her; at least it was better than sitting there and looking so bloody stupid. The minute she stood up, her place was gone so she had no option but to find Kitty. A small kitchen was partitioned off from the main room and catching a glimpse of baby pink through the open door, she surmised that her cousin must be there.

'There you are, Ella! I was wondering where you had got to. Be a pet and help pass around these sandwiches. The bread helps to soak up the booze!'

Her protests were ignored as Kitty thrust a tray of chunky doorstopper ham and tomato sandwiches into her arms.

'Here, Mac! Meet my cousin. The two of you are to offer the sandwiches around!'

A tall man followed her out of the cramped kitchen. They went in opposite directions, passing the trays around. Out of the corner of her eye Ella was aware of his large frame clad in a sports jacket, and his wavy fair hair, as like herself she tried to force sustenance on the party guests. They met in the middle, abandoning the trays on the table.

'I'm Mac by the way, one of Frank's flatmates.'

Ella grinned. He had the bluest eyes that she had ever seen, with fair eyelashes and brows, and his skin looked lightly freckled from the sun.

'I think perhaps that we should dance and let those blasted sandwiches look after themselves.'

She concurred totally and let him lead her onto the dance floor.

Ella had always considered herself a good height, in fact rather tall for a woman, yet the top of her head was only level with his chin, he was so tall. Already she knew that she was attracted to him. His hands were wide and big, yet he was no farmer's son. They were too soft for that.

'I'm from the North,' he told her. 'From Northern Ireland, a place called Bangor in County Down. The bank sent me down to Dublin to work about six months ago.'

Mac leaned forward as she spoke, listening as she told him about Mr O'Byrne and the shop where she worked, and Kilgarvan, the place that she came from. His accent was strange and it took her a while to get used to it, but over the following few hours they exchanged all kinds of information about themselves. They grew tired of dancing and Mac managed to find an armchair. After lowering himself into it he pulled her onto his lap. She had no qualms about staying there. Kitty walked by them a few times and bar a widening of her gaze did nothing to jeopardize this new flirtation. She noticed that Ella could barely take her eyes off the man, he was that gorgeous, and the two of them looked wrapped up in talking to each other.

The crowds began to drift away, the front door of the flat opening and banging closed as more and more people left. Ella longed for the party never to end, so that she could stay sitting in the chair with Mac's arms around her and his warm breath on her neck.

'Ella! Come on! We've got to go home! It's almost four o'clock in the morning and I'm knackered.'

Kitty looked the worse for wear. Her hair had come undone and judging by the way her cousin was slurring her words she'd had a whiskey or two too much. It was high time they got going before Kitty started saying she felt sick.

'I'll walk you home, girls,' offered Frank, who was half supporting Kitty.

'Sure I'll come too,' offered Mac, much to her delight. 'Brian, we're walking these beautiful young ladies home,' he called to their emigrant flatmate who lay sprawled asleep on the couch.

The streets were quiet and empty as they walked from Ranelagh, up along the canal towards Leeson Street. The night was warm and Ella flushed as Mac held her hand in his. A few stray cats prowled along the canal banks in search of vermin, and the girls were glad of their male companions. Mac said very little, and Ella hoped that he wasn't bored of her company already.

'Here we are, lads!' declared Kitty giddily as she and Frank fell into a deep huddle of kissing at the doorstep. Embarrassed, Ella looked at Mac, biting her lip, unsure of what to say or do next, and searching for the keys of the flat in her handbag.

'I'd better be going in Mac, thanks for walking me home and thanks again for the party.' She cursed herself for jabbering like a monkey.

'Ssh,' he gestured, pulling her close to him and without further ado kissing her. Disbelieving, she returned his kiss, noting that she had already broken the cardinal 'first date rule'. He tasted of Guinness and Ella wished that the kiss would go on for ever. Mac stared at her and she could tell he realized what an effect he was having on her.

'Frank, come on and let these young ladies get to their beds!' called Mac.

Reluctantly, Frank and Kitty broke apart.

'Ella, I'll be in touch, honest,' promised Mac.

Disappointed that he had made no date with her, Ella managed to open the hall door and get Kitty inside. Yawning and tiptoeing upstairs, she wondered if Mac was just saying it, giving her the brush-off, or if they would really see each other again.

Ten days passed without a word from Mac. Frank Flynn had been round to the flat twice to escort Kitty to the pictures, and had made no mention of his flatmate. Ella hadn't the courage to enquire and tried to push all thoughts of the Northern Ireland man out of her mind.

The shop was busy as Leo O'Byrne was involved

in a play at the Gate Theatre and would disappear for hours on end to rehearsals. A colleague had made some comment about him playing 'a portly gentleman' and Leon had taken total umbrage.

'I certainly would not consider myself over-weight or out of shape! What do you think, Ella?' he asked her almost daily, studying himself in the large oval mirror in the centre of the shop. She skirted around the issue as best she could, knowing how sensitive he was and not wanting to hurt his feelings.

'I think that you are very handsome and fit for a man of your age, Leo, honest!'

Almost as soon as she said the words she realized that she had said the wrong thing. Leo had put himself on a diet and was living on meagre rations of boiled eggs, tomatoes and crackers which he had read about in some Hollywood magazine, and which a friend insisted would make him drop a stone in weight in no time. Ella's stomach turned at the smell of the hard-boiled eggs, which he unwrapped in the back of the shop. She was sure the smell put off many would-be customers from entering the store. Leo himself was cranky and cross with such deprivation. Neil was keeping out of his way and barely visited the shop, having enough of Leo to deal with at home.

A delivery of tweed from the weavers in Donegal had arrived and Leo left it to her to sort out, and stock the shelves. The colours and textures were wonderful, the deep purple reminding her of the colour of the heather that grew on the hills around Kilgarvan, and the greens capturing the way the sunlight lit up a field of grass, or the rich green of hedges and ditches. The weavers had mixed the colours to capture the very essence of the land. She wondered if the wearers would ever truly appreciate where the colours had originated. On such a wet miserable Tuesday, barely a sinner came through the shop door and she concentrated on checking the stock and stacking the bales of tweed carefully.

'Ella! There's a customer for you!' Leo called.

Annoyed that Leo wouldn't deal with it himself she came out front.

Mac was just standing there in his raincoat, dripping all over the carpet. 'I thought that I'd call in and see how you are.'

She gave a slow sort of smile, hoping that he didn't guess how excited she really was at seeing him. Leo leaned on the counter watching them.

'Are you doing anything for lunch?'

She wasn't about to admit that she had wolfed down three slices of brown bread and some cheese with a cup of tea, only twenty minutes earlier.

'No. I've no arrangements made, why?'

'I thought we might go around the corner and get a bite to eat, that's if you fancy it.'

She did fancy it, definitely, and grabbed her coat and umbrella from the stand in the back.

'Take your time, Miss Kennedy and enjoy your

lunch,' suggested Leo. 'I'm not expecting a stampede of customers today.'

She shot him a look of utter gratitude before she and Mac raced through the rain to the coffee bar in South Anne Street, squeezing into a narrow booth at the back of the restaurant. They both ordered, Mac selecting a dish of their famous spaghetti bolognese while she decided on the plaice and chips.

'How have you been?' he quizzed her, touching the tips of her fingers across the table.

'Fine,' she lied, 'just fine.'

She found herself staring at him, noticing that even in daylight he looked as good as she remembered, especially wearing the navy suit which accentuated his shoulders.

'I think Frank and Kitty have become an item.'

'Yeah, they seem to be seeing each other and I know Kitty likes him.'

They grinned at each other stupidly, in the noisy atmosphere of the restaurant, before talking about the weather, and work and Dublin, and even their favourite films. An hour later, they found themselves sipping frothy Italian coffee and reluctant to part.

'I'd better be getting back to work,' she said eventually, not wanting to spoil their lunch but also conscious that in spite of his goodwill Leo was expecting her.

Mac leaned over across the table towards her. 'There's a crowd from work meeting up in

Mulligan's pub on Friday night. Would you like to come along?'

She hesitated, unsure about joining his bank crowd in some pub or other at the weekend.

'Kitty's coming along, I believe.'

'Oh, then that's fine,' She was so relieved that Kitty was going. 'I'll come too.'

Mac settled the bill and helped her into her coat before walking her back to the shop. He was overdue at the bank himself and barely had time to say goodbye before leaving her.

Leo was in a flap and disappeared for a costume fitting the minute she returned, making no mention of Mac.

Kitty and she had dressed up like two dog's dinners to go and meet the boys in the pub on Friday night and had garnered a chorus of wolf whistles from the drinkers around the bar. Frank had laughed good-humouredly, but she could tell Mac was annoyed. They jostled in the crowd and eventually he found her a bar stool, on which she tried to balance herself. On and off Mac would come talking to her but the rest of the time she was left trying to keep up with the gossip of strangers. At the end of the night when the bar staff called closing time she was actually relieved. Somebody suggested going back to a house in Ranelagh but she had no interest.

'I've to work early in the morning, Mac, and open up, Saturday is our busiest day.'

He nodded, understanding, and walked her back to the Square.

She was in two minds about inviting him up to the flat for a cup of tea, but before she could say a word he had briefly kissed her good night and disappeared off into the darkness. Annoyed with herself and frustrated she genuinely doubted that she would ever see him again. She was just so awkward and self-conscious around him. Why couldn't she just act normally?'

Amazingly, the following week he took her to the Theatre Royal, where both of them were entranced by Dublin's top variety show. She in turn invited him to see Leo's play at the Gate. Her boss had distributed a number of free passes to his friends and Mac and she cheered wildly at the curtain call at they end.

'Bravo! Bravo!' they called.

'He's falling for you!' teased Kitty.

'Do you think so?' asked Ella, still very unsure. Mac was a Protestant, six years older than her and seemed to have had his fair share of romantic involvements over the years. He had only broken up with a girlfriend from Belfast a while before.

'God, of course he is! You should see the look in his eye when he sees you, and you know he gets dead jealous if another fellah even looks crooked at you.'

Ella had to admit that was true, Mac didn't like her flirting with other men or encouraging them.

When she thought of him she felt warm inside, for somehow or other Mac seemed to have killed the desperate loneliness that had engulfed her since she came to the city. Before, she had dreaded the weekends and the evenings when she came home from work to the four walls of the flat, and the grey city streets and walls that surrounded her. Mac had changed all that. The two of them were spending more and more time together, and Mac would arrive out of the blue and take her somewhere. He owned an Austin, and on Sundays the two of them often drove up to the Dublin mountains, walking hand in hand through the Pine Forest and on Three Rock Mountain, stopping off for chips on the way home. Kitty was no longer seeing Frank and yet was discreet enough to give them some time on their own in the flat, barely batting an eyelid when she caught them wrapped up in each other on the sitting-room couch.

Mac and she were becoming more and more intimate, but Ella was determined not to rush into something too quickly. Her growing love for Mac was too important for that. She knew he felt the same and respected her. Perhaps the memory of her disastrous affair with Patrick Ryan was still too strong. But Mac and Patrick were very different types of men, and she knew that Mac was decent and honest and good and kind, and very protective of her.

She hoped that Mac would be patient for although she was madly in love with him, she was nervous of taking the next step of becoming lovers.

Kitty was back with her old flame, Tom, and Ella watched enviously the ease with which her cousin enjoyed a mad passionate reunion with him.

'Frank couldn't hold a flame to him, honest Ella he couldn't. Tom and I are meant for each other.'

Some nights Kitty didn't bother coming home, and other nights Tom and she could barely contain themselves till they got to Kitty's bedroom.

At times Ella felt lika spinster aunt rather than a girl almost the same age as her sexy cousin. I'm such a fuddy-duddy prude, she worried, and I'll die a virgin.

Dublin 1957

Chapter Twenty-one

Leo O'Byrne was beside himself with excitement, as he had landed a major part in a new production of *The Merchant of Venice* at the Gate Theatre. The producer had seen him in the previous play and had now offered him the part of Shylock, which meant he spent every spare minute rehearsing. The shop was a port of call for every actor and actress in Dublin who had a part in the same production and Ella was kept busy trying to deal with customers as well as his theatrical coterie, and at the same time keep Leo calm and relaxed. The doctor had said his blood pressure was high, but that didn't deter him a bit from performing.

'I'll be fine, Ella, don't you worry.'

She did worry, hoping that he wasn't taking on too much. The shop window needed redoing and although she dropped a few hints to Leo, he always seemed to have other things on his mind.

'Do it yourself, Ella! I'm sure you can manage to arrange a window that will attract customers.'

She looked around at their stock and came up with an idea that she thought might work. Kitty was going down home to Kilgarvan at the weekend and Ella asked her to bring one or two things back to Dublin.

Monday was quiet, with lashing rain, sending people scurrying for umbrellas and shelter, many did not come into town at all. Ella was glad of the opportunity to climb into the shop window and set it up just the way she wanted it. She was proud as Punch of the window and blushed red when Leo and Neil both remarked on her artistic talent and design skills.

Mac took her out that night to the latest Elizabeth Taylor film and sitting there in the dark feeling happy and relaxed with him Ella realized that she no longer pined for the farm and the life she had before.

'Will you come back for coffee to the flat?' she suggested, too tired to go to a pub.

Mac agreed. He got on well with all the rest of the girls, now that he was considered her boyfriend. Arm in arm they strolled through the city. It was such a nice evening that throngs of people were out walking. In the distance she could see a crowd standing near the corner of Leo's shop. She hoped everything was all right.

'Mac, do you mind if we go down by the shop?'

There didn't seem to be an accident or anything. People were just clustered on the street corner, looking and talking. Was it her window that was causing the stir? She let go of Mac's hand and pushed her way through to the window. It was just the way she'd set it out. The old broken spinning wheel that she'd found in the storeroom, set up so that it looked fine, the hanks of coloured wool, the array of knitted goods and fine tweeds, and the fluffy white sheepskin that Kitty had brought her up from home. What was all the fuss about? Seconds later she spotted the scurry of movement. One rat, no, two! God almighty, she couldn't believe it. The rats were nibbling at the back of the sheepskin. It couldn't have been cured properly. Mac was doubled up laughing, tears running down his face as she stared horrified at her handiwork. She hadn't her shop keys with her and even though she rang Leo's bell she knew full well he would be at the theatre. He'd kill her. Likely he'd sack her or she'd lose her job over such an incident. She stood there for over half an hour and the rat pair cavorted in the shop window, crowds of passers-by stopping to stare at the spectacle. In the end Mac persuaded her to come home, and regaled her flat-mates with what happened. She was expecting sympathy and a bit of support from them and instead they all got hysterics laughing.

She was awake most of the night worrying and went to work early the next morning. The flat bell disturbed Leo as he was having breakfast.

'Do come in my dear,' he said, inviting her to

come upstairs and join him and Neil for a cup of tea and some rashers and sausages.

'Leo, something terrible has happened! There's rats in the shop window. I'm so sorry but I think they must have smelled the sheepskin I put on display and come up after it!'

Leo laughed so much she thought he'd burst a blood vessel and Neil had to fetch him a glass of water.

'I'm fed up telling the Corporation about the rat troubles we have under the street but they never want to know. This time they will have to pay a bit of attention, and mark my word, no-one is putting a foot in the shop till the rat-catcher has been. I just couldn't bear it!'

The story did the rounds and even the shop girls from Lennon's would drop in and ask her about the rats. She realized how good an employer Leo was, that he hadn't forced her to leave the job and still had faith in her abilities. She could never repay all his kindness to her.

'The customers love you Ella, and in business that's what matters.'

On the opening night Ella had sat with Neil, both of them a bag of nerves, needlessly worrying as Leo gave a magnificent performance as the wily old Jew. At the end of the show he got a standing ovation along with the rest of the cast, a rare enough phenomenon, from the Dublin crowd. Next day Dublin's newspapers carried rave reviews for the play itself and the masterful Shylock as played by the well-known Dublin stage actor Leo O'Byrne. Neil and Ella felt immensely proud of him.

As the weather improved her boyfriend Mac spent almost every Saturday from Easter on crewing on a yacht out in Howth, owned by his friend Alex Barry's father. Ella was busy working and would join Alex and himself later for a drink and if Mac was not too tired go for supper. His hair had lightened to yellow gold, his skin tanned with the sea breeze, so that he looked even more handsome than ever clad in his casual sailing clothes.

'Why don't you come out with us this Sunday, Ella? Dr Barry is away and Alex has the use of the boat,' Mac offered.

'Go on Ella! You'll enjoy it. My girl Margaret is coming along too.'

Ella had never been out in a yacht. Her only experience of boats was the small pontoon that she and her brother and father had used out on the lake. Growing up in Wexford she was well used to seeing sail boats and ships come in and out of port or along the quays but she had never actually sailed in any of them.

The thought of the sea air and skimming through the water was certainly appealing and she gladly accepted.

* * *

Terri made her tie her hair back in a neat ponytail. 'Otherwise it'll be all tangled and all over the place.'

Kitty provided her with a pair of dark sunglasses, which she assured her gave her the Grace Kelly look, and Gretta had brought her home some seasick pills from the hospital pharmacy. Copying Mac's casual look she wore a pair of sneakers and a pair of white slacks, with a warm navy sweater.

Howth was busy, packed with sun-seekers and those just out for a Sunday drive or walk. They spotted Alex out on the deck of his boat the *Mary-Rose* and Mac asked one of the other regular sailors to ferry them out to it. Up close the yacht was bigger than she'd expected, and she was content to let the men pull and haul at the ropes and sail as they got under way. Alex's girlfriend Margaret was down in the cabin unpacking sandwiches, cake, flasks of tea and a few beers that she'd brought along.

'We'll have a picnic later!'

Alex's younger brother John and his friend Owen were busy jumping around the place following orders. The boat slipped out of the harbour and catching the breeze began to move, swishing through the water at a great pace. Ella breathed in the salty air as the coastline became more and more distant. They sailed out past Ireland's eye and beyond Malahide and Skerries, where the beach was crowded with day trippers. She could feel the sun warm on her skin and stretched out along the deck as Alex and Mac decided to drop anchor. Mac came to sit in the sun beside her.

'If we're going to swim, we should dip in now before we eat,' Alex suggested.

Blushing, she watched as Mac and the rest of the fellahs pulled off their shirts and shorts and slacks to reveal their swimming trunks underneath.

'Are you coming in, Ella?' Margaret asked.

Ella thanked the Lord for Kitty's foresight in making her buy a flattering two-piece swimsuit from Lennon's. After changing down below she was greeted with a chorus of wolf whistles from Mac and Alex when she and Margaret stepped up on deck.

The water was cold, much colder than expected, and she gasped with fright as soon as she jumped in. The Irish Sea felt freezing even in late May, but she was a strong swimmer and once she got used to the temperature loved the freedom of swimming in the sea.

Mac swam along beside her. They swam together, further and further from the others who were duck-diving under the water.

'You look beautiful, Ella.'

She trod water as he swam up in front of her touching her lips with his. They kissed each other, breath after breath together. He tasted of salt water and she licked it from his eyelashes and nose and cheeks. She clung to him as he ran his hands down the length of her body, the two of them drifting together.

'I love you,' he said simply, as the waves undulated around them, pulling them closer and closer. Skin against skin, limb against limb.

'I love you too,' she admitted, glad that the words were finally spoken as they made love for the first time, the ease and naturalness of it surprising her. They could have stayed there for ever, the sun sparkling on the water, except that Ella began to feel the cold.

'Come on love, we'd better get back onboard, else the others will be wondering what happened to us.'

Mac helped her to climb back in up the ladder, and Ella wrapped herself in a large towel to try and warm up. Margaret had laid out the food on deck and they were all too busy eating to pay them the slightest attention. Helping herself to a mug of hot soup, she got a fit of the giggles watching Mac stuff himself with a ham sandwich.

The rest of the afternoon they sat and sunbathed; Ella felt much too cold to swim again. On the journey homewards she snuggled up in his arms, never wanting this perfect day to end.

'You tired, Ella?'

She nodded, yawning. It must be all the fresh air.

'I think it's time you were in bed,' he whispered in her ear.

An hour later they were back at the flat and she invited him in, thankful that Kitty would not be back for hours at the very least.

Chapter Twenty-two

Ella was madly and passionately in love, her relationship with Mac growing stronger by the day. She loved the way he touched her and held her in his arms and wanted to be with her all the time. She had a permanent smile on her face and both Leo and Neil had commented on it.

'What has that Mac fellow got that makes you look so happy?' Leo teased.

'She's in love, Leo!' Neil added.

She was most definitely in love and loved. Mac was a good lover, experienced where she was not, and once she got over her shyness and feelings of guilt she longed for the opportunity for them to be alone together.

Kitty was tactful enough and tried to make sure they had some time on their own in the flat. Her cousin and boyfriend got on really well together and she was glad that all her girlfriends liked and trusted him so much.

'He's a million times nicer than that rat Patrick,'

confided Gretta, 'to tell the truth Ella none of us were really gone on him. We all thought he was rather shifty what with all that working at weekends and travelling away!'

Gretta was doing a strong line with one of the hospital interns, a strapping six-foot five-inch doctor called Brendan Casey. They both worked such long hours and appalling shifts that they rarely got to see each other.

'Probably just as well since I'm breaking my rules,' worried Gretta, who always declared medical students were only for fun and flirting and nothing serious. Their flatmate had a theory that all medical students loved dating and falling madly and passionately in love with the nurses who stuck by them through exams and repeats but the minute they qualified usually went off and married somebody else.

'But Bren is qualified,' argued Kitty, 'and doctors always want to settle down and have huge families.'

'We'll see about that!' Gretta answered cryptically.

Ella wondered what the future held for herself and Mac. He had a good secure job with the bank and had been told he would likely be promoted in the coming year, and she was blissfully happy working with Leo. There was nothing to stop them settling down in time and living happily ever after.

'He's a Protestant,' Kitty reminded her.

She was annoyed with Kitty. She refrained from

making disparaging comments about her cousin's various boyfriends, and flirtations, and double-dating, so why did Kitty have to go and say things about Mac?

'I thought you liked Mac!' challenged Ella.

'I do, I adore him Ella, but it's just that he's a Protestant and you're a Catholic, that's all.'

Ella didn't know what her cousin was trying to imply. She was a Catholic and went to Mass almost every Sunday, though of late she had refrained from taking Holy Communion, as she couldn't bring herself to enter the confessional box in Clarendon Street and tell some priest about herself and Mac. She didn't believe she was committing a sin by letting her future husband make love to her.

Mac himself rarely went to church and did not seem particularly religious, teasing her when she blessed herself passing a church or stopped to say the angelus at midday.

Religion was not and would not be a problem. When the time came she knew that Mac would do the right thing, even if that meant agreeing to raise their children as Catholic.

Bangor 1957

Chapter Twenty-three

Mac invited her to go to the North for the weekend to meet his parents. They'd been going out now for over nine months and both knew that things were becoming more and more serious. At work, at home in the flat, in bed alone at night, Ella couldn't stop herself thinking about him. Morning, noon and night he filled her thoughts and Mac told her that he felt the same about her. He had gone home for a week at Christmas but otherwise had seen very little of his family, staying in Dublin most weekends to be with her.

Ella knew that Mac was the type who never rushed into things and that his invitation meant a big step with regard to their relationship. She felt almost sick with nerves at the thought of actually meeting his mother and father and brother and sisters. What if they didn't like her or approve of her?

Kitty couldn't believe it when she heard about the following weekend's arrangements.

'My God, Ella, are you mad going up North and meeting that crowd, 'tis like a martyr going into the lion's den. You're cracked, so you are!'

'Lion's den!'

'Aye, going up North and meeting his mother and family. It's very different up there compared to here, you know that. Their Proddy son with a Catholic girl! You must be a brave woman.'

'Shut up, Kitty! Don't even say such things. Mac's not a bit like that, you know he isn't. Religion never comes into it, never!'

Ella brushed off any negative comments. She was only going to meet Mac's parents and if they were even half as nice as Mac, they'd be all right. What the hell was Kitty going on about? Honest to God you'd think she was jealous.

Mac had given her very little indication as to what a weekend in his home town of Bangor would entail but she had managed to persuade Kitty and Terri to lend her some clothes. Two blouses, a polka-dot skirt, a fine knitted cardigan, and Terri's beautiful fitted pale grey trousers with the leather belt, she'd packed them all in the small weekend case. Leo had been very accommodating and at her request given her Saturday off although it was one of their busiest days in the shop. He had not asked her for a reason or demanded any conditions. He respected her privacy and she in turn respected his. As an employee there was a strict demarcation line that she would not cross with her employer, and she knew Leo also felt that.

'Neil will just have to come in and help. You are entitled to a day off if you really need it Ella, you know that.'

Mac had collected her at the flat at seven o'clock that Friday evening and she felt nervous as she climbed into the baby Austin. Mac had to concentrate on the roads as they left Dublin behind and got on the road to Drogheda. Ella tried to pump him for information, realizing suddenly how little she knew about his family. He usually said very little about them, perhaps because she avoided talk of her brother and father, but still he could hardly expect her to arrive in Bangor with almost no knowledge of them.

'Tell me about your sisters.'

'Well, Heather is fourteen and goes to the local grammar school. Hilary has just started working in the Civil Service, the education department. She's a right brain box so she is. Heather's one of those mad-on-ponies-and-animals-type girls, you know, the sort that says she wants to be a vet.'

She could feel her stomach churning with nerves at the thought of sitting around the table with all the people he cared about. What would they think of her!

'What about your mam and dad?' she pleaded.

Mac looked puzzled. 'They're married thirty years, and still seem happy. They're a great pair, Ella. I know that you'll like them.'

'And what did you tell them about me?'

'I told them that you are the beautiful country girl who has stolen my heart,' he joked, squeezing her hand, 'and that I'm mad about you.'

'Did you tell them that I'm Catholic?'

He didn't answer for a second and she knew by the way he tightened his mouth and jaw that he hadn't.

'For God's sake Mac, why didn't you tell them?'

'It doesn't matter, Ella, it won't matter at all.'

Judging by his expression, she guessed that it would matter, matter an awful lot, and that he just wouldn't admit it.

They drove up through Drogheda and Dundalk and Newry, the border towns, the shops shut and offices closed as people minding their own business settled down home for the night. As they crossed over the border itself, neat fields and hedges edged the roadside and she wondered if it was good land, rich land. The cattle looked well fed and there seemed to be ample grazing. Following the main road to Belfast they passed fields of flax and barley, Ella noticing the straight cut of the fields and the lack of 'weeds and wildness' as her father used to call it. The farmers up north were hard workers judging by the turn of their farmland and outhouses and buildings, for there was a marked order to things.

'We'll soon be there,' reassured Mac, running the palm of his hand and his fingers across her thigh enticingly, Ella wishing he'd stop the car and make love to her and forget all about the visit.

Mac drove into a neat row of red-bricked detached houses, one the same as another, with front lawns and short driveways and garages. They were shaped in a crescent, and his parents' house sat plum in the middle of them all, the number nailed to the gate pillar.

'Here we are!' shouted Mac, all excited, jumping out of the car.

Joyce McNeill greeted them with open arms, hugging her eldest son in welcome. Ella hung back, unsure of what to say or do.

'Mummy, this is Ella, Ella Kennedy.'

'Aye, the girl you were telling us about. You're very welcome, dear. Is this your first time to visit the North?'

'Yes, actually it is.' They shook hands, eyeing each other up and down.

'Will you come in the two of you and I'll make you a nice cup of tea. Peter, did you eat before you left or would you like me to fix you something?'

'We ate in Dublin, Mum, so don't be fussing, just sit down and relax.'

Joyce ran her fingers through her permed grey hair. She was tall and thin with bright green eyes and Ella thought that Mac looked vaguely like her. She smiled to herself; sometimes she forgot that Peter John was his actual name as nobody ever called him anything but 'Mac'.

The sitting-room door opened and Ella was aware of two blond heads and two girls throwing themselves at Mac.

'You're home! Why didn't Mummy tell us,' complained the younger one, turning her pretty face into a pouting mask.

'Heather, I want you to meet my girlfriend Ella.'

His two sisters suddenly turned their attention on her. Ella sat looking at them trying to appear nice and friendly and warm. She wanted them to get a good impression of her. They both introduced themselves and she could see they were the image of their mother; Hilary's eyes were the exact shade of green.

Heather sat beside her on the rose-patterned couch asking about where she had met Peter, and how long they had been going out. Ella felt unsure of what to say or do in case it was the wrong thing.

'Don't be so rude Heather, you're just embarrasing Ella.'

Joyce disappeared into the kitchen, and Ella glanced around the drawing room, which was filled with pictures of the family. An antique cabinet held a dainty tea service and on the sideboard a large silver try held an assortment of shining silverware.

Mac's mother emerged a few minutes later with a tray with a pot of tea and two servings of tasty Welsh rarebit. Ella could spot the pieces of chopped ham mixed in with the cheese and wondered what to do. Friday was fasting day and she was meant to eat no meat, but perhaps Joyce would be offended or embarrassed if she left it behind. Mac seemed to have no idea of her dilemma and was busy eating his own. She moved it around her plate with the knife and fork. However in the end hunger got the better of her and without a word she ate every bit of it.

'Please forgive my husband, Ella,' Joyce said, 'but he is at a lodge meeting and won't be home for an hour or so. You know how men get caught up in these things.'

Ella nodded and stifled a yawn. She could tell that Joyce was anxious to talk to Mac on her own and have some time with her son. About twenty minutes later she made her excuses and disappeared off to bed leaving the two of them together.

'You're sleeping in my bedroom,' Heather told her, helping her to carry her things upstairs. 'Mummy said that I'm to have the camp bed and put up in Hilary's room. It's awful sharing with Hilary. She sits up reading books all night with the light on. Mummy and Daddy think she's studying but really she's reading all these lovey-dovey romance books. Do you read those sort of books?'

Ella shook her head.

Heather showed her where everything was before disappearing to her sister's room.

Ella climbed into bed and pulled the blankets up around her as she tried to relax. The wall opposite her bed was covered in photos and cut-outs from newspapers and magazines, all of horses. The child was obviously obsessed with them. A row of rosettes, pinned to one side, were testament to her skill as a horsewoman and her love of the animal.

Her father had horses on the farm when she was young, a plough horse called Queenie and a mare called Sheba. She had learned to ride both of them, up along the top field and down by the river, jog, jog, jog, lifting up and down in the saddle like her father showed her.

She must have dozed off but woke about an hour or two later to the sound of raised male voices coming from the room below. Mac's father must be home. Embarrassed, she lay still in the bed, not wanting them to realize that she was awake by the creaking of the floorboards. A desperate need to urinate took over and in the end she was forced to go out to the toilet across the narrow landing.

'You couldn't go for one of your own! Not good enough for you were they!'

'Hold on Dad, don't say that!'

The voices floated up from downstairs and she couldn't help but hear them.

'You brought a papist under my roof, a follower of Rome.'

'She's my girlfriend, Dad! You haven't even met her yet!'

'A Catholic, that's more than enough for me.'

Despite the warm early summer's evening she shivered. A door banged downstairs, and she just managed to slip back inside the bedroom before Mac's father appeared on the landing.

She couldn't believe it, the two of them had been fighting and over her by the sounds of it. She dreaded the next morning, having to face the family and Mr McNeill. What the hell was she going to say or do? She stayed awake for an hour or two worrying about it, angry at Mr McNeill and hoping that Mac would slip into the room and make everything all right. She waited and waited but he never came.

Chapter Twenty-four

The sun split the heavens the next morning and Ella woke to the glimpse of a blue unclouded sky, when Joyce McNeill came in with a cup of tea and some toast for her, and pulled the curtains open. Pushing her hair from out of her eyes she gazed at Joyce, wondering if she had heard the row the night before. If she did, she made no mention of it.

'Peter and his father have gone off for a walk with the dogs. They'll be back in about an hour or so. I've put the immersion on for you, Ella, in case you'd like a bath or something and you can help yourself to some more breakfast when you get up.'

Gone off for a walk, that didn't sound too bad, perhaps they'd patched things up, or maybe the row had sounded worse than it actually was. All families had rows, God knows; she should know about that if anyone should.

Joyce was wearing a pale lilac-coloured twinset with a co-ordinating pale blue skirt. She was a very feminine woman and wore a dab of face powder and lipstick even at this hour of the morning. Ella sat up stretching aware that she looked a right mess compared to the pretty woman standing at the side of the bed.

The tea was weak, just the way she liked it, and she buttered the bread and spread it with some honey from the porcelain bee jar.

'Thank you Mrs McNeill, I'm not used to this.'

'Please call me Joyce, dear.'

'Joyce.'

The older woman smiled, smoothing the pale green sateen bed cover. 'Peter tells me that your parents are dead. It must be hard to be on your own, Ella, but I believe that you have a brother down the country.'

Ella didn't know what to say.

'It's hard for a girl growing up without a mother. My own mother died just before Gordon and I got married. I cried on my wedding day just thinking of her.'

Ella didn't know what to make of Mac's mother, here fussing over her like she was a daughter.

'Heather's riding in the parish gymkhana this afternoon, you and Peter might like to come along later and see her. She's quite a good rider actually. There'll be a tea tent and a crafts and floral display too. You never know, you might enjoy yourself!'

She was up and dressed by the time Mac got back and neither of them made any mention of the night before. Mac's father introduced himself to her in the kitchen and although he was civil and polite, she knew exactly what he thought of her. He was a shorter and sturdier version of his son, but totally lacking Mac's charm and good humour. He was a dentist who worked in a practice up the town with another dentist and was just about due to retire. He had visibly shuddered when he heard her accent.

'Don't mind him!' joked Mac, 'he thinks the world begins and ends in Belfast and its environs.'

She couldn't warm to Gordon McNeill at all and was relieved when Mac suggested they take a drive into Belfast to see the sights.

Bangor itself was a nice town, situated on the coast, looking out across the Irish Sea. Sailboats cluttered the seafront, flags fluttering in the breeze, the rigging making a pleasant, ringing noise. Mac was lucky to have been brought up in such a lovely place, and Belfast was within easy reach.

She was glad to have time on her own with him. 'I heard your father last night, Mac. I wasn't snooping or anything, it's just that I woke up and I could hear the two of you arguing.'

'Don't mind him, Ella! He's caught up in some antiquated bloody religious notion.'

'He doesn't like me!'

'Like you! How could he like you or not when he doesn't even know you? He's a bigoted old bastard.'

Ella stared out of the window, not knowing what to say or do. She should have listened to Kitty.

'The old man will come round. It's just that he's so bloody stubborn and always thinks that he's right. Everything is black and white with him and there's absolutely no middle ground.'

Ella sighed, unsure, hurt by his father's reaction to her.

Mac reached over and took her hand. 'What my father thinks about the two of us doesn't matter. All that matters is how we feel about each other.'

She knew Mac was right and leaned over to kiss his cheek. She had absolutely no doubts about his sincerity and was determined not to let anything else destroy this weekend with him.

Mac took her up by Stormont, which was where the Northern Irish parliament met. It was a massive structure, facing out over a valley. They walked all around it, admiring its fine architecture, which conveyed power and might. Belfast Zoo was situated close by it. They drove back towards town, Mac showing her Queen's University and the town's student area. Then they drove up through wooded hills, where gorse and heather and pines clambered over rocks and caves.

'I used to play here at Cave Hill, when I was a lad.'

'What sort of games did you play?'

'Och, all sorts, robbers and bandits were meant to have hidden in these parts. Me and the pals were always trying to discover their gold, or precious jewels. We'd spend hours searching and climbing. Other times we'd pretend to be pirates or bandits, hiding out, ready to fight to the death before being captured. At night there were meant to be ghosts here but us brave boys never stuck around long enough to discover them.'

Ella giggled. Mac seemed so big and brave and strong now, it was hard to imagine him as a small boy running around these parts.

At the very top of the hill she gasped at the sight of Belfast Castle, which had a stunning view over the city.

'Isn't it beautiful,' murmured Mac, kissing her hair and wrapping his arms around her. She could sense how proud he was of his own place and how much Belfast meant to him. If anything she loved him even more for it.

They ate lunch in a small tea rooms off Donegal Street, enjoying just being on their own. Mac let her have a look at a few of the shops, though she had no money to spend.

'Ella, I think that we'd better get going if we want to see Heather riding in the gymkhana.'

Ella agreed. It would be fun for Heather to have her big brother there to encourage her.

They arrived in the nick of time at Hollywood House, a large Georgian mansion surrounded by fields where the gymkhana was being held. There was only one rider to go before Heather's turn and Mac's young sister was a bag of nerves. Mac tried to jolly her along and soothe her anxiety as the other girl jumped a clear round, the crowd clapping appreciatively.

'Go on, Heather! You'll be fine, sure you and that pony are just made for each other. You know that Lucy'll jump her heart out for you.'

Joyce McNeill stood at the rope barrier watching anxiously as her daughter began her round, making a well-paced entrance and a good take-off at the first jump. Ella could see that the horse was one of that brave sort that was plucky and tuned to its mistress. It sensed the need for sureness and swiftness, jumping a clear round in no time. Heather blushed as the crowd cheered her efforts. Ella and Mac sauntered off having a look around the rest of the field. Ella was glad that she was wearing Terri's polka-dot skirt as it felt cool and fresh in the afternoon heat, while the tight-fitting blouse accentuated her figure. Mac slipped his arm around her. They treated themselves to ice creams and decided it was much too hot to bother with the tea tent. Joyce had returned to her position on the floral and garden display tent and they went over to admire her handiwork. Cut flowers, pots of flowers, intricate multicoloured displays: Ella had never seen anything like it. She had a sudden surge of memory, thinking of a glass jar on the kitchen table filled with wild fuchsia and montbretia that her mother had picked from the hedgerows around their farm. Her eyes almost welled with tears at the thought of it. Mac was busy playing the interested son and talking to a group of middle-aged women who obviously knew him well. Each was trying to impress him with a display of their handiwork.

'Ella, this is Mrs Robb and June Simpson, and my neighbour Adele Kane.' Joyce began to introduce her to some of them. Ella politely admired the spires of tall delphiniums, the dahlias, the pale pink roses and the rich red ones, wishing that she knew just a tiny bit about gardening. Crops were her speciality, but these fine beautiful fiddly plants were something of a mystery to her.

She smiled politely at the women, who she could tell were bursting with curiosity as to who she was. Mac took her hand pointedly and rescued her. 'Ladies, you will have to excuse us but I believe my sister may be jumping again and we wouldn't want to miss it.'

In the centre of the field Heather and a boy of fifteen were tied for second place and would have to jump off. Heather and Lucy did it, and Heather leapt up and down with relief when the gangly boy in the white shirt knocked over a pole. Mac knew what it meant to his sister, winning a blue rosette at the gymkhana to put on her wall.

'Wait till your father hears, he'll be delighted!'

Mac had scooped her up in his arms saying how proud he was of her.

'You're my lucky mascot,' she insisted. 'You'll just have to come along to all my competitions.'

Ella noticed that Mac made no promises; at least his sister wouldn't be disappointed. Tired, the two of them slipped off home.

His mother served high tea promptly at six o'clock. Mac's brother David and his wife Judith joined them. David worked in the engineering section of Harland and Wolff the world-famous shipbuilders, while Judith stayed home to mind their six-month-old baby son Gordon junior. Ella admired the little fellow, who made no objection to being passed around between Heather and Hilary and everyone, though she noticed the baby's eyes kept following his mother, no matter what part of the room she was in.

'He's such a good baby!' mumured Judith proudly and Ella couldn't help but envy her. Mac stared at her when she took the baby and she could see David nudging him, making Mac look embarrassed.

Joyce had gone to immense trouble, perhaps trying to impress her, and the best china was set out on the dining table with the Belfast linen tablecloth and napkins.

Cold ham, chicken and salmon were surrounded by a large bowl of potato salad and plates of rich red sliced tomatoes, lettuce and scallions from the garden, thinly sliced cucumber and jellied beetroot, a summer feast. Ella passed around the home-made soda bread and sipped a cup of tea. On the sideboard there was a sponge cake layered with strawberries and cream and Judith had brought along a cake with lemon icing. The room grew warm and Gordon McNeill opened the French windows to the garden. It was a peaceful family scene and yet Ella felt ill at ease, out of place. Judith was sitting near her and at least made some conversation as Hilary, on the other side, was just ignoring her.

'David and I were childhood sweethearts. We went to school together when we were young, and I used to live around the corner from them. His mum and dad and my parents have known each other for years and they were all delighted when we got married. David's the only man for me.'

'That's nice,' murmured Ella.

'Have you and Peter known each other a long time?'

'A while. We met at a party.'

'Peter's a good sort, very different from David. It's funny how two brothers can be so unalike.'

Ella glanced across the table where Mac and his younger brother were deep in conversation. David was dark like his mother but otherwise bore a remarkable resemblance to his father, even with the same mannerisms. Mac was much taller and more handsome and as always appeared relaxed. His easy-going manner was one of his most attractive features.

'Do you live in Dublin too?'

'Aye, I share a flat with my cousin and two other girls. I'm from the country originally, a place called Kilgarvan in County Wexford.'

'I was only down south once a few years ago. We went to a place called Greystones on holidays for two weeks. I remember the fishing boats and that there were two beaches.

'You'll be coming home next month, Peter? You'll not miss the annual march.'

'I have to see Dad, it depends on work and a few things.'

Ella could almost feel every eye in the room on her. She hadn't a clue what they were all talking about.

'It's the annual Twelfth of July march,' explained Judith. 'Gordon and Peter and their father usually take part in the big march through the town or in Belfast. They put on their suits and bowler hats and their orange sashes and there's marching bands and the drums and afterwards there's usually a big picnic with everyone bringing food and deckchairs. It's a big day out.'

'What's it for?'

'It's something to do with King Billy winning the Battle of the Boyne.'

'And routing the Catholic king and his followers.'

'Dad!' warned Mac.

'Oh all right then, routing his enemies! You'll come home for it!' insisted Gordon McNeill. 'You haven't missed a parade since you were a wee boy and you don't go breaking traditions like that, no matter what . . .'

'Gordon!' warned Joyce.

'I'll try Dad, honest I will.'

Ella studied the slice of strawberry cake on her plate, not fully understanding the discussion. It was a warm evening and the boys had set up some deckchairs on the back lawn. Hilary disappeared as she had made arrangements to meet a few friends and Heather occupied herself playing with the baby on a rug on the ground.

The grass was freshly mown and Ella thought there was nothing to beat the smell of cut summer grass. They made small talk as the sun set over the well-tended garden with its boxed hedge and rose bushes and tidy flower beds. Gordon McNeill seemed to make a point of ignoring her, burying himself behind *The Times* newspaper, and she wondered what she could have possibly done to provoke such ire. The others seemed oblivious to it, but she knew Joyce was embarrassed and apologetic.

On Sunday morning they all rose early.

'We're going to Sunday service in our local church,' explained his mother, 'but there's a Catholic church about a mile away if you should want to attend. I believe there is a Mass every hour.'

Ella would have loved nothing more than to stay in bed and sleep, pleading that God would understand and forgive her. But whether because of Mac's bigoted Catholic-hating father or the concerned look in his mother's eyes, she was determined to go to Mass. She got herself up and dressed early and was fasting for Communion, the fact that she took no breakfast drawing stares from the rest of the family.

Mac seemed surprised at her religious zeal but said nothing. He drove her to the church before going off to join his family at the Presbyterian chapel at the other end of the town.

'Will you be all right, Ella?'

'Mac, it's a glorious day. I'll walk back when Mass is over. The walk will do me good,' she said, kissing him goodbye.

The church was crowded, the large congregation joining in the familiar hymns as the priest began to speak in Latin. Ella prayed to God to make everything right between herself and Mac. The routine and familiar rhythm of the Mass made her feel relaxed and no longer an outsider. Another few hours and Mac and she would be back in Dublin and things would return to normal. The visit hadn't been that bad, maybe the next time things would be better and his family would get used to her. The people of the parish were good people, hard-working, decent people worshipping their God on a Sunday and she was glad that she had joined them. She wondered if any of them knew or were acquaintances of Gordon and Joyce's, but somehow or other she doubted it.

As she walked back she felt the first drop of rain and although she ran for cover got caught in the heavy summer shower that drenched the ground. Her blouse stuck to her and her skirt was clinging damply to her hips and thighs; her light sandals got soaked through. Her hair looked like rats' tails plastered to her head. She was undecided what to do and made up her mind to walk back to the house once the rain eased off, hoping that she could manage to get in and change before the rest of them returned. She had just turned into their driveway when she heard them arrive behind her.

Hilary and burst out laughing and Ella was tempted to punch the two of them with their perfect fair hair and slim-fitting summer dresses. Why did Mac have to have such good-looking sisters! He just ruffled her wet hair and told her she looked even more beautiful than ever and that he had a thing for bedraggled-looking country girls.

An hour later her hair was still a mass of waves when she sat down with them for Sunday lunch of roast lamb and potatoes. They had barely finished their dessert of strawberries and cream when Mac began to make excuses about leaving.

'I want to be on the road fairly soon, Mum, as it's a long drive back to Dublin.'

Ella went upstairs and packed the rest of her things away and checked to make sure that she had left Heather's room tidy. They said their goodbyes in the hall, his parents hugging him.

'You'll be up for the Twelfth?' his father reminded him. 'Sure that's only a few weeks away.'

They shook her hand awkwardly, making no mention of seeing her again.

'Drive safely Peter!' urged his mother.

Mac and she had only just got into the car when Ella remembered that she had left her washbag in the bathroom.

'I forgot something Mac, I'll be back in a minute.'

She raced back up to the front door, which his parents had just closed. She was just about to knock when she heard Joyce McNeill's voice. 'Thank the Lord that bloody little Catholic bitch is out of my house, Gordon. She'll not set foot across this door again!'

Reeling, she stood where she was, unbelieving. She could hardly breathe with the shock and the pain of it. She stood for a second not moving then she was aware of Mac sitting in the car, smiling, waiting for her. She turned back towards him. 'Honest to God I'm going daft! Sure I remember packing it earlier. Come on Mac, let's get on the road!'

Mac talked. She was too tired to talk, even to think.

'Ella didn't you hear me! I said the next time you

come up with me things will be better, the old man will soften and at least you and Mum seem to get on OK.'

She just nodded in agreement, knowing that there never would be a next time. Joyce McNeill had seen to that.

Chapter Twenty-five

The letter was waiting for Ella when she came home from the North. Carmel must have gotten one of the nurses to post it for her as it was stamped with the name of the famous TB hospital in County Wicklow. Ella couldn't believe it when she read that her sister-in-law had been admitted to the famous Oldcastle Sanatorium with tuberculosis and was in a room on her own in isolation. Poor Carmel, she always hated being on her own. What would Liam do with his wife in hospital and two small children and the farm to mind? Maybe Aunt Nance and her cousins and some of the neighbours might be able to help out, though even Ella knew how reluctant people were to get involved with a family where one member had TB. Liam had apparently had to scrub the house from top to bottom and had burnt most of the linen and some of Carmel's clothes in an effort to get rid of the infection. She thought of the two little girls and how much they must be missing their mother and how awful it must be for Carmel to be away from them. She imagined that she had troubles, but they were nothing compared to what her English sister-in-law must be going through.

'Don't you be worrying, Ella,' said Kitty, 'they're trying out all kinds of new antibiotic treatments for tuberculosis at the moment and the doctors and nurses down there know exactly what they're doing. They'll want to get Carmel well and strong and clear so she can get back home to the farm as soon as she's able. Honest, she's in the best place.'

Brendan, Gretta's boyfriend, had said almost exactly the same thing when he called at the flat and Ella tried to accept their assurances of Carmel's recovery. She knew Carmel loved getting letters and sat down and wrote a big long letter straight away, telling her all about her visit to the North but leaving out the bit about Mac's parents as Carmel had enough to be worrying about without her mentioning how much they upset her. She promised herself to try and write to Carmel once a week while she was ill in the sanatorium and visit her just as soon as she was allowed.

She'd confided in Kitty about what had happened at the McNeills', and of course Kitty had gone and told Gretta and Terri straight away too. Her flatmates were all appalled at the story as they sat eating a pan of burnt Denny sausages and lumpy mash that Terri had managed to ruin.

'What a wagon!' jeered Terri, chewing the blackened sausage.

'Poor you going to have such a pair of in-laws!' Gretta agreed. 'Thank God Brendan's mother died about five years ago and his father is so busy working in the practice down in Tipperary he's not time to be worrying about anyone.'

'What'll I do?' Ella asked.

'What does Mac say?' enquired Kitty.

'He doesn't say anything, because I didn't tell him.'

'Didn't tell him! They're his bloody parents!' Terri was incredulous.

'And don't you dare tell him either,' Kitty advised. 'Men all adore their mothers and think butter wouldn't melt in their mouths. No fellah wants to hear that the mammy who gave birth to him and raised him and loved him is an old cow, none of them do! For God's sake Ella, don't even mention it to Mac.'

'I suppose he won't believe you even if you tell him anyways,' argued Gretta. 'You'll be the difficult girlfriend, and she'll be the poor sweet innocent mother.'

'Mac's not like that!'

'They're all like that!' laughed the three of them.

'She's an old rip!' Terri was indignant. 'I wouldn't put up with it, but if you love him . . .'

'I do.'

'Then you have no option but to let herself and that old bigot of her husband get away with it.'

She was quieter than usual when Mac and she went to the pictures later that week to see Cary

Grant in the latest Alfred Hitchcock film, and wondered if he had heard any more from his parents, but if he had he didn't let on. She told him how much she had enjoyed seeing his home town but avoided any mention of them, and when he kissed her in the moonlight walking home through town all worries about the differences in their religions were pushed to one side. If it didn't bother Mac she wasn't going to let it affect her either. They were in love and that was all that mattered.

Mac went home for the Twelfth of July for four days.

'You sure you don't mind, Ella?'

There had been no mention of her joining him and even if he had asked she would have made some excuse or other not to.

'So you'll be marching and parading and the like,' she slagged him, wrapping her arms around him and nibbling the corner of his ear.

'It's our tradition,' he said seriously, pulling her into his arms and demanding a kiss in return. 'And some traditions should never be broken.'

'I'll be busy here. Leo and Neil are going to London for a few days to see some friends and have got tickets to some shows in the West End. You know the two of them, they'll be in their element while I'm looking after the shop.'

'London, that's a good idea, maybe in a few months' time we could go over and have a proper weekend away ourselves.'

Ella loved the idea of seeing London, and London with Mac would be even better. There she was worrying herself silly about things with Mac and herself, and here he was, planning to take her away to England for a break. She was a right eejit to think that Mac would ever let anything come between them.

Chapter Twenty-six

They couldn't help but hear it; every morning Terri was sick as a dog in the bathroom, vomiting while the rest of them stood outside on the landing pleading with her to let them into the lavatory. Often they had to go downstairs to use Dessie, Con and Louis's bathroom in the flat below, enduring the indignity of male underwear strewn everywhere and a filthy toilet with a urine-stained floor.

'For Christ's sake, let me in,' pleaded Kitty, 'before I wet my pants.'

The young hairdresser looked awful, her face pale and blotchy, and although Gretta hadn't said a word, and Ella and Kitty were trying to be discreet, they all had a fair idea of what was the other girl's problem.

Terri spent a lot of her time crying and refused to talk about what was going on, while Gretta warned them not to upset her and that she'd tell them in her own good time. For the first time ever

Ella noticed Terri's dark roots, as she hadn't touched up her hair colour and her nails were the same colour as Ella's own, totally bare and unvarnished. Terri was tired all the time and lay on the couch for hours with her feet up when she came home from work, too exhausted to go dancing or to the pub.

In the end it was Gretta who persuaded her to let her have a urine sample to bring to work to be checked, and when the result came back Terri had howled so loud that old Mrs Mulvey in the basement had come up all the way upstairs to ask if everything was all right. Ella wondered what Bill Brady was going to do about the child he'd fathered and any mention of him seemed to set Terri to crying even louder. Poor Terri had to face going into work in the hair salon every day and pretend nothing was the matter with her or else she'd lose her job.

She got hysterical one Sunday morning when they were getting ready to go to Mass. 'My mammy and daddy will kill me when they hear about the baby. I'm disgraced, so I am. Ruined!'

The three of them didn't know what to say or what advice to give and could only reassure Terri that no matter what, they were her friends and would stick by her and support her while she had her child.

'No, I'll go away. Go to London. I'll get the

mailboat over and no-one need ever know this has happened,' she codded herself.

'She's talking about going to London and getting rid of it!' worried Gretta. 'We can't let her do anything like that.'

'What about Bill?'

Ella had got to know Bill and had always considered him the type that wouldn't let a girl down. He'd always seemed decent enough and had no children, so surely he'd want this child.

'What did Bill say, Terri?'

'I haven't told him yet.'

'But why?'

'He's got a wife in England already!' she sobbed, crying afresh. 'As God is my judge, Ella, I only found out long after I got involved with him. They got married during the war and split up not long after when she went off with some other fellah. They never got round to getting a divorce so I can't marry Bill!'

'But you've got to tell him!' all three of them insisted. 'Not in a pub, not in a restaurant but somewhere quiet where the two of you can sit down properly and discuss it, Terri.'

'You've got to glam yourself up and look absolutely amazing,' urged Kitty, 'before you drop the bomb and tell him!'

Ella was nervous for Terri. The country was full of homes and institutions for unwed mothers, forced to give their children up, and orphanages full of illegitimate offspring that nobody wanted.

She couldn't imagine Terri in one of those places.

Filled with trepidation the three of them disappeared off to the pictures leaving Terri in a sexy button-through dress with an off-the-shoulder neckline and a neat waist and full skirt, immaculately groomed, with the flat as clean as they could get it in a few hours, ready to break the news. They were all too terrified to go back and dillied and dallied deliberately in O'Connell Street, buying chips and window-shopping as they walked home.

'We're getting married!' Terri announced, hugging them all on their return. Tears of relief streamed down her face. 'Bill's got to organize a few things first and sort out his legal situation, but I'm going to be Mrs Bill Brady. They've already started divorce proceedings.'

Kitty poured them all a gin to celebrate and Terri sat on the couch with her mascara smudged and her eyes red, crying with happiness and relief that her child would have a father.

Terri and Bill got married in early October. Their wedding was a small affair held in Donnybrook church in town, with only a handful of guests. The priest had been in school with Bill and was glad to be of service in their dilemma. Terri hadn't wanted to get married down home where all the O'Mearas' neighbours would notice and remark on her condition. Her parents had been invited to the ceremony and small reception but had chosen to stay away; a brother who lived in Clontarf was the only one there to support her. Terri looked blond and radiant, despite being six and a half months along. The priest was kind and made no mention of her obvious condition during the ceremony. Ella, Kitty and Gretta were all on tenterhooks until Bill and Terri had both said the words 'I do'.

'Thank God they're married!' sighed Kitty.

Ten of them had lunch in the Shelbourne afterwards, and Ella thought she had never seen a prettier bride. Bill's brother and his wife had joined them and they all toasted the happy couple with champagne. Only when Bill and Terri had waved goodbye and set off for their honeymoon in Killarney did it dawn on her that she had no idea of how Mac would react if she found herself in a similar situation.

Chapter Twenty-seven

Mac had offered to drive her the whole way down to the sanatorium in Wicklow to visit her sister-in-law.

'Are you sure you don't mind, Mac?'

'I wouldn't offer Ella, if I didn't mean it.'

She loved the way Mac said what he meant and did what he wanted and didn't play games the way a lot of people did, pretending one thing and doing another; also there weren't that many men prepared to give up a day off for an act of kindness. She knew from Carmel's letters that she was bored and fed up. Only next of kin were allowed to see her and since all her family were in Liverpool that meant that Liam and her uncle and aunt had been her only visitors. She had asked Ella to come down to the sanatorium as she wanted to talk to her.

'We'll stop off somewhere along the way for something to eat and if we get a chance have a bit of a walk,' suggested Mac, putting her coat and her basket of small gifts for Carmel on the back seat of the car. She loved the way he took charge of things and organized her and was actually looking forward to the day's outing with him. He was a good driver and she relaxed totally in the car with him as they drove along the country roads, empty on a Sunday morning. Visiting time in the hospital wasn't until the afternoon so they'd driven up to Enniskerry and walked hand in hand all along its winding country lanes. Ella savoured the autumn day and collected pine cones and chestnuts.

They discovered a small hotel in the centre of the old-fashioned village, overlooking the square, and joined the crowd of people there having Sunday lunch of roast lamb and mint sauce with potatoes and baby peas, followed by a large helping of the chef's delicious bread and butter pudding. Then they'd got back in the car and set off for Wicklow. Ella felt nervous, unsure of what to expect once they got there.

Oldcastle Sanatorium was visible from the main road surrounded by a beautiful grey stone wall that gave it a sense of enclosure and peace, separated as it was from the rest of the world. Mac turned into the driveway and drove up the wide avenue, flanked on either side by lush shrubs and neatly clipped hedges. The gardens and grounds were well cared for and they noticed a number of patients walking around them, exercising slowly. The main building itself was low with glass-sided corridors and wards that seemed to stretch in all directions; an older building had been converted into offices and a laboratory. Ella couldn't believe the size of the place and remembered how Carmel had said all the wards were full. Tuberculosis remained a scourge, with many people and families affected by the devastating diagnosis of consumption and the isolating treatment needed to clear it.

'I'll stay in the car while you visit her,' Mac said. 'You take your time, I've got the Sunday newspapers and a book to read, so you just take as long as you want with her, Ella.'

She kissed him, thinking how good and kind he really was, tempted to stay in the car park with him all afternoon.

'Go on!' he teased.

She asked at the front desk and the porter there directed her to the room where her sister-in-law was. Along the way she tried to avoid staring at the gaunt-faced, bright-eyed patients who walked past her in the corridor or who rambled outside on the rich green lawn.

Carmel was sitting up in bed, looking prettier than before, alone in a small room looking out over the grounds, a glimpse of blue sea far in the distance.

'Oh Ella, I'm so glad to see you! I'm that happy that you could come down from Dublin to visit.'

Carmel's voice was light and wispy as if she found it hard to breathe or raise her voice, and without thinking Ella hugged her.

'Ow! Ow! be careful. I had an operation a few weeks ago on my side and it's still sore.'

'Operation!'

'Aye, they took away a bit of my lung and a few of my ribs.'

Carmel felt all bones, and Ella was shocked by the change in her. 'Carmel, I should have come down to see you earlier. I didn't realize how sick you were.'

'It makes no matter, Ella. I wasn't allowed visitors then. I'm feeling much better now, honest I am. A bit sore where they cut out my ribs, but otherwise not too bad, and the doctors say I'm improving now that they're trying out the fancy new medicine on me.'

Ella pulled up a metal chair and sat down near the bed. She busied herself unpacking the few treats she'd brought down. Carmel loved the rich pink nightdress Ella and Kitty had spotted in Clery's and appreciated their thoughtfulness. There was a coffee cake, a few bars of chocolate, some fruit, two bottles of red lemonade, a small bottle of freesia-scented cologne and some magazines.

'You've brought me far too much Ella, far too much!'

Despite her protestations, Ella could see the other girl was not used to being made a fuss of, and was pink-cheeked with surprise.

Ella told her all about Mac, and that he was sitting outside waiting for her.

'I'd like to meet him, Ella. He sounds a real dreamboat. Tell him thank you for driving you down to see me.'

'You will once you're better, I promise.'

Ella looked around the spartan room, wondering how her sister-in-law could possibly occupy herself and keep her sanity. 'Carmel, what do you do all day?'

'Sleep mostly. I'm right tired a lot of the time. Some days I walk a little bit or the physiotherapist comes in and I have to do some exercises with her. Mostly I listen to the radio and think about home.'

Ella was filled with pity for her sister-in-law and didn't know how she stuck being confined in such a small place, away from everything.

'In a few weeks' time when I'm a bit stronger I'll move into one of the wards. The women there are great fun and then, God willing, another month or two and I'll be going home.'

'Of course you will.'

A pretty nurse with red hair came in and took Carmel's temperature and pulse, discreetly removing the sputum-filled jars on the bedside locker.

'Catherine, this is my sister-in-law Ella.'

'Ah, the girl you were telling me about who works in Dublin.'

Ella smiled politely.

'Carmel and I have long chats, don't we, Carmel.'

'I'd be lost without Catherine,' admitted Carmel, squeezing the nurse's hand.

'Go on out of that! I'd better go and see to a few of my more troublesome patients. Would they were all as good as you!'

Ella studied the drawing on the wall behind the bed. It showed a house and trees and three figures, drawn crudely in coloured wax crayons, one tall elongated figure with a cap on and two other smaller ones, standing in front of it all.

'Mary did that. It's Liam and herself and baby Sally.'

She could see that, recognizing the porch and windows of Fintra.

'I'm not in it,' whispered Carmel, drawing in a shuddering breath. 'She's left me out of it.'

'She's just drawing now, what's happening to her now!' exclaimed Ella, trying to reassure her. 'Look, there's her picture of you in the hospital, lying in a big bed!'

Carmel bit her lip, trying not to cry. Ella did not know what to say.

'You'll be back home before you know it, Carmel, honest you will, you and Liam and the children will be back to being a family again.'

She had to laugh. Here was she, a spinster with no husband or child of her own, advising a settled married woman what to do.

'That's why I wrote to you, Ella. I wanted to see you, wanted to talk to you.'

Carmel was overwrought, worried and afraid.

Ella could see it her eyes and anxious state. Maybe she should go out and find that nurse again, the one Carmel liked.

'Ella, if anything happens to me, I want you to promise to help look after my children.'

Promise, how could she promise that? 'Liam would look after them, Carmel. Anyway this is daft talk. You were saying yourself that in a few months you'll be going home. You shouldn't be upsetting yourself like this, Carmel. Honest you shouldn't!'

'You lost your mother when you were young, Ella. You know what it's like! I just want my girls to have someone there to care for them and love them if anything should happen to me.'

'Liam would take care of them, Carmel, you know that. He's their father!'

'I know, Ella, but Liam told me what happened to his father when your mother died. I don't know how he'd cope on his own Ella, honest I don't. You're his sister.'

Ella sighed. She hated hospitals, hated them. She remembered the day her father brought her to the County Hospital. They'd said her mother would only be in for a day or two, and not to worry, she'd get better. A nurse in the corridor had asked her name and hearing she was Helena Kennedy's daughter told her to run as fast as she could up to the ward as her mother was dying. She'd barely recognized her beautiful mother, the poison from the septicaemia raging through her body following her appendix bursting. She'd held her hand till the very end. Her father, ravaged with grief, cursed the doctors and nurses.

'This is crazy talk, Carmel, crazy. You're in one of the best hospitals in Ireland, with good doctors and nurses, and you're getting better. Nothing's going to happen to you. Don't even dream of thinking of it!'

No matter what she said, or how much she reassured the patient in the bed, she could see that Carmel was fretting and utterly refused to be placated.

'Please Ella, please!'

She hated being pushed into a corner but couldn't let the sick girl get herself into such a state. 'Oh, all right then. I promise to help with the girls and Liam should anything happen to you. But it won't!'

Carmel leaned back against the pillows, her eyes closed. 'Thanks Ella! Thank you. I can rest easy now.'

Ella couldn't believe what she'd let herself be persuaded to do. Already Carmel looked more relaxed and Ella, anxious to change the subject, began to chat about the shop and Leo and Neil and the new play at the Abbey Theatre that Leo had a small part in. She could see that Carmel's eyes were closing and she was beginning to drift off to sleep.

'I'd better go.'

'No, don't go, Ella. Liam will be in to visit in a

while if Nance or one of the girls are able to mind the children.'

Ella had no intention of meeting her brother and having any sort of a discussion with him and pulled on her coat. 'No, Carmel, I have to go. Poor Mac is waiting ages outside.'

'I'm sorry, Ella. Listen, thank you for coming, and for everything.'

Ella stood awkwardly at the door.

'Take care of yourself!'

She hated leaving Carmel there on her own, and walked quickly along the corridor and out of the hospital, not wanting to be there if Liam came.

She could see Mac in the distance in the car park. He had his head thrown back, dozing, and jumped up the minute she pulled the car door open.

She flung herself on top of him kissing him wildly, so relieved to be out of the hospital. The elderly man and woman in the car parked beside them glared at them. She felt raw and emotional and longed to be in his arms, far from this awful place.

'Where to, madame?' he joked, reading her mind.

'Home. Mac, please just take me home.'

Wexford 1957

Chapter Twenty-eight

Ella returned to Kilgarvan for Christmas, glad to be with her aunt and uncle and cousins for the usual Christmas festivities. Uncle Jack had cut down an enormous fir tree and Slaney and Marianne had festooned it with coloured glass baubles and red ribbons. Holly branches laden with berries decorated the hall and the mantelpiece. The Christmas candle burned in the window as Aunt Nance fussed around them all as usual, treating them as if they were a group of twelve-year-old girls. Teresa and Finbarr had gone to his parents for Christmas dinner but had called in with gifts for them all. Connie was expecting again and was the size of a house. Aunt Nance was sure it was twins this time. There were twins on Jack's side of the family after all. Brian and Anna announced their engagement and were building a house on an acre of land that Uncle Jack had given them. Ella had never seen her cousin look so happy and content. The wedding would be in June, and she and Mac were invited.

'It's a good match,' declared her aunt 'Anna's a grand girl and knows what farm living entails and will help Brian run this place when the time comes.'

Mac had gone up North to be with his family and she didn't expect to see him for at least a week. He'd dropped in to the flat with her Christmas present, a beautiful gold chain that she had put on immediately, and she'd given him a hand-woven tweed sports jacket that she'd ordered through the shop. They'd gone for a Christmas drink to Davy Byrne's, joining a crowd of his friends from the bank and Kitty and Tom, the pub so crowded they could barely move. She missed him already and the holiday week had barely begun.

'Ella, I've invited Liam and the children to join us for Christmas dinner,' Aunt Nance told her on Christmas Eve. 'I couldn't have your poor brother and those dotes on their own in the house with Carmel still away in the sanatorium.'

Ella sighed. Her aunt was good and kind and would always welcome those who needed a place on Christmas Day. It wasn't her place to object and make a scene or fuss about how awkward it might be.

Kitty and she had visited Carmel only two weeks before, and she knew how much Carmel longed to be home for Christmas. She was in a women's ward now and seemed brighter and livelier somehow, planning what the girls would wear and the presents.

Liam arrived up at Rathmullen after they'd returned from midday Mass, the smell of the ham and turkey filling the house. Ella had greeted him along with everybody else, shocked at how much her brother had aged and upset by the barely disguised pain in his eyes.

The little girls were beautiful, each different from the other, one like Liam, one like Carmel. They both wore dresses with smock stitching, one in berry red, one in rich ivy green, with warm woollen tights. Her cousins were mad about them and scooped them up for tickles and hugs. Ella stared at them, filled with regret that she had not seen more of her little nieces. Mary came over shyly and introduced herself, Sally following on and insisting on a 'kissee'.

Liam lifted her up into Ella's arms. 'Sally, this is your Auntie Ella.'

The plump arms went around her neck, and she couldn't resist burying her face in the soft curling fair hair and baby skin.

'She's so beautiful Liam, they both are. You and Carmel are lucky.'

'Lucky! I wouldn't call myself lucky,' he said gently, his eyes meeting hers.

'I'm sorry, Liam, about Carmel, I truly am.'

'I believe you went to visit her. Thank you for that, Ella. I appreciate it.'

They stood there in the midst of the rest of the family, too proud to say too much to each other, Sally putting her arms out for her daddy.

Santa had come that morning to Fintra and Mary told them exactly what everybody had in their stocking. There were more presents under the tree and the little girls tore at the wrapping paper, squealing with excitement at the dolls she'd bought them and the colouring books and jigsaws that Kitty had purchased in Pim's.

Uncle Jack said grace and they all crowded around the two tables that had been pushed together as Aunt Nance served the dinner. Ella ate so much she thought that she'd burst, and laughed to see Kitty's face, guessing that she'd stolen an extra glass or two of sherry in the kitchen while she was helping her mother. Thankfully Liam was the far end of the table sandwiched between her uncle and Slaney, so she was able to avoid getting into deeper conversation with him. The minute the pudding was served and the meal was over Liam had made his excuses to leave as he was driving up to see Carmel and bringing the girls with him. They hadn't seen their mother for months and Carmel would be in a state waiting for them.

Ella watched as he wrapped them in their coats, buttoning them up well, checking each had her mittens and tucking hair in under knitted caps, before leaving the house. Aunt Nance had followed them out to the hall and had a gift ready-wrapped for Carmel, and a pudding in a bowl for herself and the patients to share.

While Liam was thanking her Ella showed the girls the wooden crib that Uncle Jack had carved when he was a young boy. Mary had picked up a little sheep, cradling it in her hand. It had been a favourite of Ella's too when she was a small girl, and she said nothing when Mary slipped it into her pocket, not wanting to give it back. She was sure Uncle Jack would understand her little niece borrowing it.

'Take care, Liam, and give Carmel all our love, and tell her we're all praying for her.' Aunt Nance clutched him to her large chest and hugged him tightly. Ella, more reserved, kissed him lightly on the cheek. He had made absolutely no mention of her visiting home or seeing the girls again and she in turn had not asked.

The rest of the Christmas Day continued with Marianne organizing charades from the Hollywood movies, everyone guessing the wrong answers, and shouting out of turn, and Slaney getting everyone to tell spooky Christmas ghost stories before they went to bed.

Tom surprised Kitty by arriving down unexpectedly on Stephen's Day. Uncle Jack and Aunt Nance made a great fuss of him and Slaney declared 'He was a fine thing!' Ella wished that Mac wasn't so far away and could be here with the Kavanaghs too. On the way back, the next day, Tom had stopped off in Oldcastle so the three of them could visit Carmel.

'The girls are beautiful, Carmel. They're a credit to you and Liam,' Ella said sincerely, glad to see her sister-in-law looking much brighter and noticing the little sheep perched on the side of her locker.

'They were as cute as kittens on Christmas Day in their dresses. We're all mad out about them Carmel, you know that!' confided Kitty, sitting down near her.

Carmel sat up in the bed, coughing slightly. 'Tell your mother thanks for inviting them and Liam to your place for Christmas dinner. Your mother is a good kind woman, Kitty.'

'We all know that, Mammy's the best. Anyways you can tell her yourself next week when she comes to visit you, Carmel.'

'When will you be going home?' Tom asked politely from the far end of the bed.

'After the cold spell. The doctors say I'm much improving and they'll let me home real soon.'

Ella dozed in the back of the car as Kitty and Tom chatted, glad to see that the up and down and on and off stage of their relationship seemed to be calming down, with Kitty finally content to be a one-man woman.

The flat was icy when they got back to Merrion Square. Gretta was away in Cork and Lesley the nurse who was sharing the room with her must be on duty.

'Light the fire Ella, before we fecking freeze,' bossed Kitty. 'We're back in Dublin now!'

Dublin 1958

Chapter Twenty-nine

Mac told her in January that he'd been transferred. The bank was sending him to work in their branch up in Ballymena and he'd be moving back up North in less than two weeks' time. Ella couldn't take it in or believe it. She couldn't even begin to imagine her life without him.

'They can't just do that Mac! They can't! What about us?'

'There'll still be us!' he laughed, rubbing the tops of her arms. I'll come down at weekends to Dublin and you'll come up North some weekends to me.'

'I have to work on Saturdays in the shop, Mac, you know that.'

'It will sort out, Ella. I know it will. Bank staff are always being transferred and everyone survives it. Things will be a bit more difficult for a while, that's all.'

'Could you not just tell them you want to stay in Dublin?' she argued.

'Are you mad, Ella? This is a promotion! The bank is my career, so for the moment I go where they tell me, like it or not. Anyway, Ballymena is a good town, my father says there are all kinds of new business developments there and lots of house-building, so maybe I'll be able to afford to rent or buy a house there with my increase in salary.'

Even with an increase in salary, she didn't like it, not one little bit. She feared what might happen if Mac was not around; she did not want him to go and leave her. Promotion or not, Mac shouldn't have accepted the bank's offer without talking to her about the consequences for their relationship.

Terri's baby was born at the end of January. Terri looked exhausted and pale in Holles Street Hospital when they went to visit her. Bill, choked with emotion, held his newborn son in the crook of his arm for them all to see, proud of his wife and baby as he gave them a blow by blow account of their hospital dash.

Ella was filled with envy seeing the two of them with their child, wondering what lay ahead for herself and Mac.

Mac made the move back up North, Frank being good enough to tell him he could sleep on the couch in the old flat whenever he was in Dublin. For the first month he was back down religiously, going out to dinner with her and taking her dancing and making up for not seeing her during the week. Her body ached for him and Kitty and Tom went off to watch a rugby match in the rain in order to give them a chance to truly be together, Ella crying and clinging to him when the time came for him to leave.

'Absence makes the heart grow fonder,' Gretta consoled her, 'and Mac will realize just how much he misses you too!'

February brought ice and sleet and hail, and although Mac phoned her, the weather was too bad to travel. He had an awful cold and fever by the sound of it and she comforted herself with the thought of him sitting at a fire with a hot drink on his own reading the papers.

At Easter she managed to persuade Leo to give her a few days off from the shop and was thrilled with the thought of spending them with Mac. She got the train to Belfast and the two of them nearly made a disgrace of themselves at the station. Mac kept telling her how much he missed her and loved her, and she tried to console herself that even though he had to work during the day at least they had the evenings together. She was bored hanging around Ballymena waiting for him and walked all over the town getting to know it. Mac was already part of the community; there, people stopped to say hello to him in the street and greet him while she felt a total outsider.

'You'll get to know them Ella, just give them time.'

He was staying in a digs around the corner from the bank and she had to stay in a small local hotel close by. After work he drove her out by a building site where he told her he had paid a deposit down on a three-bedroom home with a garage that was being built.

'It should be ready in the autumn,' he proudly declared. Ella felt annoyed that he hadn't even discussed the purchase with her.

'Why didn't you tell me about the house, Mac?' she demanded.

'I wanted to surprise you, anyway it's a good investment. Paying money out for digs is a waste and I'll likely be working here for the next few years, so a place of my own will be great.'

She tried to make the most of her time with him but felt awkward and shy with his new colleagues who left her out of their conversations and talked incessantly about the bank's treasure hunt and social club. She herself was conscious of the fact that here in the North with Mac she just didn't fit in. People were polite and civil to her but she was still an outsider.

She noticed Mac missed the next two weekends and when he did come down was apologetic but insisted on bringing Frank and his girlfriend to dinner with them.

She slept in one Sunday missing the Belfast train, and rolled over in the bed asking herself how in God's name she had not woken when the alarm clock had gone off, imagining Mac waiting at the station for her. He had been decidedly cool when she did phone and told her he was going sailing in Bangor the next weekend. She had absolutely no intention of returning to his home town and didn't know what to say or do about his sailing plans for the summer.

Gretta had tried to talk to her about him but she wasn't interested in what the other girl thought of their situation, as she was the one who had to deal with it. She had to accept that the stretches between their visits were getting longer and that the old closeness between them seemed to be disappearing. Mac was still the essence of good manners but she suspected he might be seeing someone else.

'Mac, you'll be down for my cousin Brian's wedding in the beginning of August.' She could tell immediately that he had totally forgotten about it. 'All my cousins and family will be there, Mac, they're all dying to meet you and it's about time you saw Rathmullen and Kilgarvan, the places that I grew up.'

'I'm sorry, Ella. I can't make it to the wedding.'

'Can't make it, Mac?'

'I'm sailing that weekend in the Bangor Cup.'

'Feck the bloody Bangor Cup! You told me that you'd come with me to Brian's wedding Mac, you know you did!'

'I'm sorry, Ella! I can't.'

She knew by the way he said it and the way his lips barely brushed hers when they parted that evening, it was over. It just hadn't worked out and never would. There was too much to divide them. There had been no huge arguments or upsets, no mention of religion. Mac and she had just let the love they had for each other gradually die, neither of them willing to fight hard enough to save it. She didn't want to see him again and was too wounded and raw to even pretend to.

Kitty made her usual forthright comments. 'Ella, you're as well off not having that Protestant bastard in your life and those awful in-laws!'

Ella would still have given anything to be able to turn the clock back to the times when Mac was her world and they'd made each other happy.

Gretta and Lesley insisted on her coming out with them on their nights off, and Julia dragged her along with the girls from Lennon's to a dance or two.

Leo and Neil tiptoed around her being the souls of discretion while her relationship crumbled and then became suitably supportive, telling her that the perfect man was somewhere out there and she had yet to find him.

Brian's wedding had been wonderful, the sun splitting the heavens when they'd all come out of Kilgarvan church. Anna Delaney looked as pretty as a picture on her special day with a stunning white bridal gown and long train which her three bridesmaids carried. Carmel was home. She'd put on weight, so that her face now looked round and full, and she was glad to be reunited with all those she loved and cared about. Liam fussed about her and made her sit down and not tire herself out with the dancing afterwards in Casey's Hotel. Ella was glad for both of them that things were finally returning to normal. She sipped her glass of wine, watching the happy couple waltz across the floor. Mac should have been here with her; instead here she was on her own yet again.

As summer turned to autumn Leo confided to her his plans to retire and sell the business. She was devastated.

'But you're too young to retire, Leo!'

'I lie about my age,' he admitted, fixing her steadfastly with a glimmer in his eye, still not telling her how old he really was. 'It has always been my plan, Ella. I've no intention of ending up a grouchy old man behind the counter, trying to cajole customers in to buying. That's not my style, you know that.'

The business was thriving, and tourists and foreigners were already beginning to find the way to the store. Leo couldn't just close it down like that.

'Neil and I have always planned to travel. Neil wants to see places, write about them. I like doing my bits and pieces of acting, and I'll always find something to keep me busy. Radio work, theatre work and the money from the shop will be my pension.'

It was all worked out. She offered to buy it off him, realizing that the money still sitting in her account wouldn't even come close to what the shop was worth.

'Let me talk to the bank. Maybe I could get a loan,' she pleaded. 'Please Leo, you owe me that!'

She had met Frank, Mac's old flatmate who worked in the bank, telling him of her proposal. He had gone through the figures with her.

'I'm sorry Ella, but you won't get the loan. Even investing all your own capital you would still be borrowing a huge amount, and though I shouldn't say it, the bank won't look as favourably on a woman getting a loan They just won't give it to you.'

'But it's a great shop, a great business and I know I can make a go of it!'

'I'm sorry Ella, honest I am.'

She felt so frustrated and angry she didn't know what to do.

'You can always come back and work in Lennon's,' Kitty consoled her.

'I've had a large offer from one of the building societies,' Leo informed her the following week. 'They obviously have had their eyes on this patch of mine for a long time.'

'I thought that you were selling the shop as a going concern, Leo.'

'Well, that had been my intention, but this offer is exceptional, Ella. I'd be a fool not to take it.'

Ella had hoped to get a job with whoever took over the shop. Now even that opportunity was gone if there was going to be a totally new business there. She was at her wits' end not knowing what to do.

'They have premises leased in the street around the corner and apparently their lease is up. The landlord wants to put up the rent and isn't willing to sell, though they offered to buy him out. Anyways the premises are small, too small, as they plan to expand and here is exactly what they want. What's more they have no objection to my keeping the flat upstairs.'

Ella had to accept that her job was all but gone and that she needed to find something else. She knew the little building society office and could see the sense in them moving. After work that night she walked there. There wasn't much to it, one window, but though the space was small it did seem to go back a fair bit, which would give storage space. She stood in front of it, passed across the street from it, studied it from either side. How had she never noticed number twenty-six before? Excited, she ran back to Leo's. The shop was shut but she rang the bell. Leo O'Byrne had a great sense of business and she would trust his judgement.

The three of them went straight away to see it and tried not to look conspicuous as they peered in the office window. Neil opened a bottle of red wine when they got back to the flat, and they sat on the couch planning how much the shop could possibly be worth and if there was space for rails and shelves and a counter. The suppliers knew her already, and Leo would introduce her to any who didn't and vouch for her. She was hoping they might give her credit. Leo promised to find out the name of the landlord first thing in the morning and arrange for her to see him. He would suggest that he was interested in the shop for himself in order that whoever it was would see her.

Neil walked her home. Her feet were almost lifting off the ground with excitement, and she was dying to see what Kitty thought of it all.

Chapter Thirty

The shop was hers! She still couldn't believe it. Overnight she'd become the keyholder and a woman of property right in the centre of Dublin.

The building looked small and dingy at the moment, not really like a shop at all, but there was no denying its potential and the great location just off Grafton Street. The front window bowed out into the street, which would be a big advantage for displays, and there was space at the back for storage and a toilet and tiny wash-hand basin. The premises had cost her almost all her inheritance, as the landlord had insisted on her taking out a five-year lease. She'd got the shakes withdrawing the money from the bank, thinking of how hard her father had worked to accumulate such a sum. She'd paid it over to the solicitors' firm who acted for the landlord. As soon as she had signed the agreement they had handed her over two sets of keys.

Standing in the middle of her new business

premises she was suddenly overwhelmed by what she'd gone and done. Jesus, Mary and Joseph, was she mad to have thrown nearly all her money into this venture! She had no husband, no boyfriend, no family to back her up if this should fail. She was totally on her own.

Kitty, Gretta, Julia, Bill and Terri had all come along offering their advice. They washed the walls and helped repaint the building society's grey decor in a creamy colour. Bill had sent one of his site carpenters over to build the wooden shelves and counters she needed and Tom had turned up trumps doing all the electrics in his spare time. Leo had been true to his word and helped her with ordering her stock and dealing with the suppliers. Her premises were far smaller than his, and she had to make decisions about what to stock and not to stock, and what kind of shop she wanted it to be. One counter was glass-fronted, as with so little space the sweaters and cardigans that were stored inside it could also be displayed. She decided against a fitted rail for the skirts and blouses and waistcoats as if she was very busy she could push a moveable one in against the shelves to make more space.

'What are you going to call it?' Kitty asked her.

Ella wasn't sure. Everything had happend so suddenly and she'd had to move so fast getting everything organized that she was undecided.

'The Tweed Shop.'

'But you stock more than tweeds!'

'The Hand-knit Shop.'

'But then what about all your lovely tweed and rugs and shawls?' argued Gretta.

Ella hadn't a clue and the signwriter was coming the next day.

'Might I be bold enough to make a suggestion,' Leo offered. 'I always found using my own name an advantage. People knew who they were dealing with and that I was the proprietor.'

'You think I should put my name above the door?'

'Of course I do, Ella.'

'Ella Kennedy.' It sounded good enough.

'Write it in that lovely loopy convent writing of yours,' added Kitty.

She tried it in various sizes.

'Now that's perfect! Give it to the signwriter to copy. Your signature is your mark!'

She opened the following week, nervous as hell as she turned the key in the lock and undid the bolts and turned on the lights. It looked lovely, just the way she wanted. The wood was warm and inviting, and a large mirror hung against the wall opposite the window for customers to admire themselves in and to give the illusion of the shop being bigger than it actually was. Only half the stock she'd ordered had arrived, but she managed to spread it around so that the shop looked full, with most of it on display. The Donegal weavers had done her proud and sent in bales of their beautiful tweed with over a month's free credit. The knitters had hand-knitted shawl-collared cardigans and ribbed waistcoats as well as their usual sweaters and cardigans, and had even provided a few in small sizes for children. So much work went into the Aran patterned hand-knits that they were expensive, but the knitters more than earned their pay.

'Offer them top rates, half a crown or a quid extra than the other shops and you'll get the best knitters working for you!' advised Leo, guiding her yet again.

She'd bought a metal cash box with a lid and tray, cash books and receipt books and an order book. They all looked so new and empty that she itched to write in them. Mindful of her times in Lennon's when she was on her feet all day she'd also bought a stool which she hid behind the counter.

That first morning she stood and sat behind the counter for hours without a solitary soul appearing or even enquiring about a single item. Disappointment lowered her spirits and filled her mind with horrible thoughts of future ruin and embarrassment. Kitty popped in at lunchtime, bringing her a tomato sandwich and a cherry bun.

'Thought you might fancy something to eat,' she grinned, flicking the cash book open.

'Not a dicky bird, Kitty! Not even one person came in to look at anything.'

'For heaven's sake, Ella! You're only open a few hours. Give people a chance to see the shop.'

Ella was impatient and hated sitting around watching and waiting for people to come in. Was she missing something, doing something wrong? Her mind was in turmoil, and she felt full of doubts.

Kitty and she even went through the charade of her cousin pretending to be a customer, slipping on a crew-neck Aran and then pretending to pay for it in the hope that someone might be encouraged to step inside when they saw Kitty leave.

Neil and Leo had popped over mid-afternoon. Ella was near to tears when she saw them.

'We bought you these.'

Ella unwrapped a pair of black china cats.

'They're for luck!' Neil added. 'Put them in the window.'

She placed one on either side of the window, the cats reminding her of the farm cats that sat in the sun down home in Kilgarvan. They had only been there a second when the first customers crossed the threshold of the shop. Ella felt almost tempted to hug them or offer them a glass of champagne or something equally celebratory. Her friends disappeared as she concentrated on showing the fine selection of warm mohair rugs to the middle-aged man and woman who wanted a useful gift for an elderly aunt. She could have cried with relief when they bought one. By closing time she had dealt with five customers and sold three items. Hardly a flying start but it was a start! Exhausted from the stress and strain of the new business she was delighted to accept Kitty's offer of tea out.

Dublin 1959

Chapter Thirty-one

The business was slow to get going and Ella found herself constantly worried about money. She was doing her damndest to attract business and was forever changing the window in a bid to get customers' attention. The city streets were busy and every day there seemed to be more developments of shops and offices springing up everywhere, old tenement housing making way for tall new office buildings. The city was beginning to expand outwards with more and more houses being built for the increasing number of Dubliners, the likes of Bill Brady making their fortune as the suburbs of Dundrum and Churchtown and Templeogue and Stillorgan got built. The signs were good but she just had to learn to capitalize on the increasing business in town and stake her claim in her own particular type of market. She wasn't prepared to sell her goods below cost as everything in the shop was handmade or crafted and she believed that the knitters and weavers and designers all deserved a decent return for their effort and hard work. She herself hadn't made a penny since she opened and she wondered how long could that go on.

'Give it time, Ella dear!' advised Leo, repositioning strands of traditional brightly coloured woven crios belts. 'Rome wasn't built in a day, you know, and it takes time for the public to decide what it likes and doesn't.'

'You're in business now, Ella, so you've got to take the good days with the bad ones, just like the rest of us,' Bill Brady remarked when he called in to check on the carpenter's work.

She knew that everyone was right and that she shouldn't expect so much.

Leo and Neil threw a going-away party in the flat before they flew off down to the South of France. Neil's publisher had a relation who was prepared to let out his house down there and the two men had jumped at the chance of having a place in the sun.

'It'll be the perfect setting to write and paint and maybe Leo will finally get started on writing that play he's always talking about.'

Ella had never seen Neil so excited and animated, obviously relishing the thought of leaving Dublin and its narrow-minded society behind, whereas Leo, after a few glasses of red wine, was all emotional, imagining himself almost like the writer James Joyce leaving Ireland to go into exile.

The small flat was crowded and as they mingled with their guests, Ella realized just how many people had been helped along the way by Leo's generous nature and spirit. She'd really miss both of them and promised to keep them up to date on the shop and how it was doing.

By the end of the first month she just about broke even, not including her own salary; in the second month, which was better, she showed a small profit and took a nominal amount of salary. At night at home in the flat she totted up receipts, filled in order books, checked dockets and made an enormous effort to keep her books the way Frank had advised. There was a satisfaction in seeing at the end of the day how much you sold and filling in the lodgement dockets. There was no time for romance or going out late dancing when she'd a business to run.

The customers began to come. Wealthy country women wanting a certain shade in a tweed, to get a suit or skirt or coat made. Men looking for warm sweaters to protect them when they were fishing, like they protected the men of Aran in times gone by. Americans visiting Dublin for a day or two and wanting to bring back something from Ireland, studying the waves and patterns and stitches that represented the cottages, fields, hills and seas of the country. Parents wanting to buy the warm hand-knitted scarves and hats and jackets for their children. Her small shop kept a cornucopia of handmade, goods, and attracted an ever-larger number of customers. She was still working single-handed but realized she would likely need someone to help her if business kept on improving, even if it was only part-time. The satisfaction she got was enormous and it reminded her very much of the sense of achievement she'd felt when she'd stood and looked at a field of barley or potatoes, or cabbages that she'd planted or sown.

Tom had finally asked Kitty to marry him. Their years of fighting and flirting and breaking up and making up were over at last. Kitty was like the cat that got the cream, flashing her three diamonds at anyone who cared to study them. Ella wished them happiness but knew that theirs would always be a stormy relationship for Tom was rather vain and self-centred and not used to considering others. Aunt Nance and Uncle Jack had come to Dublin for a celebration meal in the Hibernian Hotel. The next day, she was delighted when they came to see the shop, her aunt insisting on buying five yards of crock-of-gold tweed and a warm heavy-knit cardigan.

'My old one is in tatters, between the dogs and those three grandchildren of ours.'

'Martin and Helena would be very proud of you Ella,' her uncle told her. 'Very proud!'

Ella had all but given up on romance and considered herself unlucky with men. After Mac she didn't think it worth getting into a relationship with anyone else. Perhaps she was destined never to marry and have a family. She thanked God for her two darling nieces and all her cousins' growing brood. She got an immense joy from visiting them and watching them grow. Likely she'd end up an old maid on the shelf, a spinster aunt consoling herself with her business and godchildren.

'You'll never guess who Tom and I met at the races?' Kitty announced all excited one Saturday night after returning from the Phoenix Park.

Ella gave up, not interested in playing Kitty's usual childish guessing games.

'Someone from down home. Someone you know!'

'Kitty if they're from down home it's pretty obvious I'd know them.'

'It was Sean, you know, that neighbour of yours.'

'Sean?'

'Yeah, the one you used to have a crush on when you were young.'

Ella stopped what she was doing. Sean Flanagan back in Ireland. It had been so long since she'd even said his name, imagine! Likely he was married and had a family by now.

'Was he with someone, Kitty?'

Her cousin was busy unrolling her nylons, and getting changed into her nightdress. 'I don't know. He was with a crowd. Tom and I noticed them up in the stand. They were shouting their heads off when their horse was coming in. Did I tell you I'd two winners today myself?'

She was going to ask Kitty if he'd enquired about her, but obviously he hadn't bothered. Sean Flanagan had come back home. He was just an old boyfriend, ancient history as far as she was concerned, but somehow or other it unnerved her knowing that he was even in the same country as her.

Chapter Thirty-two

Once or twice she'd imagined she had passed him in the street, seeing a man of his build and hair-colouring or spotting a flash of a smile or look of an eye that reminded her of him. It hadn't been and she wasn't even sure if she was disappointed or relieved about it. The shop was busy, doing better than she'd ever expected, and she had little time to be mooning about over somebody from the past.

She wanted to increase her customer numbers, and she decided to get a brochure made for the business, intending to distribute it in the hotels and places of business in town.

'I'll model for you!' offered Kitty, pulling on a heavy ribbed knitted jacket and prancing round the shop as if she was a Chanel model. The Aran knit looked wonderful with her russet hair and her marvellous cat-green eyes. A photo of Kitty like that would probably sell more sweaters than anything else.

'All right then, you can be one of my models.'

'How much will I get paid?'

Ella laughed. 'You'll be famous modelling, think how proud Tom will be to say his fiancée is a model!'

'How much? Remember I'm saving to get married.'

Ella had to agree a few quid, which she reckoned was money well spent. She was actually beginning to make profit from the shop, which she had on deposit with the bank.

Slaney had come to Dublin for an interview, and looking very grown-up and glamorous joined in the photography session. After a little persuasion one of the lads in the flat below agreed to model the men's jumpers. Ella got a few hundred sales brochures printed and then set about delivering them to the various information desks and city-centre hotels. Some she placed up front boldly on racks, others she dropped discreetly beside the sales information for the expensive shops. She crossed her fingers in the hope that these would bring her even more business. She was just coming out of the Gresham Hotel on O'Connell Street, where the receptionist had been particularly frosty, though she'd still managed to slip a few into the rack at the porter's desk, when she almost crashed into a hotel guest as she tried to make a retreat.

'Ella! Ella Kennedy!'

They were standing on the steps, facing each other, Ella realizing that this time there was no mistaking Sean Flanagan. Without thinking they hugged each other, the smell and feel of him immediately coming back to her.

'Sean, it's good to see you.'

She genuinely meant it. He looked well. The passing years had been good to him; he'd filled out, and seemed broader and stronger-looking than ever. His skin was tanned, hair clipped neatly, and she noticed he was wearing a well-tailored suit, with a pressed white shirt, something she was unused to seeing him in.

'God, you look great Ella, honest you do!'

Even his accent had changed. There was a slight American twang to it and he was even more attractive than she remembered him.

'How are you, Sean?'

'I'm fine, doing grand. I've been away in America.'

'America!' She tried to sound surprised.

'Aye. I was working at all sorts of things for a year then I started working for this motor company, learned a lot about the motor industry. What about you? I heard you were working in the drapery business.'

'I still am.' She wasn't going to go and brag about having a shop of her own.

'What are you doing here?'

'Oh, I just had to leave something in the hotel, what about you?'

'I've some American friends over. We're having dinner.'

Through the hotel doorway Ella was aware of a middle-aged man and smartly dressed blonde young woman looking towards them. Waiting for him. For a second neither of them spoke, and she found herself hoping he'd ask where she lived or something.

'Listen Ella, I'd better be going, I think our table is ready.' He was turning around, obviously anxious to join the others, the woman waiting inside the door for him. She wasn't going to have him cut her out of his life again.

'Sean, I'm sorry but I have to dash as I've a date. It's great to see you.' She turned so fast she almost fell on the hotel step, his hand steadying her. Almost pushing him she managed to get away. 'Enjoy your dinner!'

She walked so fast she was out of breath by the time she got to O'Connell Bridge, stopping and cursing herself as she leaned against the stone parapet overlooking the river. The Liffey was at full tide, the dark water slapping against the quay-sides as a lone beggar man played a tin whistle. Why was she such a fecking eejit! Sean Flanagan was a nothing! He meant nothing to her. She should have known that their paths would cross sometime. Dublin wasn't that big a city and no doubt she'd bump into him and his American girl-friend again. Being stupid about it didn't help at all.

* * *

She decided against mentioning it to Kitty as she'd only start slagging her about him again; besides she was all up in a heap as Slaney was staying with them again. Slaney filled them in on all the gossip from home and Ella was glad to hear that Carmel was keeping so well. Her younger cousin had managed to land a job as an air hostess with the state's airline Aer Lingus and was training and being fitted for a uniform.

'It's the best job ever, Ella. I get to meet all sorts of interesting people and fly all over the world.'

Ella wondered what Aunt Nance and Uncle Jack thought of their youngest daughter's job. Growing up almost overnight, Slaney had now become an absolutely stunning-looking young woman but was still as funny and charming as ever.

Slaney answered the door. 'Ella, it's somebody for you.'

Ella got up reluctantly from the couch, yawning. She'd been packed out with customers and had had two commercial travellers in that afternoon showing her new knitwear lines, both of which she was uncertain about stocking. She was looking forward to a quiet evening in just chatting or listening to the radio and getting a good night's sleep.

Sean was standing there, waiting for her. 'Hi Ella! I got the address from Kitty.'

She could have kicked Kitty. What the hell was she doing telling Sean where they lived?

'We didn't get the chance to talk the other night, and we need to talk.'

She could see Slaney standing listening to them and knew Gretta was due in at any second.

'Do you want to go out? We could go for a drink or a drive, whatever you want.'

Running back into the flat she grabbed her coat and handbag, making sure she had her keys.

'I'll be back in later, Slaney.'

It was a nice evening, too early to go to a pub.

'Let's go for a drive,' he suggested.

Sitting in close proximity to him in the car as they drove out of town and towards Sandymount Strand reminded her of those drives he used to take her on before in his father's car, the two of them ending up having a loving session down by Lough Garvan. She wondered if he remembered that too. He paid her lots of compliments and she was only glad that she hadn't been wrapped up in her plaid dressing gown when he'd called.

It was so strange she felt shy and awkward with him, even though she'd known him most of her life, and she could sense he was equally ill at ease with her. He pulled the car in along the seafront looking out over Dublin Bay, Ringsend, the gas works and Blackrock and Dunlaoghaire all glimmering in the dusky light.

'Ella, I don't want it to be strange and difficult like this with us. I always thought we were friends. Good friends.'

'Friends, friends don't go off without a word and not bother telling you where they're going or never bother writing so much as a letter or card!' she blurted out angrily.

He sat back, inhaling heavily. 'I was upset after your leaving, you know that.'

She didn't want her time with him to develop into a tit for tat row. Neither of them deserved that.

'Sean, come on, let's get out and walk.'

Ella wanted to be out of the confines of the car and the danger of being so near him again. The sea air outside was rather chilly and she was glad she'd brought her coat. Sean pulled out a packet of cigarettes and lit one as they walked the length of the strand. A dog howled somewhere in the distance, and they passed a young couple engrossed in embracing each other. Ella felt almost envious of their closeness.

'Was that your girlfriend the other night?'

Sean laughed, shaking his head. 'Joan is Abe's wife! The man I was having a dinner with. She's a good bit younger than him but that don't matter back in Chicago.'

'Oh!' She must have sounded relieved.

'I did have a girlfriend. She's back in the States. She didn't want to leave home and live in Ireland, so.'

'I see.'

'What about you?'

'There was someone, he's from the North of Ireland.'

Sean was staring at her intensely, his eyes looking down into hers.

'But it just didn't work out.'

'So here we are,' he said, touching her face.

She couldn't remember which of them moved first but in an instant he was bending down kissing her. She was used to the feel of his lips and responded eagerly, not believing herself but not wanting to stop either.

Breaking away she could see the flicker of triumph in his eyes.

'Well at least that hasn't changed!' he said honestly.

It had been such a long time, yet she responded to him the same way as before, realizing that Sean still had the power to make her want and care for him. They walked on further, Sean taking her hand in his, the way old lovers do. Ella felt embarrassed and unsure of what would happen between them. This time she was not going to let him hurt her like before.

They walked and talked and ended up sitting in the car for hours, filling in those missed years, avoiding talk of the time her father had died and she'd come to Dublin and he had disappeared from her life. He finally drove her home at midnight, sitting outside in the square till one in the morning, both of them reluctant to part. Ella eventually kissed him goodnight softly on the lips before running back up to the flat where she lay awake for most of the night thinking about him.

Chapter Thirty-three

Sean Flanagan was back in her life and Ella could hardly believe it. He asked her out for drinks and invited her to lunch and to dinner, bending over backwards to please her. His gentle easy-going manner had become more sophisticated, which made him almost irresistible. She accepted graciously, unsure of what she was letting herself in for, afraid that he might break her heart again.

'I think you're fecking mad!' was Kitty's contribution to the debate about whether she should or should not agree to going out with him again. 'Remember nearly five or six years ago and how he treated you. Don't forget what happened then, Ella, sure he didn't bother even coming to Dublin to see you. He'll let you fecking down again!'

'I know,' she chastised herself.

Slaney was totally captivated by him and flirted with him every time he called to the flat. Ella reminded him she was Kitty's little sister.

'I think Sean's kind of handsome like one of

those Americans and he seems so nice and polite and charming, and he's got his own business. God Ella, he's a right catch!'

Ella burst out laughing at her young cousin's summary of his attributes, but had to concur.

There was an easy friendship between herself and Sean, since they had known each other for so long and came from the same background. They could talk on and on for hours, time running away with them as they remembered those days back on the farms in Kilgarvan with affection.

'You must have found it hard, Sean, leaving Wexford and going out to America?'

'Aye, I did, Ella, but when my reason for staying had gone, I suppose that made it a whole lot easier.'

He gazed at her intently and she realized that he was referring to her. She took a deep breath, not wanting to talk about the time he'd hurt her so much, a time she'd been so vulnerable and alone and had needed his love.

'The past is the past,' he said softly, kissing her the way he always had.

She acknowledged just how much she had missed him over all the years and how important he was compared to Mac and the others she had loved.

They drove out to Rathfarnham one evening and he showed her the large vacant site he had recently purchased, a collection of ramshackle sheds on one corner, and concrete foundations and building work begun on the other. He'd sunk most of the money he'd earned in Chicago and Detroit into its purchase and development.

'This will be the huge forecourt and sales area, here where they're busy building will be the showrooms and offices, and over there on the far side we'll have the garages for car servicing and maintenance and repair work.'

She could feel his sense of excitement as he walked her round explaining everything about the dealership contract he'd been awarded for Ireland. 'Those guys trust me, Ella. I worked on both sides of the fence in America and they know that I know the motor industry. Ireland is virgin territory! Things are changing, Ella. With Sean Lemass and Taoiseach this country will turn around and make something of itself.'

Ella noticed that a main road ran to the front of the site, but otherwise there was just a country lane and some housing development and fields. As if reading her mind he explained that the city was spreading out very fast, and that people wanted cars, though they mightn't all know it yet; but in a year or two or three they would. He already had an option on a smaller site down in Cork.

Ella had never seen Sean so excited and assured in all the years she knew him. America had changed him; it had made him stronger and tougher and more focused on what he wanted. She couldn't help but wonder if that also included her.

Sean in turn had been most impressed when he

saw her shop, standing out on the street admiring the sign that swung over the door.

'Sean, for God's sake come in and stop staring like that!' she joked.

He was so tall and big he seemed to fill the space and she watched as he looked all around running his hand along the counter and taking out some of the knitwear to look at it.

'It's only a small shop, Sean.'

'It's lovely Ella, a great business. I'm so proud of you.'

He pulled her into his arms and almost lifted her off her feet as he hugged her. 'As they say in America, you're some girl!'

'Put me down Sean, a customer might come in!' she teased.

Ella was relieved that he liked it and understood that she had a life of her own. She too had worked hard and wasn't going to be dependent on him, waiting for him to decide their future.

Their dates and meetings became more frequent. The two of them drew closer but Ella was still unsure, wary of letting herself become more deeply and intimately involved with him, of letting him hurt her again. This time she wanted things to be different.

Wexford 1959

Chapter Thirty-four

Kitty was in a frenzy organizing her wedding to Tom Donovan which she'd decided she wanted held at home in Rathmullen. Ella agreed to become a bridesmaid along with Slaney and Marianne. Aunt Nance and her cousins kept coming up and down to Dublin buying outfits and presents for the bride and groom. Ella tried to keep things calm as possible although Kitty was in a highly emotional state and there always seemed to be extra people in and out of the flat.

The wedding was held on the fifth of July. Aunt Nance was red in the face with all the preparations necessary to fit so many people into the old farmhouse. Meanwhile Uncle Jack sat back and smoked his pipe and politely chatted to all the relations and guests.

Kitty looked absolutely beautiful in an almost off-the-shoulder fitted lace top and a full skirt that made her look like Scarlett O'Hara. Under her long tumbling veil her green eyes flashed with happiness. The bridesmaids' dresses were much simpler, each with a wide collar and nipped-in waist and full swing skirt in a pale lavender-blue colour. Looking at herself in the mirror Ella could see that the colour showed off her skin tone and accentuated her dark eyes and hair colour.

Tom's family were good sorts. His mother, a widow from Drogheda, was delighted to have a daughter-in-law like Kitty as she only had three sons. Nance showed her all around the house and kissed Tom warmly at every opportunity, telling Rita Donovan she'd raised a fine son.

The parish church was packed with all the neighbours and the invited guests. Terri as usual had caused a stir wearing a huge pink and cream hat, and a pale pink suit.

'She looks like an ice cream!' said little Mary admiringly.

Beside them sat Gretta and Brendan who had quietly got engaged and were moving to London where he'd been offered a new medical posting.

Kitty had almost broken down in tears when she came to take her marriage pledge, Tom squeezing her hand encouragingly. Ella felt delighted to witness her cousin's marriage to the man she had loved all along. At the back of the church she caught a glimpse of Sean Flanagan taking it all in.

Friends and relations crowded into the farmhouse, where the Kavanaghs served roast beef and all the trimmings to their guests. Tables had been set up in every room, so everyone could mingle. The best man, Tom's brother Eamonn, stood up and led them in a toast to the bride and groom.

Kitty and Tom made a very good-looking couple and Ella hoped that they'd be happy living in their new home in Dundrum. She'd miss her giddy cousin so much and would have to make do with Slaney as a flatmate, though Slaney was often away, the airline crew overnighting in different destinations. With the flat across the landing vacant when Gretta left, she would likely end up living on her own, something she supposed she'd have to face anyway.

Sean was deep in conversation with Bill Brady at a table in the corner of the sitting room, no doubt talking about building and property. Terri looked interested, sipping only a lemonade as she'd confided to them she was expecting again. Ella sighed to herself. She'd miss her friends, so much was changing with Kitty's marriage. The only good thing was that she had agreed to Kitty coming to work with her part-time in the shop which meant at least they'd get to see each other most days. She badly needed someone to help her and Kitty, who'd had to resign her post in Lennon's because she was a married woman, needed a job.

Her nieces Mary and Sally ran around the sitting room and garden in their pretty floral dresses, Connie's eldest boy screaming and chasing after them. She couldn't help but notice that Carmel scarcely had the energy to catch them. Liam kept fussing over her and fetching her drinks and food and making sure she had a seat.

Teresa and Constance barely batted an eyelash when she introduced them to Sean and were as nice as pie to him, no matter what bad things they'd heard about him before. Sean mixed easily with everyone; she was glad that Kitty had relented and invited him, and she was able to relax and enjoy the wedding party without needing to worry about him.

'Weddings are great!' she giggled, hugging Gretta and Slaney and Kitty. 'Everyone should just go and get married!'

'I fully agree, Ella,' Sean added, coming up behind her. The others laughed as she rushed off to the kitchen on some pretext or other.

The only person she avoided was her brother. They were still not on proper speaking terms, for too much had happened between them to ever be close again. From afar he looked tired and as if he'd lost weight. They'd been through a tough time; Uncle Jack told her he was killing himself on the farm and had borrowed heavily for some new-fangled equipment, a loan he was having difficulty paying back to the bank. She noticed that Liam had the car and went home early to do the milking.

Carmel was in good spirits, chatting to them all and joking with Sean about the times he used to call to the house for Ella. Sally hopped up on her knee for attention. When her sister-in-law grew tired she noticed that it was Sean who offered to drive her and the children home to Fintra.

Later that night when some of the crowd had dispersed and the older guests had gone home or to their beds, Marianne and Slaney cleared a space in the kitchen for dancing and for anyone who fancied getting up to sing.

Sean had pulled her onto his lap and kept his arm firmly around her waist. 'I've scarcely seen you all day, Ella. This time you're not going to get the chance to run away,' he warned.

She didn't want to and they stayed up till all hours joining in the singing and dancing.

Sean held her close in his arms long after everyone else had gone home. Eventually she sneaked upstairs and he made his way back to his parents' farm.

Chapter Thirty-five

Kitty was scarcely back from her few days' honeymoon in Paris when the bad news came that Carmel was ill again. Aunt Nance had gone to visit and had phoned them to say how worried she was.

'You should go home and visit her,' urged Kitty. 'I can manage on my own in the shop, honest.'

Ella got the train down to Wexford and went straight from the station to the county hospital. Carmel was in a small room of her own, off a busy crowded ward, and was too weak to talk to her. Her sister-in-law looked desperate, her eyes huge in her pale face, her hair lank and greasy, coughing non-stop. She had developed pneumonia. Ella could imagine how disappointed and fed up Carmel must be feeling at the thought of being sick and in hospital again, and having to leave her children, and what if she had to return to Oldcastle!

'I know it's awful, Carmel, but you'll get better.

The last time they got you better in Oldcastle. It'll be the same this time.'

She could see a single tear trickle down Carmel's cheek as she nodded, trying to pretend everything would be fine when they both knew that it wouldn't.

She spoke to one of the nursing sisters, and from what Gretta had already told her realized that everyone was very concerned over Carmel's condition.

'I don't know what's going to happen to Liam and the girls now that I'm sick again,' Carmel whispered in a low voice.

'Liam's strong, Carmel, you know that! He'll manage. Don't you go worrying yourself over everything. You have to save your energy and concentrate on getting better. I'll go and see Liam, I promise. You know it must be awful for you to have married into such a stubborn pig-headed family! You're far better than the both of us.'

Carmel smiled and Ella hugged her instinctively, only then realizing how thin she'd recently got.

Coming out of the hospital later that afternoon Ella was tempted to phone Rathmullen. But instead she decided to get the country bus that went to Kilgarvan. It was crowded with country women returning from shopping and a few schoolgirls from the convent secondary school. She nodded at a few who recognized her. The driver stopped to let her off before the village. She hopped down, almost regretting her decision the minute the bus pulled away along the country road. She had packed a weekend bag and began to walk along the familiar paths that led towards Fintra, noticing how beautiful everywhere looked. Her bag was heavy and she could feel her hands getting blistered from the rubbing of the leather-covered handle as she walked. There were thistles in one field, tall and upright, and she noticed that the hedgerow hadn't been trimmed. Swans grouped together on the distant lake, dabbling their beaks in the water. The dairy herd gazed at her mournfully as she passed.

From a distance her heart leapt as soon as she saw home again. The sunlight splashed the white walls, the windowpanes glittered in the light; only up close did she notice the weeds patterned her mother's old flower border and dandelions burst through the cracks in the pathway. The paint was beginning to peel from the front door and window frames. She stood for a second unsure of what to do or even if she was doing the right thing. What would she say or do if Liam told her to get off his property like he'd done the last time? He had a fierce temper and was far too proud for his own good. He had a sick wife in the hospital and although he needed someone to help might think that she was interfering.

Knocking before she had time to change her mind, Ella stood on the doorstep of her old family home unsure of what kind of reception she might receive. Mary answered the door, her pretty face creasing into a huge grin the second she recognized her.

'Daddy, it's Auntie Ella!' she called.

Liam himself came out a second later, pulling the door wide open. She wasn't at all sure what his reaction to her presence would be. They stood looking at each other for a second, neither saying a word.

'So you heard!'

Ella nodded. 'I visited her in the hospital earlier on, Liam.'

She could see her brother trying to contain himself. 'I suppose you'd better come in then.'

'I want to help Liam, really I do.'

The little girls looked at her in the kitchen unused to seeing her there, not knowing what to make of it, little Sally's eyes almost popping out of her head, whispering to Mary.

'I was going to get the tea.'

'Here let me help Liam, what were you getting?'

'Bread and honey, that's what Daddy always gives us when Mammy's in hospital,' Sally blurted out.

'Sometimes Daddy cooks us beans on toast or a sausage or a rasher,' added Mary loyally, glaring at her sister.

'Some bread, that's all.'

Liam looked weary, she could see it in every muscle and bone of his body. He put on the kettle and took a pan of bread from the bread bin. Ella could see the two pairs of eyes watching his every move, dependent on him.

There was a bowl of eggs on the dresser and she wondered if the flour bin was full. Lifting the lid she was glad to see that Carmel still used it.

'Is there milk?'

Liam shrugged. 'There's always bloody milk!'

'What about if I make us some pancakes!'

'With sugar on them!' insisted Sally.

Mary looked at her father. 'We like bread Auntie Ella, honest we do.'

She caught Liam's eye. 'I think pancakes would be nice for a change, Mary, and anyhow I want to see if Aunt Ella can actually cook them.'

Ella got out the heavy black pan and set it to warm as she mixed the batter, praying the pancakes would turn out. The golden butter had melted as she dropped the circles of batter into the pan and watched the pancakes take shape, tossing them quickly out onto the waiting plates. Mary sprinkled them with sugar and the girls and Liam ate them as quickly as they could. Ella eventually got some for herself. Liam made two big mugs of tea and they sat at the table talking.

'Do you want me to run you into the station or up to Rathmullen later?'

Ella looked at Mary's eyes watching them. 'If it's all right with you Liam, I'd like to stay.'

'We managed fine the last time on our own!'

'I know that, but it would only be for a day or

two. I just want to help.' She could see him considering her offer, trying to make up his mind what to do. 'I could stay with the girls while you go and visit Carmel.'

'Aye, I suppose. I was going to get the young O'Grady one to come up and sit with them.'

Relieved that he had accepted Ella tidied up, changing the girls into their night clothes while he was out. It was strange to her to see the rooms now crowded with all the children's toys and clothes. The old house had become a family home again. They wanted a story, they wanted to be tucked in and they both demanded a good-night kiss. She thought of Carmel and knew how much she and the children must be missing each other.

She stayed till the end of that week phoning Kitty to check that all was going well in the shop. She was exhausted between the cooking and cleaning and helping in the dairy and found herself yawning and nodding off at night. Carmel was too sick to transfer as the condition of her lungs had worsened.

Ella had gone in one afternoon to visit her with Aunt Nance and Uncle Jack, telling her all about the children and their antics, noticing that Carmel was so drowsy that her eyes kept on closing. They were trying her on some new sort of antibiotic treatment and everyone was praying that it would work. Liam was beside himself and walked the fields at night as she watched from the windows, frightened for him.

'She's not going to make it this time Ella! She's not!'

Ella didn't know what to say, hearing the despair in his voice.

Her brother had been right, as Carmel lost her battle for life that weekend. Liam was distraught with grief and Ella absolutely filled with sadness at Carmel's death. Liam was the one who sat down with his small daughters and told them that their mammy had been too sick and had gone to heaven. Seeing the misery in his eyes and hearing the gentleness in his voice earned him a new respect from her. Mary bawled her eyes out, and little Sally neither believed him nor understood at all.

It was a simple funeral in accordance with Carmel's wishes. She'd already discussed it with Father Hackett. Her mother and two sisters and a brother came over from Liverpool, still shocked by the news.

Ella did her best to organize the house and the funeral the way her sister-in-law would have liked it, regretting that they had not got to know each other better or become the firm friends they might have been. Kitty had closed the shop and come back home. Brian and all the girls were as supportive as they could be. Sean Flanagan appeared, kissing her cheek gently in the church, holding her elbow at the graveyard and following her with his eyes back at Fintra.

She was aware of his presence the whole day as she served meals and poured drinks and held Sally in her arms when she fell asleep. Sean stayed there, watching her.

Chapter Thirty-six

Liam had slept for almost two days, the blankets pulled up over his head, barely stirring, not wanting to eat or drink or talk to anyone. On the third day Mary and Sally stood outside the bedroom door in their nightdresses.

'Your daddy needs you girls,' Ella whispered. 'He's sad and lonely without your mammy but he's a lucky man because he's got the two of you.'

'Maybe Daddy needs to sleep some more and he'll be angry with us for waking him!'

Ella could see how concerned Mary was about doing the right thing. 'He's had a really long good sleep, Mary, and now it's time for your daddy to wake up. Tell him breakfast will be ready in about fifteen minutes.'

She opened the door, watching from the landing as the children sneaked into the room. Sally, curious, clambered up onto the bed first, ignoring his protests and orders to go outside and not disturb him, then pulled the blanket off and asked her daddy to 'Wake up! Wake up! like Ella told her to. Mary fetched his clothes and shoes from the wardrobe and told him about breakfast.

Ella stayed downstairs out of the way and eventually was rewarded by the sight of Liam dressed and shaven sitting across from her, as the girls ate the toast and scrambled eggs she'd prepared. Soon, she hoped, she'd be able to go back to Dublin.

'I don't want the bloody place, Ella, honest to God I don't!'

'You're in shock, you're just saying this because of Carmel, Liam. This is your home now and the girls need you.'

'I can't stay in this place, Ella. If I'd never brought Carmel back to Fintra she'd have never got sick. She'd still be alive.'

'You can't say that, Liam. Carmel told me herself that lots of neighbours where she grew up in Liverpool had TB! Her getting it might have had nothing to do with coming here to Ireland, honest it mightn't.'

'I don't give a shite about that, any of it! I'll sell off most of the bloody place. 'Tis cursed anyways! It killed our mother and now my wife. It's too hard a life for a woman. I'll go back to sea.'

Ella stared at her brother. She could see it in his eyes, he was getting set to run again. Ready to take off and disappear just like he'd done before.

'What about the girls?' she reminded him.

'Naturally, the girls will come into it. They'll be looked after while I'm away.'

'They've lost their mother, Liam. You can't just run off and leave them, they're too small.' She could see it, he wasn't thinking straight. He was in pain and wanted to remove himself from it.

'Christ Ella, what am I going to do?' Her brother sat with his head in his hands. 'It's all turned out such a mess!' He was trying to control his emotions, overwhelmed with grief.

'It's all right Liam, it will be all right.' She put her arms round him and held him, cuddling him like she would Mary and Sally. 'It's all right, Liam pet.'

Tears welled in her own eyes, words of consolation useless as her brother cried.

'I'm sorry Ella, sorry for everything,' he said afterwards. 'I should have shared this place with you, no matter what the bloody will said. I knew how much Fintra meant to you. Carmel was always telling me how unfair it was.'

'You got the farm,' she reminded him. 'You were the one chosen to inherit it.'

'A hundred bloody acres! Ella, you wanted to buy it off me years ago, buy it off me now. I don't want the shagging place.'

Ella gazed around at the green fields, and the expanse of good farm land that her father and his father before him had worked, the potato drills, the pasture land, acres of flat fields and hillside slopes, tillage, the yard and outhouses, not knowing what to say. She had wanted to own it so much, grieved for it, but now that circumstances had changed so much she wasn't sure.

'I owe money to the bank, Ella. Theo O'Grady and the Flanagans have been asking me to sell off bits of land to them for years.'

Ella stared at him in disbelief. Now he was prepared to sell the place, break up her father's landholding. She wouldn't stand for it!

'You could buy it and move back here where you belong.'

Ella didn't know what to make of his proposition. Back here with a landholding of her own she'd be able to have her own small farm and watch the girls grow up, but what about the shop and her life in Dublin and Sean Flanagan?

'Liam, you're upset and tired. We can talk about this tomorrow or the next day when we've both had time to think.'

Kitty had sent word from Dublin asking when she was coming back. Sean Flanagan had been in and out looking for her and demanding to know when she was returning from the country. Some of the commercial travellers had made appointments to see her, and Kitty couldn't fend them off much longer. The shop had been busy and the stock levels were low and in need of reordering.

'I'll be back soon,' she promised her cousin.

*   *   *

She had taken the girls for a walk down to see the new calves in the lower field, the animals sucking at their fingers as Sally and Mary squealed with delight. The calves butted and nudged for attention, as the girls dipped their fingers in a little milk. They were such dotes, so different from each other, and she was broken-hearted at the thought of them not having their mother Carmel there to raise them, remembering the awful loneliness of her own childhood after her mother's death. How history had repeated itself with Liam now in the same situation her father had faced. Liam was a good father, she had seen plenty of evidence of that, and she would do everything to help her nieces, giving them the love and support and care they deserved, just as Aunt Nance had helped to raise her.

After all, it was what she had promised Carmel. She petted and tickled the calves one last time and tried to stop Sally climbing onto one of their backs by explaining that the calf was still only a baby.

'Will we go down and say a prayer at The Grotto!' she suggested, leading them back down towards the roadway.

'Mammy loved this place,' Mary confided, as they stood in front of the high rock formation, the hillside's quiet broken only by a thrush in a nearby tree.

'Then we'll say a special prayer for her here.'

Mary knelt down looking up at the statue of our Lady amongst the stone and rocks, Sally, bored after a few seconds, hopping up and down along the rail and step making up some secret sort of game. Ella let the still and peace of the place wash over her as she prayed. Mary had her hands joined, concentrating.

'Are you all right, pet?'

'I'm praying to Mammy, in heaven and that Daddy won't go away and leave us too!'

'He wouldn't do that,' she said reassuringly.

'He wants to go back to the sea, I heard him telling Uncle Jack,' she murmured softly.

'Your daddy wouldn't do that!'

'What'll happen to Sally and I?'

Well, probably the same thing that happened to me, pet, when my mammy died; your daddy will stay and mind you and look after the farm. It's what my daddy did. And what Liam will do.'

Mary seemed satisfied with that answer.

'And I'll always be close by to love you and help you both,' Ella promised.

The girls looked at her understandingly, Mary hugging her tightly. Walking back towards the farmhouse Ella made her mind up, knowing that with her help and the loans paid off Liam could stay here at Fintra and raise his children. It was their home.

On the Friday evening Sean Flanagan had driven into the farmyard, surprising her as she trimmed the girls' hair in the kitchen. He parked his big car at the back door. Sally was wriggling and squirming about like a puppy dog as Ella cut some of her long trail of curls.

'I waited for you back in Dublin.'

'I'm sorry, Sean, but I just couldn't get away. Liam needed me here.' She could see Mary watching them, and calling her brother, put on her coat and slipped outside with Sean.

The night was still, only the sound of their footfall breaking the silence. The grass was already damp with dew.

'Remember how I used to walk you home,' Sean reminded her as they crossed through the fields.

She remembered all right, the kissing and the fumbling and the play-acting and how much she'd loved him even then. Now they were grown-up! This time he kissed her lightly.

'Ella, what's happening between us?'

She closed her eyes, not knowing what to say or do. 'I don't know,' she whispered, for truthfully she didn't know. She told him about her brother's offer to sell her part of the farm and for her to move back down to Kilgarvan.

'Is that what you want?'

Ella stood there overlooking the lake, unsure.

'I'll buy you the bloody farm, every bit of it, if that's what you want, Ella. I'll sell the garage and give up what I'm doing. I'll come back to Kilgarvan and be the farmer you always wanted, if that's what'll make you happy!'

Ella couldn't believe it. The garage was his life,

346

all his ambitions and plans were tied up in the place and yet he was prepared to drop them all for her.

'I should have done it years ago, married you! Christ we've wasted so many years and here we are again.'

'I would have married you then.'

'But we had nothing!'

'That didn't matter, Sean.'

'Aye.' He breathed in. 'I know that now.'

She could hear the slapping waters of the lake below, the moonlight reflected in its surface as Sean kissed her, just the way he used to before, neither of them wanting to break apart.

'You're driving me crazy, Ella, I can hardly work with thinking of you. At the wedding all I could think of was you up there at the altar. When I see you there with Liam's children all I want is our own children. You were and are the only woman for me. There never has been anyone else,' he admitted.

She smiled. It had been exactly the same for her.

'Will you marry me, Ella?' he finally asked.

He had his answer as she nodded, and flung her arms around him.

'Do you want the farm?' he asked her later.

'No, Sean. All I want is the two of us together wherever that may be.'

'What about Liam?'

'I've already agreed to lend him the money to pay off his debts provided he stays. His children need him. I don't want to buy Fintra but I don't want him to sell it either. This is Mary and Sally's inheritance. Carmel would want them to have this place, where they were born and will grow up. An acre or two in return would be enough for us, somewhere we can build a house so we can come down and see the girls, watch them grow up, and for our children to come and visit their cousins.'

He kissed her slowly. 'You're a good woman, Ella.'

Even in the darkness she felt at peace, glad of all the good things in her life: the promises kept, the land of her father safe, the new life she'd built for herself. Sean was back and now there was someone to share it all with.

THE END

THE MAGDALEN
by Marita Conlon-McKenna

A powerful adult saga of love, betrayal and lost innocence by Ireland's bestselling children's novelist.

The wide open spaces of Connemara, filled with nothing but sea and sky, are all lost to Esther Doyle when, betrayed by her lover, Conor, and rejected by her family, she is sent to join the 'fallen women' of the Holy Saints' Convent in Dublin. Here, behind high granite walls, she works in the infamous Magdalen laundry whilst she awaits the birth of her baby.

At the mercy of the nuns, and working mostly in silence alongside the other 'Maggies', Esther spends her days in the steamy, sweatshop atmosphere of the laundry. It is a grim existence, but Esther has little choice. The convent is her only refuge, and its orphanage will provide shelter for her newborn child.

Yet despite the harsh reality of her life, Esther gains support from this isolated community of women. Learning throught the experiences and the mistakes of the other 'Maggies', she begins to recognize her own strengths and determines to survive. She recognizes, too, that it will take every ounce of courage to realize her dream of a new life for her and her child beyond the grey walls of the Holy Saints' Convent.

'This book pulls no punches. . . Marita Conlon-McKenna is breaking new ground with *The Magdalen*' *Image*'

A Bantam Paperback

0553 81300 5

CITY LIVES
by Patricia Scanlan

Devlin, Caroline and Maggie. Women in their prime. They have it all. Careers. Success. Marriage. They are the envy of their peers. But at what price?

Just when Devlin has everything she has ever dreamed of, a callous betrayal shows her that there's no room for friendship and loyalty in business. Can she be as tough as she needs to be in a world of deceit and double-dealing, where honesty and integrity are rare commodities?

Caroline, fed up being a victim, is no longer shy, unsure and needy. She's about to take a step that will change her life. Then tragedy strikes, and her plans change completely. But when one door closes. . . another opens.

And Maggie, alone, unsupported and unhappy in her marriage, has to make a choice that will put her children's needs before her own. Has she the strength to do what she has to do?

City Lives is the story of three women who have one great certainty in their lives. Their friendship. The enduring bonds of loyalty and love will carry them through the worst of times and the best of times.

CITY LIVES:
'Another entertaining tale of big business and female bonding'
Woman's Own (Best Book)

A Bantam Paperback

0553 81291 2

A SELECTION OF FINE NOVELS AVAILABLE FROM BANTAM BOOKS

50329 4	DANGER ZONES	Sally Beauman	£5.99
50630 7	DARK ANGEL	Sally Beauman	£6.99
50631 5	DESTINY	Sally Beauman	£6.99
40727 9	LOVERS AND LIARS	Sally Beauman	£5.99
50326 X	SEXTET	Sally Beauman	£5.99
40497 0	CHANGE OF HEART	Charlotte Bingham	£5.99
40890 9	DEBUTANTES	Charlotte Bingham	£5.99
40895 X	THE NIGHTINGALE SINGS	Charlotte Bingham	£5.9
17635 8	TO HEAR A NIGHTINGALE	Charlotte Bingham	£5.9
50500 9	GRAND AFFAIR	Charlotte Bingham	£5.99
40296X	IN SUNSHINE OR IN SHADOW	Charlotte Bingham	£5.9
40496 2	NANNY	Charlotte Bingham	£5.99
40117 8	STARDUST	Charlotte Bingham	£5.99
50717 6	THE KISSING GARDEN	Charlotte Bingham	£5.99
50501 7	LOVE SONG	Charlotte Bingham	£5.99
50718 4	THE LOVE KNOT	Charlotte Bingham	£5.99
81274 2	THE BLUE NOTE	Charlotte Bingham	£5.99
40973 5	A CRACK IN FOREVER	Jeannie Brewer	£5.99
81300 5	THE MAGDALEN	Marita Conlon-McKenna	£5.99
81257 2	PROMISED LAND	Marita Conlon-McKenna	£5.99
17504 1	DAZZLE	Judith Krantz	£5.9
17242 5	I'LL TAKE MANHATTAN	Judith Krantz	£5.9
40730 9	LOVERS	Judith Krantz	£5.9
17174 7	MISTRAL'S DAUGHTER	Judtih Krantz	£5.9
17389 8	PRINCESS DAISY	Judith Krantz	£5.9
40731 7	SPRING COLLECTION	Judith Krantz	£5.9
17503 3	TILL WE MEET AGAIN	Judith Krantz	£5.9
17505X	SCRUPLES TWO	Judith Krantz	£5.9
40732 5	THE JEWELS OF TESSA KENT	Judtih Krantz	£5.9
81287 4	APARTMENT 3B	Patricia Scanlan	£5.9
81290 4	FINISHING TOUCHES	Patricia Scanlan	£5.9
81286 6	FOREIGN AFFAIRS	Patricia Scanlan	£5.9
81288 2	PROMISES, PROMISES	Patricia Scanlan	£5.9
40941 7	MIRROR, MIRROR	Patricia Scanlan	£5.9
40943 3	CITY GIRL	Patricia Scanlan	£5.9
40946 8	CITY WOMAN	Patricia Scanlan	£5.
81291 2	CITY LIVES	Patricia Scanlan	£5.
81245 9	IT MEANS MISCHIEF	Kate Thompson	£5.
81246 7	MORE MISCHIEF	Kate Thompson	£5.